BOUND

BOUND

SASHA WHITE

HEAT
NEW YORK, NEW YORK

THE BERKLEY PUBLISHING GROUP
Published by the Penguin Group
Penguin Group (USA) Inc.
375 Hudson Street, New York, New York 10014, USA
Penguin Group (Canada), 90 Eglinton Avenue East, Suite 700, Toronto, Ontario M4P 2Y3, Canada
(a division of Pearson Penguin Canada Inc.)
Penguin Books Ltd., 80 Strand, London WC2R 0RL, England
Penguin Group (Ireland), 25 St. Stephen's Green, Dublin 2, Ireland (a division of Penguin Books Ltd.)
Penguin Group (Australia), 250 Camberwell Road, Camberwell, Victoria 3124, Australia
(a division of Pearson Australia Group Pty. Ltd.)
Penguin Books India Pvt. Ltd., 11 Community Centre, Panchsheel Park, New Delhi—110 017, India
Penguin Group (NZ), Cnr. Airborne and Rosedale Roads, Albany, Auckland 1310, New Zealand
(a division of Pearson New Zealand Ltd.)
Penguin Books (South Africa) (Pty.) Ltd., 24 Sturdee Avenue, Rosebank, Johannesburg 2196,
South Africa

Penguin Books Ltd., Registered Offices: 80 Strand, London WC2R 0RL, England

This is an original publication of The Berkley Publishing Group.

Copyright © 2006 by Sabrina Ingram.
Cover photo by Malek Chamoun/Picture Quest. Cover design by Lesley Worrell.
Text design by Stacy Irwin.

First edition: July 2006

Library of Congress Cataloging-in-Publication Data

White, Sasha, 1969–
  Bound / by Sasha White.—1st ed.
      p.   cm.
  ISBN 0-425-21274-2
  I. Title.
  PS3623.H57885B68   2006
  813'.6—dc22   2006003457

PRINTED IN THE UNITED STATES OF AMERICA

10 9 8 7 6 5 4 3 2 1

The strongest way to be BOUND is by emotion.

This book is dedicated to my family. My mom, dad, and big brother, for their blind faith and support in all that I do, and to Beth and JJ for keeping me sane while I do it.

Also, a special thank-you to my family at BP's, especially Dani, Kevin, Kelly, and Tanya for your friendship.

PROLOGUE

Everybody has a dark side. I just never expected mine to come out in my sexuality. But in that quiet time before I drift off to sleep or when I shower, always in the dark, images come into my mind that shock even me.

When I stand under the water, the needle-like spray aimed directly on my nipples, I imagine myself tied to a bed and being teased mercilessly. I want to be brought to the brink of orgasm again and again. Women are supposed to be multiorgasmic, and ever since I set eyes on Joe Carson, I've wanted to test that theory.

I imagine him walking into the room and demanding I get on my knees. Once in this position, he decides he likes my breasts, and he instinctively knows how much I like to have them played with, so he starts to roll the nipples between his fingers while talking to me.

Telling me what he wants. He wants me to suck his cock, and he wants to spank my ass, and he wants to fuck my pussy. He also wants to fuck my ass, but he knows that it may be a while before I let him do that.

I admit it. I'm an addict.

I'm addicted to the freedom that I find in the darkness.

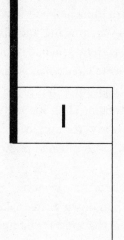

What the hell had I done?

I ran naked, still dripping from the shower, through my tiny apartment. Picking up strewn clothes and notebooks along the way, I stacked magazines neatly in the corner and stashed my latest erotica novel in the kitchen cupboard. I was getting ready to pull out the vacuum cleaner when I stopped dead in my tracks.

This was crazy! Vacuuming was taking things a bit too far. It wasn't like Joe cared if I was good housekeeper or not. He was coming over for one reason and one reason only. To finish what I'd started at work earlier that day.

Heat pooled low in my belly and my insides trembled at the enormity of what I'd done. Masturbating for him via the casino's surveillance system at work had sure started this . . . thing off with a bang.

Well, actually, the masturbation thing had only been a bang on my part. The thrill of knowing he was watching me, and his heavy breathing into the phone while I played with myself, had set me off good.

His bang had come a short time later when we met in the surveillance room. And it wasn't enough for either of us. It was like my first taste of chocolate, I wanted *more*. Then Joe had told me to go home and get cleaned up, to "be ready" for him in an hour. My heart had pounded and my just-seconds-ago satisfied body had tightened in anticipation.

Now I was running around like a crazy person.

I looked around the room, then down at my naked body. Rigid nipples poked out, and I could feel the constant dampness of my excitement leaking onto my thighs. He said be ready. What was ready?

My body couldn't be any more ready. My mind, well, it was functioning on autopilot, if at all, and my apartment looked like a twenty-six-year-old single girl lived there.

Clothes might be good.

Dashing to my bedroom, I glanced at the clock as I headed for the closet. Five o'clock. His shift was over now, and the casino was about ten minutes away, so I had at least that much time to get ready. What sort of clothes did one put on when you knew they were going to come off right away?

Scanning my closet I found no sexy peignoirs or silk robes. Not a big surprise there. Spotting a stretchy knit top, I snatched it off the hanger and pulled it on without a bra. My breasts were small enough that a bra would be prudent, but not necessary. For private company that I really wanted to look sexy for, the bra wasn't needed. After stepping into some bikini underpants, I added a pair of baggy cotton drawstring trousers.

The look was summer, lightweight, and casual. Now all I had to do was achieve that attitude.

Sucking in a deep breath I strolled into the bathroom and looked into the mirror. Big brown eyes stared back at me, looking a little glassy.

"Breathe, Katie, breathe," I muttered to my reflection.

I grabbed the blow dryer, did some quick work on my hair, and finished just as the buzzer signaling Joe's arrival sounded. A final glance in the mirror by the door showed me to be a casual-looking all-American girl with long blond hair and big Bambi eyes. I wondered if anyone looking at me would be able to tell that I was so aroused I could barely think straight.

The door to the apartment swung open slowly and I stood there, unsure of what to say or do as six feet plus of solid muscle walked inside like he owned the place. Thick black hair that was a touch unruly made my fingers itch to touch his wavy locks, but those distant, ice blue eyes seemed to suggest that wouldn't be a smart move. Right now those eyes were guarded, but hot, as they ran over my still form.

Joe Carson.

The man I'd been fantasizing about ever since I first saw him two months earlier when he'd hired on at the casino I work in. At twenty-six years old I'm no virgin, but I can honestly say I've never had much luck in the sex department either. None of the guys I'd ever been with were anything to brag about. Until today, I'd never had a male-induced orgasm. When I needed to get off, I relied on myself.

Then Joe showed up.

I could count him among my lovers now. After all, he'd fucked me so good only that afternoon and gave me such an intense orgasm that I'd promised to do anything for him. Now he wanted to hold me to it. Okay, so I told him he could do anything *before* he gave me an orgasm. The chance to live out a sexual fantasy with my dream man had been too much to resist.

"Hi, Joe." At least my voice sounded natural, if a bit breathy. "Can I get you a drink? I have water, diet pop, or pear cider?"

"No, thank you." He shook his head and advanced toward me, the hungry gleam in his eye making my pussy throb. "I just want you."

My pulse jumped and my knees weakened. He stopped when he was only inches from me, swallowing up my personal space. I looked up at him and licked my lips nervously, reveling in the tidal wave of sensations.

"You look very nice." He reached out and brushed his knuckles over the tip of one breast then the other, making my nipples tighten and stand out. His words, when he spoke, were soft and cajoling with a bit of steel buried beneath. "But I told you to be naked for me when I arrived."

Instantly I was back in the surveillance room, eager to please, and ready to do anything for him.

"Sorry." I smiled at him sassily, fighting to remain somewhat normal. "Getting dressed after a shower is habit."

He quirked a dark eyebrow. "Do you want me to leave?"

"No."

"Then get naked." He turned and lowered himself into the overstuffed armchair just inside the door. "Now."

Gone was the tender lover who, earlier that day, had held me up and cradled me against his chest until my orgasm receded, and I could stand on my own. In front of me now was the enigmatic security guard that I'd been drooling over for two months; the one that came to me in my dreams and used my body as his personal playground.

I bit down on my bottom lip and stifled the urge to ask him what he had planned. Instead, I crossed my arms at the waist and pulled my shirt over my head. Joe's casual posture never changed, his expression remained detached except for his eyes. They darkened at the sight of my naked breasts, and my confidence swelled. The tension in the air got thicker, and my insides grew heavier, weighted with arousal. The urge to tease him was strong, so I ran my hands over my breasts, cupping them to tweak the nipples between thumb and finger.

"If you're happy doing that I don't need to be here." He made to get up from his seat.

"No!" Before he could stand fully, I pushed my pants and underwear from my hips, and stepped out of them, heart racing. "I'm naked. Don't go."

He stepped closer, until we were close enough that his breath danced across my cheek. He stared into my eyes, searching for something. "Are you sure you want to do this?"

My heart pounded and a tingle of something almost like fear whispered through me, blending easily with the lust simmering in my veins.

"Oh, yes." My words were soft, almost a whisper.

"I noticed you my first day at the casino. The way you walk and talk as if ice wouldn't melt on your ass." He stepped back and unbuckled the utility belt around his waist. He dropped the belt and all its security gadgets on the armchair and planted his hands on his trim hips. "The things I've wanted to do to you. I've dreamt of fucking you in every position imaginable. I've jerked off to the thought of coming all over your pretty face."

The crude words entered through my ears and flowed down my body, stroking my insides and heating me up until I could feel my nether lips swell and dampen. No one had ever talked to me like that before. No one dared to. But I loved it. The words heated my blood and melted my insides, and I wanted everything he described.

"I never dreamt you'd actually be into it. Then, today, out of the blue, you decide to give me a private peep show at work." He chuckled and gave his head a small shake. "There's no way in hell I'm going to ignore that."

"I'm glad," I said softly. "I've never done anything like that before, Joe."

He looked at me for a long silent moment.

"I believe you. But . . . after I fucked you, you said something else." He reached out and stroked his fingertips over my belly, up over my ribs, and along the undersides of my breasts. "You told me you were mine. My slut, to do with as I pleased."

Heat crept up my neck and I mentally cursed my fair skin. I'd said that in a moment of passion. As if he could read my thoughts, his full lips lifted at one corner. "Did you mean it?"

Something soft flickered the depths of Joe's eyes, a flash of uncertainty maybe, and then disappeared. A shiver skipped down my spine and I pressed my thighs together. He was so aloof, yet so intense. I'd seen him prowl the casino floor, and my fantasies had gotten darker and darker. Matching the almost primal aura that surrounded him.

He may be dangerous, but he didn't scare me. At that moment my only real fear was that he'd walk away.

"I meant it."

By no means am I a submissive personality. My father's early death made sure I knew how to look after myself and my mother, too. I'm a supervisor at work, and my whole life people have told me I'm a natural-born leader. Part of me even fantasized about being a dominatrix. The part that made Joe say "please" when I'd teased him over the surveillance camera that afternoon.

But when he'd pulled me into the office, and it was just the two of us, it had been as if he'd seen deep inside me, to the place where even I was scared to look . . . and I'd been able to deny him nothing.

With him standing in front of me, looking at me with eyes so hot they scorched my skin, it was too easy to sink back into that place.

"You're so pretty, almost like an angel." He spoke in a soft firm tone as he did a slow walk around me, trailing his fingers over the planes of my naked body. He tweaked my nipples and I gasped. "Ever since I arrived in Chadwick, I've been told what a sweet girl Katie Long is. You're the town's Golden Girl aren't you?"

A warm hand skimmed across my back and patted me on the ass lightly. When I didn't answer him, the hand smacked my rump sharply, the slap echoing through the room.

"Aren't you?"

"Yes," I muttered, focusing on the flare of sensation at the slap.

Stopping directly in front of me, Joe cradled my head in his large hands and lifted my face to his. "Well, now you're *my* girl, my angel. And we're going to see just how good you can be."

With that, he took my mouth.

His tongue came out and licked across my bottom lip before spearing between them and invading. His tongue dueled with mine, conquering it completely, and imprinting his flavor on my taste buds. My hands clasped his waist, and I leaned into his hard body to rub my nakedness against the coarse material of his uniform.

One of his hands slid to the back of my head and he pressed forward, bending me backward slightly. Excitement rose up in me as his mouth ate at mine, our harsh breathing the only sound in the room. One of my arms wrapped around his waist, holding tight to him while the other slid between our bodies to measure his hardness through his pants.

A low growl vibrated against my lips a second before he gripped my shoulders and pulled away. My low whimper echoed in the room, and he shushed me.

"Not so fast," he whispered. Firm hands spun me around and his voice purred in my ear. "Take me to your bedroom."

Biting my lip, but glorying in the liquid fire pulsing through my veins, I led him to my room.

"On the bed," he commanded.

I scrambled to the middle of the bed and watched as he stripped off all his clothes, revealing a body to die for.

Wide shoulders, a muscled chest, a light dusting of fine dark hair led my eyes on the path across a hard stomach to the small patch of tight curls surrounding a cock that made my mouth water. I licked my lips and forced my eyes to travel the rest of his body. Muscled thighs and defined calves, dusted with the same dark hairs.

Yummy.

My insides clenched with anticipation when I measured the size of his cock with my gaze. He was long and thick, the head shiny and tempting. Joe stood there for a minute, watching me eat him up with my eyes. The longer I looked the more I saw. There was one wicked-looking scar bisecting the front of his shoulder to his chest, with a few smaller ones on his abdomen and left thigh.

Seeing him standing there, rough and ready, glorious in his complete maleness, it was clear to me that he was a hard man, in more ways than one. When my gaze traveled back to his face, he climbed on the bed and laid his body atop mine.

I gasped at the first contact of skin against skin. He was so warm and hard and rough against me. Pressing me back into the mattress he pinned my wrists by my head and kissed me deeply. I wiggled and tried to spread my legs, to get him aligned so he pressed more fully against my sex, but his legs framed mine, and he wasn't moving.

Hard cock pressed into my belly, rubbing there and driving me deeper into a fog of lust as his lips traveled across my jaw to my ear, teasing me. My whole body shuddered as a bolts of pleasure shot straight to my pussy. He noticed my response and breathed hotly into my ear, causing more shivers.

"Ohh, I found a hot spot," he purred.

Another breathy moan eased from my lips as he nipped at my

earlobe sharply, then skimmed his lips across my chin to the other side, where he repeated his seductive torture.

I writhed beneath him, my moans turning to whimpers. His hands left mine, and immediately I reached for him. He slid down so his hands could cup and fondle my breasts. He squeezed them, fingers and thumbs working the nipples expertly. When his mouth closed over one nipple and he sucked it avidly, I actually cried out loud it felt so good.

Never before had a man made me actually cry out in pleasure! I'd faked it a few times, but I wasn't faking it with Joe. The man was magic.

Wanting more, my fingers burrowed deep in his soft thick hair, holding him to my breast. When he shifted and went to work on the other rigid tip with his mouth, his fingers still pinching and pulling at the abandoned one, my restless hands slid down to his shoulders. His muscles bunched and flexed beneath my hands, my fingers turning to claws as his teeth worried the nipple and pleasure/pain washed over me. It hurt, but in such a way that arrows of pleasure shot straight to my pussy.

"Yesss," I hissed, only to jerk and pull back slightly from a sharp bite.

"You like a little bit of pain with your pleasure, huh, angel?" Joe's husky chuckle echoed through the room, and his other hand abandoned its teasing to trail down my side. His fingertips skimmed over my ribs, my waist, my hip and back up.

"Joe . . ." I moaned, on fire for a firmer touch.

He lifted his head and quirked an eyebrow at me. "Yes?"

"Touch me." My voice had a bit of a whine to it that I wasn't sure I liked.

He shifted his weight to the side a bit, and cool air washed over my overheated skin. He tilted his head and I followed his gaze to where his hand hovered over my hip. So close, yet so far from where I wanted it.

Where I *needed* it.

"Say *please*."

I froze and he looked up at me, a gleam in his eyes. In that moment I realized that I might've bitten off more than I could chew.

"Please," I whispered, blood roaring in my ears.

His hand lowered and rubbed at my hip before traveling down my outer thigh and up my inner thigh. Flirty fingertips brushed against my swollen lips and he smiled. "That's my angel."

My eyelids dropped, and a heavy sigh of pleasure escaped me at his words of praise. How could those two words, which I normally hated, sound so good coming from him? His fingers delved between the folds of my sex and brushed my clit, and all rational thought fled. The little button was hard and aching, and I knew it wouldn't take much to get me off.

He diddled there for a brief minute before playing the finger around my entrance. My hips jerked, and he thrust his finger in deep. Rubbing the heel of his hand against my clit, his finger moved inside me. Soon, another finger joined it, and my body stretched pleasurably.

"Oh yes."

"That's it, baby." His lips brushed across mine. "Tell me what you like."

"That . . . I like that."

My hips gyrated and I spread my legs wider to give him better access. One of his legs covered mine to keep them in place, and the light restriction made my juices flow even faster. I was so wet that I could *hear* the squish of Joe's fingers moving in and out of me. "More, Joe. I need more."

Our lips were still touching as he spoke. He licked at them, nibbled on my bottom lip, and demanded the words from me. "What do you say?"

"Please!"

"That's it. Tell me how good it is. Tell me what you want, and I'll give it to you." He slid a third finger inside me, pressed the palm of his hand against my clit harder, and I came apart.

"Ohhhh—"

Joe's mouth slanted across mine fully, cutting off my cry as my insides clenched around the intruder. My back arched, pressing me against his hand firmly, and I think that all that was keeping me together was him by my side.

When my shudders subsided, Joe's kiss gentled, and he withdrew his hand to rest it on my belly.

"Very good girl," he whispered. "Now let's see how that feels when I'm inside you."

Sliding his body on top of mine, he entered me smoothly. My sated body instantly jumped to attention, and tension gathered low in my belly.

His forearms rested on the bed alongside my head and shoulders, trapping me as he bent his head and nuzzled into the crook of my neck. He kept his legs on the outside of mine, giving me very little room to move. Forward and backward, his cock slid in and almost all the way out before filling me up again.

With a whimper, I struggled to spread my legs wider, to take him deeper into me, but he didn't give an inch. My legs were only wide enough that the slow and steady movement of his hips had the length of his cock rubbing against my clit with every thrust.

I lifted my head off the pillow and licked at the corded muscle between his neck and shoulder. His pace increased a bit. I nibbled on the muscle. His hips pumped faster, deeper. Opening my mouth against his skin I sucked at the sensitive spot and scrapped my nails down his back.

A low rumble echoed in my ear and my body reacted to the

sound instinctively. My head went back, giving him easier access to my vulnerable neck and I reached down to clasp his butt cheeks, silently urging him to fuck me harder and faster.

But he didn't.

He nipped at the flesh of my earlobe and kept his maddening pace.

"Joe," I panted his name out on a breath. "Please!"

He lowered his body more, so his chest grazed my sensitive nipples, and I was completely surrounded by him. Trapped in an erotic cage created by his hot, hard body. His forehead rested against mine, and he gazed deep into my eyes. "Not this time, Katie."

The intense blue fire in his eyes seared my soul. I could see passion, excitement, pleasure and . . . His eyes closed and his face tightened, he thrust deep and his cock jerked inside me. Warmth flooded my insides and he jerked hard against me, his pelvic bone grinding against my clit and sending my world off its axis once more.

The earth righted itself, and Joe tried to pull away but I held him tight to me and whispered, "Stay."

My body was drained, my mind was blank, and for some unknown reason, the last thing I wanted to do was let go of him.

2

I was stomping across the small parking lot of my apartment complex, digging in my purse for keys that I'd probably left inside behind my locked door, when I saw old Mrs. Beets across the parking lot. She was waving and calling my name in that nasal screech unique only to her.

"Katie. Yoo-hoo! Katie Long!"

Rummaging a bit more frantically at the bottom of my bag, I finally found the keys and flashed the blue-haired old lady a big, false smile.

"I can't stop to chat right now. I'm late!" I called out and jumped into my car as fast as I could. "And even if I wasn't, I don't want to talk to you, you nosy old bat," I muttered while buckling myself into the seat.

Pulling out of the lot, I headed for my mom's place. Twinges of re-morse prickled at the back of back of my brain, and I couldn't stop my-self from apologizing. "Okay, I'm sorry I called you an old bat, even though you didn't hear me. It was uncalled for. You're not that bad, just extremely nosy, and I really don't need the third degree right now."

Mrs. Beets couldn't hear me. I knew this, but it made me feel better to say it just the same. Well, better about calling her names, but not about the sharp left turn my life had taken the night before.

I glanced at the dashboard clock and grimaced slightly, I was late. I was never late. My mom was going to be in a snit if she wasn't on time for her hair appointment. I shoved the clutch to the floor and shifted gears to climb the mountain road, trying not to pay attention to the satisfying aches that made my body pleasantly heavy in a way that only the well fucked would understand.

Memories of what caused the aches, and had made me so exhausted I'd slept through my alarm clock, flittered through my head, and I fought the rising tide of panic in my chest. Instead, I pretended life was perfect and flashed another fake smile. This time it was directed at Matt, the mechanic who sat in front of Morgan's Gas Station all day every day, watching the world go by while he waited for his next customer.

What the hell had I done last night?

It felt as if I'd grabbed a tiger by the tail and tugged. The tiger would be tall, dark, and dangerous-looking Joe, and the tug would be the show I'd put on for him yesterday afternoon at work.

I still couldn't believe it wasn't all a dream. Only the stiffness of my muscles and the tenderness of my pussy convinced me that it had been real.

A huge sigh forced its way up and out. It'd been a long time since I'd put anything in the "questionably smart" category of my life. I was due.

The steep incline of road leveled out just before I hit the center of town. Like most small towns in British Columbia, traffic was pretty sparse on the streets of Chadwick, but the sidewalks were full of people strolling the small downtown area and enjoying the summer sunshine. I drove past the small park and couldn't stop a grin from spreading across my face at the sight of the kids splashing around in the wading pool.

My cell phone rang just as I turned off Main Street and onto Pine Road. Reaching over blindly, I found my phone on the top of the junk in my purse and flipped it open without looking at the caller ID. I already knew who it was.

"I'm almost there, Mom. I just turned onto your road."

"You're late, Katie. You said you'd be here by ten o'clock and it's almost quarter past."

"I had a late night last night and overslept a little." Late was a very polite way to describe the almost sleepless night I'd had. "I'm sure Mary will hold your appointment if we're a few minutes late. Come on out, and we'll be there before you know it."

I folded the phone back up and pulled into the driveway of my parents' two-story home. Except it wasn't my parents' home anymore. It was just my mom's since Dad had lost the fight with cancer almost fifteen years ago. I saw the curtain in the window shift and knew she would step out the door in just a moment, ready for her appointment at the beauty parlor, and unhappy with me for being ten minutes late.

The good girl in me made it impossible to say no to her when she asked things of me. No matter how many times I tired to subtly tell her I wasn't her personal driver, and that she could drive herself, or even take a taxi, she couldn't grasp the concept of doing anything on her own. I guess it was partly my own fault because she'd been so lost after Dad died that it had been easier to do for myself, and her, than to remind her that *she* was the adult.

Lydia Long stepped out of the house and hurried down the

driveway. "I can't miss this appointment, Katie," she said as she buckled herself into my passenger seat.

Shifting gears I backed onto the street, using the fact that I had to look both ways to avoid her gaze.

"You won't miss it, Mom. Why are you so worried about it? It's not like Mary doesn't do your hair once a month and will always make room for you in her day."

"I have a date tonight and I want to look my best," she answered with a girlish giggle.

Ahh, that explained a lot. Every time Mom met a new man she started acting like an infatuated teenager, demanding and exuberant at the same time.

"Well, I know if you tell Mary you have a date she'll fit you in no matter what." It was true, too. When Mom told the other ladies at the beauty parlor she was seeing someone new, they would *all* turn into giggling teenagers.

"Why don't you see if one of Mary's girls can do your hair, too, Katie dear?" I could feel her critical gaze roving over my simple ponytail and I tensed. I knew what was coming next. "You have such beautiful hair and you never do anything with it. Maybe if you did your hair once in a while you'd be able to get a boyfriend, too."

Sigh. Here we go again.

At fifty-six Mom was from a generation when women were all about marriage and family, and she had a hard time understanding that there could be more to life than finding a husband.

"I had a boyfriend. It wasn't all it was cracked up to be, Mom. I'll just stick with the manicure I have scheduled."

I pulled into the strip mall on Burke Street and parked in front of Mary's Place, just as Brad Marks was stepping out of the hardware store.

Speak of the devil, or in this case, the ex-boyfriend, and he shall appear. My gaze swept over his wiry frame and I felt nothing. With his short blond hair and clean-cut features, he was attractive; I couldn't deny it. Yet, he hadn't been attractive *to me* for a few years now.

Mom waved at Brad and jumped out of the car. She started to close the door behind her but stopped and poked her head back into the car. "That was a long time ago, Katie, and I don't blame him for breaking up with you. You never did appreciate him the way he deserved."

She shut the door before I could remind her that it was me that dumped Brad, not the other way around.

I closed my eyes and prayed for patience and tolerance. Traits that were desperately needed if I was to get through the rest of the day without strangling her.

Not that it mattered; it was inconceivable to my mother that a woman would break up with a man for any reason. I should know. She let every one of her loser boyfriends walk all over her before they walked right out the door. "Any man was better than no man" was her motto, and she lived by it.

Making one last plea to God, I opened my eyes and saw her flirting with Brad on the sidewalk. She gestured to me in the car, and they both turned expectantly.

Pasting a fake smile on my face, I eased out of my car and started toward them. The ache of stiff muscles being used again caused a warm flush to flow through my body. Joe had made good use of my body, and complete willingness the night before. And the lingering aftereffects were making it impossible not to remember the intimate, dirty details with every step I took.

"You're going to be late for your appointment, Mom." I reminded her when I stopped in front of them.

She glanced at the beauty parlor window, saw Mary waiting for her and rushed away, throwing a quick good-bye over her shoulder.

"Your mom's quite a whirlwind isn't she, Katie?" Brad winked at me, a fond smile tilting his lips up at one corner.

He looked good. At thirty-four he was close to the same age as Joe, but he didn't have the hard-lived look that Joe did. Brad's wholesomeness also didn't make my heart race the way Joe's rough looks did.

"She does get more energetic when there's a man around," I agreed. I didn't really want to talk to him. I just wanted to go somewhere and think about the events of the day before, but politeness and proper social courtesy were bred in me so deep that I couldn't just walk away.

"How are you, Brad? Things going good at the store?" Brad had gone to college after he graduated from school here in Chadwick, and then he'd returned to work in his parent's hardware store.

When Brad returned from college and a few years in the big city, he was twenty-five. And I thought he was the most worldly guy around. I'd go into the hardware store with excuses to ask him for help with something. He'd flirted with me, but he never took me on a date until I'd turned eighteen.

He was a good guy. It always surprised me that nobody gave us a hard time when we became a couple, me being eighteen and him being twenty-seven, but we were accepted. The sex had never been anything spectacular, but the companionship was nice. After four years together, it became clear to me that no matter what I said or did, Brad had no intention of ever leaving Chadwick again. Then I really started to lose interest.

He wanted to take over his parents' store, get married, and raise a happy little family. I wanted more for myself than this town had to offer, and no man was enough to make me stay.

Only familial guilt and sense of responsibility could do that.

"I'm doing good, Katie. You? Still working at Black's?"

Yeah, it's a decent job." Black's is the casino just outside the town limits. I worked in the cash cage, counting the buckets of change and stacks of bills that people throw at the slot machines and gaming tables. I couldn't stop a grin from spreading across my face. After a glance at the watch on my wrist I gestured to the beauty parlor, letting Brad know I had to run.

"I like it there. It's never dull, and I get to meet all kinds of people," I said as I waved good-bye.

People like Joe. The man whose hands I could still feel on my body.

How was I to know that Joe's idea of good sex was total domination? Or that I would like it so much?

———————

Reading erotica had opened my eyes to a lot of possibilities out there. Sex with Brad, when were together, had never been what I would call adventurous. It had always left me feeling a tad bit . . . empty. Like I was standing outside the bakery staring at luscious chocolate éclairs eating a fat-free bran muffin.

After a night of drinking with my best friend, Julie, where we'd talked about sex and orgasms and men versus women, she'd practically dared me to hit on Joe, and I'd gone for it. When Joe had come to escort me to the vault with the cash trolley my overactive imagination and libido had combined to free my fantasy dominatrix.

The elevator had arrived to bring me back up to the cash office, and a plan had begun to form in my mind. The heat thrumming through my veins had told me to stop being a chicken shit, and go after what I wanted, and then maybe, I'd get it.

The girls were fine when I got back to the cash cage, so I'd told them I had paperwork to do, had gone into the office and locked the door. The whole time I strolled around my desk in the office I'd been aware of the security camera in the corner. And the fact that Joe was the one sitting in the surveillance room. I'd pretended to see something on the floor just so I could bend over to pick it up, thus giving him a nice view of my round arse, barely covered by my plaid kilt, before I'd stepped behind my desk and sat down.

It took me a few more minutes to get up the nerve to follow through with my plan. I'd shuffled papers and pretended to concentrate on work. Then I let my hand trail from the side of my neck around to caress my throat in a teasing way. With the hope that he was watching my hand, I'd played with my collar, then the buttons on my shirt. I undid one button, then another, and trailed my fingers across the upper swell of my breast.

My nipples hardened and poked out obviously. To tease myself a little more, I ran my hands lightly across them, circling the rigid tips until I was sure I could follow through with my plan.

Before I let myself think too hard I'd leaned forward and picked up the phone. Punching in the extension for security, I sat back in my chair and waited for Joe to pick up.

My eyes were closed and I was playing with my nipples again when he answered on the third ring.

"See anything interesting now?" I'd asked, referring to the fact that he'd told me surveillance was boring.

"Definitely." His answer had been firm, his voice deep.

A shiver had skipped down my spine, and a naughty chuckle had escaped. It was time to reel him in.

My fingers had traced from my nipple to my blouse buttons. Closing my eyes, I'd imagined he was right in front of me instead of in the basement watching me on a monitor.

"Do you want to see my breasts? They're aching for attention right now." I'd never done phone sex before, and while I figured the visuals would be enough, I needed the verbal. I needed to close my eyes, and imagine it was all a dream. I slipped another button from its hole and moved on to the next one. When my blouse was undone I let it hanging open, with my breasts still covered.

Joe still hadn't said a word by then. But I wasn't going any further without active encouragement. "If you don't answer, I won't show them to you."

"Show me," he'd ordered.

"Say *please.*" Just giving the order had made my heart race. To tease him some more I'd slid my hand under the flap of my loose shirt and cupped a plump breast.

"*Please,*" he'd practically growled.

To oblige him, and myself, I'd shrugged my blouse aside, undid the front of my bra, and showed him what I had. I could hear his sharp intake of breath and it had been a heady thing.

"This feels so good. My nipples have been aching ever since we were in that elevator. You saw them when we got to the basement, didn't you? It was the sight of your tight ass that got me revved up. Did you know that?" I couldn't help but talk to him. To tease him as my hand cupped and fondled first one breast then the other.

"Seeing your handcuffs on your hip, and imagining what you would do to me if I let you cuff me to my bedposts. I fantasize about it being a little rough sometimes. I think you'd enjoy that. I know I would." I pinched a hard nipple with my thumb and forefinger. I rolled it around, starting to pant as pleasure sparked throughout my body.

I could hear Joe's breathing deepen and speed up a bit but it wasn't enough. I wanted more. The plan to tease him, to seduce him, had been forgotten. At that point in time all I'd wanted was to come with him watching.

"These are your fingers I feel lifting my skirt." I taunted him as my fingers walked up my thigh, gathering my skirt and baring more for him. The soft groan that had echoed over the line when he saw that I had no panties on was music to my ears. "You like that? It gives me a thrill to know that while I look so innocent, and everyone thinks I'm so innocent, underneath I'm just a horny little girl looking for a man who can satisfy her. A man that will look at me and see what I'm truly like."

I'd brushed my fingers over the coarse curls between my thighs. "I'm wet here," I'd told him. "Aching, too, but I think I'll stop now. Wait until I get home and have my vibrator handy."

"No!" he'd called out. "Don't stop."

I'd froze. Waiting for the magic word.

"*Please.*"

That word, from his lips, had me ready to do anything. "Does the camera have a zoom on it, Joe?"

"Yes."

I'd told him to zoom in, and braced my feet on the edge of my desk. My legs were spread crudely open and when I dipped my fingers between my thighs and spread my swollen pussy lips open I knew he could see everything. "Can you see how wet I am? How hungry my cunt is?"

A groan had echoed through the phone, making the inner walls of my cunt clench in response. It was then that I knew the dirty talk was a huge turn-on for him. He liked to hear those bad words come from my innocent mouth. I'd stayed in that position, fingered my clit, and talked dirty to Joe until I'd come for him.

When I was done, the seduction plan had flooded back into my head and I'd tried to be sexy. I'd set my feet back on the floor, straightened up a bit, gazed straight into the security camera, and licked my fingers clean.

"Well?" I'd asked.

"Who knew little Katie Long from the cash office was such a bad girl?"

And he'd hung up.

I was at a loss, I'd wanted Joe with a hunger I'd never felt before, but I wasn't about to put myself out there any more than I already had.

Turns out, I hadn't needed to.

3

"Oh. My. God."

Julie stopped dead in the middle of the lounge floor, a tray full of drinks balanced skillfully in her right hand, the fingers of her left hand wrapped around my arm. "You did it, didn't you? You really did it!"

The shock on my best friend's face was outdone only by the excitement in her voice.

"Did what?" I tried to play innocent.

With my long blond hair, big brown eyes, and wholesome smile, most people fell for it. Not Julie Anderson. She had been my best friend since grade school, and she knew me too well to believe I was innocent of anything.

"You made your move. Somehow, you finally got up the nerve to hit on Joe, and he took you up on it, didn't he? Oh yeah, and from the glow in your cheeks he was every bit as good as he looks." She let out a husky chuckle, and a wicked glint that I knew only too well appeared in her amber eyes.

Julie knew Joe had been the star of my fantasies ever since I'd first set eyes on his six-foot-plus, solidly muscled body. It wasn't just his body that gave me a hot flash, or the way he looked in his security uniform, with the big nightstick and handcuffs on his hip. It was the energy that radiated off of him.

Maybe I'd been hanging around Julie's New Age roommate too much lately, but beneath Joe's wavy black hair and intense blue eyes was a quiet strength and a vibe that sucked me in and made me forget everything but him.

"Would you hush?" I warned her. "I don't need the whole world to know." I skimmed the crowd in the small lounge and gave the bartender a small wave.

"Relax," Julie scoffed. "You know the people that come here don't care what you do when you're not here, even if it is something wild with 'Big Bad Joe.' All they care about is that you cash out their winnings. That's why you work here." She paused and eyed me shrewdly. "Well, that and the fact that it drives your mother absolutely batty."

Julie called Joe's invisible energy his "bad boy" vibe, but that didn't do it justice either. First of all, he was no "boy," bad or not. He was definitely all man, and the bad part? Well, something told me it was more than bad. It was almost . . . dangerous.

Watching him walk the casino floor was like watching an animal hunt. A sleek, sexy, panther prowling through the urban jungle. When he first arrived at Black's, his eyes were always shuttered. I never had a clue what the man was thinking or feeling, but I always got the feeling he *saw* everything. Even when I'd seen him smile and joke around with the other guards, I sensed he kept himself on a tight leash.

I recognized that kind of self-control. It was the sign of someone who was hiding his true self, and it only made him more attractive and intriguing. It had made me want to see what it would take to make him lose it and what it was that he hid.

I'd dreamt of having all that energy focused on me, but the reality of it had been way more than I'd anticipated. When we were in the surveillance office yesterday, I'd gotten a look behind those shutters and the intense emotions there had both scared and thrilled me.

"No one cares," I muttered to Julie, glancing around the dimly lit lounge. "Except her."

Julie peeked over her shoulder and saw Renee, my arch nemesis since grade school, standing at the oak bar watching us intently.

"Yeah, she cares. But she can't hear us from over there so give!"

Before I could open my mouth and say anything, Louie, one of the many regulars who thought the world revolved around him, called out to Julie in a whiny voice, "I'm dying of thirst over here, sweetheart."

I ignored him and eyed Julie. "Are you almost done?"

"Yeah, Renee's already started taking over the tables; this is my last round." She gestured to the full tray in her hand.

"Go finish up and cash out." I waved her off. "I'll wait outside and tell you all about it on the way to your place."

"You're on," she said as she started off in Louie's direction. "And know this . . . I want all the dirty details!"

I nodded and headed for the back exit, my eyes scanning the interior of the casino as I hurried through it. No way was I going to give Julie all the details of the night before. I wasn't *ever* going to tell anyone the complete details! I'd share some of the good stuff with her. She was my best friend, and if it weren't for her I wouldn't know half the shit I knew about sex. Even Brad had considered me too much of a lady for anything other than the missionary position.

Well, okay, every now and then I'd taken control of the situation and climbed on top of him. He'd always been helpless to stop me when I did that.

The point is that Julie, and maybe her roommate Lillian, were the only people who would believe that I had the nerve to try and seduce someone like Joe. No one else knew that I had a bit of wild streak in me.

Usually, when I picked Julie up at work, I'd have a seat at the bar and wait for her. But today I wanted some quiet time with my thoughts before I had to answer Julie's questions, so I hotfooted it outside. Besides, if I waited outside for Julie, my chances of running into Joe were pretty slim.

As much as I hungered for a glimpse of him, I wasn't ready to face him just yet.

I tossed my purse into the back seat of my little Hyundai and leaned against the driver's side door.

Black's Casino was on the outskirts of Chadwick, hidden from the main highway by the birch and pine trees that populated the Selkirk mountain range of southern British Columbia, giving the near-empty parking lot a quiet, almost serene feel. It was late afternoon, and the sun was still bright overhead, so I tilted my head back and let the July heat seep into my body while I struggled to shake off the tension of dealing with my mother all afternoon.

My life would seem pretty damn good to anyone looking in from the outside, but that didn't mean it *was* good. Living the life others thought you should live, instead of the life you wanted to live, could be stressful. Sometimes I felt like an actress stuck in a role I didn't want. Hell, I was an actress. And a damned good one!

I just wasn't getting paid for the role I was playing.

With Joe, I hadn't been acting. He'd stripped me of any pretense and left me with no thoughts, only feelings. Raw feelings that were new and daring and way intense.

"I need you to come with me, Katie."

Hearing his voice I looked up from the file cabinet with a flirtatious smile. But it faded fast when I saw his blank expression. I asked what was wrong, but Joe just shook his head and repeated that he needed me to go with him.

We told the girls in the cage I was leaving; Sara and I had already done our count and changeover so my shift was over anyway.

When we stepped into the elevator, Joe moved to the back and I stood directly in front of him. The doors slid closed and the lift jolted and descended to the basement level. Joe stood silently, his intense eyes full of blue fire as they locked with mine. Recently sated arousal unfurled in my belly and my juices started to flow again.

I was determined to have him make the next move. I'd put myself out there once, and I wasn't going to do it again. The elevator stopped with a loud chime and the doors slid open.

"This way," Joe said, and took off down the hall.

At the door to the surveillance room he stepped in and motioned me to follow. Tom got up from the corner monitor and left the room, closing the door behind him.

We were alone.

Joe took my belongings and set them on the table in the corner, then stepped closer, making the air between us thicken with sexual tension.

"That was quite a show you put on for me," he said softly. He planted his hands on his hip, cocked his head and ran his eyes over my face, my neck, my cleavage . . . my nipples poking rudely against my top.

"Is that what this is about? Am I in trouble?"

"You are definitely in trouble." He grabbed my shoulders and spun me around to face him. "Assume the position."

Adrenaline pumped through my body, laced with the heat of arousal, and an excited whimper escaped when I placed my hands on the wall. Joe's chest pressed against my back as he reached around me, grabbed my wrists, and stretched my hands higher. I was in the perfect position for a good frisk.

Sure hands skimmed down my arms, across my shoulders and back before settling on my hips. He gripped my hips, and kicked my feet apart. I'd dreamt of this so often I didn't know if I could stand the reality. Joe's hands skimmed across my ribs and up to cup my breasts.

Another moan slipped out and I bit my lip to stay silent.

"Oh, you're enjoying this, aren't you? You've been hiding your true nature for too long, Katie. With a thorough search, who knows what else I might uncover?"

He bent down, a warm hand encircled each of my ankles, and began a slow unhurried trip up my legs. Heat followed wherever he touched. His fingers skimmed over my calves, lingered at the back of my knees and then continued up and under my skirt.

Teasing fingers brushed over the bare flesh of my inner thigh before shifting to cup my butt cheeks. He kneaded them for a minute, his breath hot on my sensitive skin, then his thumbs delved into the crease of my ass. My back arched automatically, thrusting myself deeper into his hands.

When a small moan echoed through the room, Joe abruptly stood up. He pressed his body against mine, and his lips brushed against my neck when he spoke.

"You're such a tease, you drive me crazy," he growled, nipping my earlobe. "The things I want to do to you . . ."

I could feel the struggle in him. In the tension of his body, the growl of his voice. I could feel it in his unfinished sentence. Bad Boy Joe still had doubts about me.

"Anything," I whispered.

Gentle fingers pinched my chin and turned me so he could see my eyes. His were full of lust, yet tinged with a fine layer of doubt.

"Anything," I repeated, not backing down. "I'm all yours, to use any way you want."

My words freed us both. He reached for my left wrist, and pulled it behind my back. A shiver racked my body at the touch of cold metal encircling my wrist.

"Give me your other hand," he commanded.

Once both of my hands were locked behind my back, he brought me to stand in front of the bank of security monitors. He kicked Tom's chair out of the way and pressed my hips against the countertop.

He reached around me, flipped a switch, and images of me bending over in the cash office filled all the screens.

"Look at that ass. I want that ass." He bent me forward and lifted my skirt, baring my nakedness. He shifted to the side and pressed his groin against my hip. We watched the images on the screen and he rubbed the rough palm of his hand over my cheeks briefly, before dipping his hand between my thighs.

Bolts of pleasure shot through my body at his touch and another, louder, moan filled the room. "You are a little slut, aren't you?" Joe chuckled and thrust his fingers deeper into my hole.

I swallowed more passion sounds and pressed my forehead against the counter. I'd never been so vocal before, but this time I couldn't help it. I'd never been so fucking turned on before either.

"Admit it, Katie," He leaned forward and whispered in my ear. "You're a horny little slut, aren't you?"

I didn't answer him. Not with words. But I spread my legs wider, arched my back, and let out a quiet whimper. The next groan that echoed through the room wasn't mine.

Joe shifted his weight and his hands left me. I heard metal jingle and clothes rustling. I heard the thud of his utility belt hitting the floor, then felt the hot hardness of his cock slide between my thighs and along my wet slit.

He wrapped one of his hands in my hair and pulled slightly, tilting my head so that I had to watch myself masturbating on the monitor six inches in front of my face.

"Look at you on there. A man would have to be a saint to turn down that invitation." The thick head of Joe's cock probed my entrance and with one forceful thrust he filled me up and I squealed in pleasure. "And I'm no saint."

The walls of my cunt clenched around his cock. "And I'm not an angel," I gasped. I turned my head and tried to look at him over my shoulder. "But I am your horny little slut."

His guttural groan filled the air and I knew my words had pleased him. "Mine, eh? To use any way I want?"

He gripped my hip tightly with one hand, holding me still for his pistoning hips. He was fucking me fast and hard, and I was on the edge. I could feel my orgasm gathering low in my belly.

His other hand shook free of my hair and traveled down my back and over my rump. I felt a fingertip probe surely at my exposed anus and a whimper escaped me. He pushed a bit and the finger breached my virgin hole, sending intense sensations radiating throughout my body and shattering the ball of lust in my belly.

It was sensory overload. The images of myself masturbating all around us, Joe's cock hitting deep inside me, my cunt spasming around him as he continued his forceful fucking. Another orgasm washed over me and I felt his cock swell, throbbing fiercely as hot jets of come flooded my insides.

A primitive groan reverberated off the walls seconds before Joe fell forward and rested his forehead between my shoulder blades, his cock still twitching inside me.

I remained still for a moment, then flexed my cuffed wrists, and stroked his belly with my fingertips. It was a small touch, but I couldn't stop myself. That small touch cemented my connection with him.

Joe pulled out of me and helped me straighten up again. My knees were so weak I stumbled against him and his arms surrounded me.

"My slut, huh?"

I turned in his arms, not caring that I was still handcuffed and come was dripping down my thighs. "Yours. To do with as you please, whenever you please."

A strong hand cupped my cheek, his thumb stroking my bottom lip before he kissed me, possessing my mouth completely and letting me know that he was in charge. When he pulled away again, my head was swimming with desire and it took me a minute to remember where we were.

He stepped behind me and undid the handcuffs. When they were off he looked me in the eye.

There was no doubt clouding his expression this time, and I smiled. A smile that turned triumphant when I heard his next words.

"Then go home, clean up, and wait for me. I expect to find you naked, and ready for a complete body search. Because I intend to discover all your secrets."

———————————

The back door of the casino slammed shut and footsteps crunched across the gravel parking lot, pulling me from my memory of the afternoon before.

"Yahooo! Free at last!" Julie's cry echoed through the air and a couple of birds took off from a nearby tree.

I climbed behind the wheel and started the car. "Do you need to hit the store first or should we go straight to your place?" I asked while she settled into the passenger seat.

"Home, James." She fastened her seat belt before fixing a steady gaze on me, "Spill! What happened with Joe . . . and start from the beginning."

Fighting a blush, I blurted out, "I masturbated for him on camera." A move I still couldn't believe I made. I mean, I know I'd been determined to get his attention, but was masturbating for him via the security cameras at work really the smart way to get it?

It might not have been the smartest way, but it had sure been the most effective way!

"What?" Julie gaped. Funny how I felt a tingle of pride at being able to shock her and a twinge of embarrassment at my actions at the same time.

"Yeah, at work, no less."

"You didn't!"

"I did." I pretended to concentrate on the road so I didn't have to meet her eyes. "The idea hit me when we were on our way to the vault with the deposit, and I went with it. The fact that he might record the whole thing never occurred to me."

"He taped it?"

"Uh-huh, and then he pulled me into the office and played the tape for me before telling me he was coming to my place after work."

I didn't bother to tell her that I'd been bent over the desk with my hands cuffed behind my back, and Joe buried deep inside me at the time. Or that it had been the most arousing, erotic, and passionate experience of my life, comparable only to the rest of the night spent with him.

"Did he show up?" Then she waved the question away. "Never mind, I can tell just by looking at you that he did. Well? Tell me more! Was it better than you thought? Was it wild? I bet *he* didn't treat you like too much of a lady to get down and dirty. That man was made to get busy."

I glanced over and saw her fanning herself dramatically. Seems I wasn't the only one who got hot just thinking about Joe.

"He showed, and he spent the night. But he was gone when I woke up, and I'm not sure how I feel about that."

"What's not to be sure about? You had a good time—you did have a good time, didn't you?" When I nodded, she continued on with a wicked grin. "If the *opportunity* arises to do it again . . . go for it. If not, what's the big deal? It's not like you're looking for a serious relationship."

She was right. I wanted to get out of this town. The last thing I needed was a relationship that might tie me down. Figuratively, or literally.

4

When we got to Julie's apartment Lillian was already home, the guacamole was made, and the ciders were cold. You'd think beer would be the drink of choice, but living in B.C., the land of fresh air, orchards, and roadside fruit stands, the ciders were the perfect drink. Plus, they had higher alcohol content.

Julie dashed into her bedroom to change out of her work clothes, while Lillian and I got settled at the kitchen table.

"How's life, Lillian?" I asked. "Anu's Kitchen keeping you busy?"

"Business is good. I need to hire some part-time help soon. I can make enough stock to keep up with the demand, but I can't make the stuff if I'm manning the booth at the mall."

Six months ago Lillian had moved to Chadwick from Toronto to open a kiosk booth in the mall. She sold herbal lotions, shampoos, oils, and soaps that she made herself, along with candles, crystals, and funky jewelry. Sort of a mini–New Age shop.

When she'd moved to town, she'd answered Julie's ad in the newspaper for a roommate. It was a good thing, too. I'd been contemplating giving up my own apartment and moving in with Julie myself so I could save money faster, even though both of us had known that if we wanted to stay friends we couldn't live together for very long.

So when Julie came out of the bedroom dressed in sweats and a tank top and shared what seemed like a private smile with Lillian, I told myself the twinge in my gut wasn't jealousy. After all, they were lovers, and lovers had secrets. Plus, why would I be jealous of someone who'd saved me from hating my best friend?

"Okay, girls. Get ready to hand over your money." Julie rubbed her hands together and gave an evil chuckle as she joined us at the table. We each had neat stacks of cash in front of us and our favorite munchies in bowls next to us. Mine held peanut M&M's. How anyone could resist peanut M&M's was beyond me.

"Everyone got fifty dollars? Tonight's game is Texas Hold'em." The command in Lil's naturally husky voice cut the small talk short and got the game started. We took turns calling whatever variation of poker we'd play, and I was pleased with Lil's choice. Texas Hold'em was a good game to win big, or lose big. I planned to win.

Once we each put our money in the jar, Lillian handed us our chips and we stacked them neatly in front of us. Then she dealt the pocket cards while I peeked at my oldest friend and my newest one. Silky black hair draped down Julie's back to her waist, her Native Indian ancestry clearly seen in her high cheekbones and dark eyes. She looked more like a tomboy than the town troublemaker of her reputation. Lillian had long chestnut curls and serene features that rarely showed the wicked thoughts she shared only with us. And me, well, I was the token blonde.

To look at us, we were all completely different, and in reality, we *were* completely different. Julie was adventurous, Lillian was mystical, and I was quiet and reserved. But when you put us together in a room, we balanced out, and helped to bring out the best, and sometimes the worst, in each other.

Our poker nights were a good example of this.

They'd started out as a fun way to relax and have a few drinks together without feeding the town gossip mill. At first none of us had known the rules and we'd had to keep a cheat sheet on hand. But after almost six months of the bi-weekly get-togethers we knew a couple of ways to take each other's money. Our competitive natures had made us serious about it, too.

I sat back in the cheap vinyl chair and surveyed my cards. The queen of hearts and jack of spades. Not bad, not great, a possible straight if I was lucky.

"Five dollar buy in." Julie grinned and tossed a fiver in the center of the table. I saw her bet, so did Lillian and the flop was dealt.

A jack of hearts, eight of spades, and three of diamonds.

Julie threw another two dollars in the center of the table. Ignoring the evil eye she sent my way, I saw her bet and raised it five more. I had a pair of jacks. That was worth starting off strong.

Lillian laid her cards facedown. "I've got nothing. I fold."

Julie met the bet and raised it another two dollars, avoiding my gaze as she did it.

I watched Julie's face closely for a minute. "I think you're bluffing, Jules. I see you, and raise five more."

Her cheeks flushed just a bit. Lillian dealt the next card, the ace of hearts. Looking me straight in the eye Julie raised the bet with another five-dollar bill. "Guess what Katie did at work yesterday, Lil?"

"What?"

"She masturbated for Bad Boy Joe on the security camera."

"You're kidding!" Lillian laughed and grinned at me with pride. "Good for you, girl. Take charge and get what you want! You did get what you wanted, didn't you?"

I knew Julie was trying to get me flustered by bringing that up, and it worked. Thoughts of getting what I wanted from Joe made my blood heat and all the tiny aches and pains from a night of nonstop fucking come alive.

"Yeah, I got what I wanted." I shrugged, not wanting anyone to get a hint of just how much I'd gotten from Joe.

Julie was the adventurous one of our group, but when she smirked at me, I couldn't help but call her bluff. After all, there was more to poker than the cards.

"All in," I said, pushing my stacks in the center of the table. Geez, what had gotten into me? Betting everything in the first hand of the game was not the smart, safe way to play, even if I did have a pair of jacks.

I took a sip of cider, munched on an M&M's, and met Julie's gaze head on.

"Take it," she said, tossing her cards down.

"Whoo hooo!" I crowed and reached for the pot. This was going to be a good night.

"What did you have?"

I shook my head. "Like I'm going to tell you? That would defeat the purpose of the game, wouldn't it?"

Julie growled, then looked to Lillian for support.

"Your deal." Lillian finished gathering all the cards and passed them to Julie. "And she's right. If you wanted to see her cards, you should've bet."

"Fine," she said. She shuffled the cards and started the next round. "Did you find out why he was in Chadwick?"

There was a lot of speculation around the casino as to why Joe was there and where he came from. When asked directly, he said he was from Vancouver, and that was that. Of course, lack of a real answer made people think there was more to the story. That maybe it was none of their business never occurred to them.

I shrugged and looked at my cards. "We didn't talk much."

"Jimmy thinks he's a burnt-out ex-cop." Jimmy was the daytime bartender Julie worked with sometimes.

"Could be."

"Renee thinks he's ex-military."

"That could be true, too."

Julie reached over and snagged a handful of M&M's from my bowl. "She's having fantasies of a Navy SEAL team coming to visit him and having a gang bang with her."

We all laughed at that. I didn't say anything, but the scars on Joe's body came to mind. I didn't know why he'd come to Chadwick, and I wasn't sure I even cared. There was obviously something more to him than just being your run-of-the-mill security guard, but whatever it was, it was his business.

I'd wanted him. I'd made a move. We'd had a good time.

That was it. It was over. We hadn't shared secrets or even your basic pillow talk really. It was time to concentrate on real life. And to play cards.

The next hand wasn't so good for me, but I won with a king for a high card. Lillian had folded again and Julie only had a jack high card. If the river card had been a ten, she would've won with a full house, but luck was on my side. It was then that I realized just how much I enjoyed the risk-taking.

"Julie, do you know a card player named Brandon? He was there on the weekend."

She shook her head, a small furrow between her brows.

"I think he won pretty big." I shuffled and dealt as she thought about it. "Big good-looking guy? Blond hair, perfect smile, drank rye and ginger?"

"Okay, yeah, him."

"What about him?"

I folded before I dealt the flop for Lil and Jules. "He was telling me about a regular card game he hosts for friends once in a while in Hemlock. Some of the players come up from Chewelah and a couple from Kelowna. He rents a room at the Hartman Hotel, and they play all night."

"And?" She looked at me and waited for the rest.

"When I mentioned I played a little poker, he asked me if I wanted to try and get in on a game."

"Why would they go to Hemlock Lake to play cards? It's not much bigger than Chadwick." Lillian quirked a delicate eyebrow.

"I don't know. I don't plan on finding out either. But it was sort of flattering to be invited to join."

She rolled her eyes at me. "He's never played cards with you, Katie. So basically he invited you because you're pretty, not because you can play cards."

Pain snapped through me when I bit the inside of my cheek to keep quiet. "So what? That could work to my advantage."

Julie's head snapped up at that. "Does that mean you're thinking about it?"

I shrugged and changed the subject.

———————

It was just before midnight when I left Julie's apartment. The three ciders I'd drunk had helped ease the tension from spending the morning with my mother, but not so much that I worried I shouldn't drive. Three ciders in five and a half hours weren't enough to impair my judgment. For whatever reason, God had blessed me with the ability to drink like a fish and remain in control. Proof of that was the wad of cash I dumped on the passenger seat as soon as I was seated in my car.

I straightened all the crumpled bills out and added them up. I'd cleaned house.

Just over two hundred dollars now resided in my purse. It was really getting too easy to take the girls' money from them. After winning the Texas Hold'em, Lillian had been the one to suggest a couple hands of five-card draw, not me. I almost felt guilty, but reminded myself that playing for cash had been their idea to start with, and if they couldn't be bothered to study the game like I had, it wasn't my fault.

Turning the engine of the car over, I started for home. I was so tired, all I wanted to do was curl up in bed and sleep forever. The day with my mother hadn't been all bad, and the night with the girls had been fun. It was nice to be around people I knew cared for me, but at the same time, the more time I spent with all of them, the more alone I felt.

Like Brad, they wanted such different things from life than I did. They were happy here in this place where almost everyone knew not only their name, but also what their favorite food was, and what day they did laundry on. I wasn't. I hated that everyone knew the details of my life, yet none of them seemed to know *me*.

Unrolling the window and turning off the car radio, I let the wind whip my ponytail around while I enjoyed the peaceful drive and lack of traffic.

I pulled into the parking lot of my apartment complex and shut off the car. Tilting my head back, I closed my eyes and reveled in the utter silence of the mountain night. After a minute of silence the crickets started chirping and the wind blew, rustling the branches of nearby trees. Somehow, I summoned the energy to roll up the window and climb out of the car.

When I strolled towards the apartment building, I noticed a figure move in the shadows next to the entrance, and my heart stuttered. Then the shadow stepped into the light and my nipples puckered, heat pooling between my thighs.

It was Joe.

5

Looking at him, I became aware of the fact that I'd never seen him in anything but his uniform before. Well, that or completely naked. In that moment, I realized that it didn't matter what he did or didn't have on, even without the big nightstick and handcuffs on his hip, he was devastatingly sexy.

My eyes roamed over his six-foot frame, and I licked my suddenly parched lips. A scuffed leather jacket hung open to show a plain black T-shirt stretched lovingly across his delicious muscles. Tight, faded jeans rode low on his hips cupping an impressive package and molding to powerful thighs. Tightening my grip on my keys, I strolled forward and tried to ignore my body's instant response to his presence.

"Hi there," I greeted him softly, stopping directly in front of him. "Are you waiting for me?"

A silky black eyebrow lifted and his lips tilted slightly. "I don't know anyone else who lives here."

My cheeks heated, and I turned to enter the building so he wouldn't see me blush. Why the hell I was suddenly feeling so shy I didn't know. It wasn't as if he hadn't seen me blush all over already.

He followed me into the building, neither of us speaking as we went up the stairs to the third floor. When I reached to unlock my apartment door my hand was shaking so much I fumbled it. On the third try the key finally slid into the lock.

The door swung open and I strode into my small apartment on shaky legs. It was as if a switch had been flipped the minute I was within five feet of Joe. The fatigue I'd felt minutes earlier disappeared, and my body was vibrating from the inside out, awake and ready for action.

"Where were you?" he asked, voice careful and controlled as he took off his jacket and tossed it on a nearby chair.

"Why is it your business?" My voice was flirty and I gave him a small smile when I replied.

He stopped his visual inventory of the room and focused on me. "You told me yesterday you were *my* slut. If you're out fucking around with someone else, I'm going to punish you."

The stiffness I felt from last night disappeared, and every nerve ending came alive, throbbing and pleading for attention.

"Punish me?" I raised an eyebrow at him, trying not to let him see just how much his words affected me. I know I'd sorta committed myself to him sexually, but really; there was no "relationship" here. Was there? "I don't think so."

"Where were you?" He stepped closer. So close his breath floated across my cheek and my nipples rubbed against his chest when I sucked in a deep breath.

"I was at Julie's." The words were out of my mouth before I could bite them back. "You going to punish me for that?"

"Last chance to back out, angel." He trailed a finger gently down my cheek, lingering near the corner of my mouth. "I want you as mine. You said you were mine. I don't take this lightly and I don't want you to either. That means punishment, as well as rewards. What I say goes. Are you sure you can handle it? That you can handle me?"

My tongue darted out and sampled the flavor of his skin before I spoke, confident and sure. "I've been wanting to handle you for a long time, Joe."

His closeness was driving me crazy, and I gave into the urge to touch him. Lifting my hands I started at his shoulders, then down over his pecs, circling his flat nipples through his T-shirt until they hardened. His hands grabbed my hips and pulled me tight against him. His erection burned a hole through our clothes and my pussy clenched in excitement. I lifted my gaze, looked into his eyes.

He was struggling with something, some inner demon. He wanted me; I knew it the same way I knew I'd do anything to please him. Instinctively. But he was fighting it. He was fighting himself, and he was fighting me.

My knees went weak and my heart kicked in my chest. I couldn't let him get away, so I threw down the gauntlet. "I'm not backing out. Are you?"

The flames leapt to life in the depths of his eyes, and he lowered his head, claiming my mouth with a hungry kiss. His tongue thrust between my lips and took possession as my hands crept up over his shoulders and around his neck, gripping him tight.

My heartbeat raced and a tidal wave of lust swept over me. My hips gyrated against his, one of my legs lifted to wrap around him and pull him closer so his denim-covered erection rubbed against my cleft. A whimper escaped and echoed through the silent room.

One of his hands skimmed over my back and neck and gripped my ponytail. He gave it a tug and pulled my head back sharply, exposing my neck to his hunger.

Sharp teeth nipped my sensitive skin, a large hand covered my breast, cupping and squeezing it through my shirt. A moan bubbled up out of my mouth as I panted, trying desperately to regain some sense of control.

"Joe, wait."

He released my hair and my breast only to whip my shirt over my head and duck his head to suck a rigid nipple into his mouth. His strong arms wrapped around my waist and he bent me back, his mouth going from one breast to the other, sucking, nibbling and even biting not so gently on the hard nubs until I was gasping and trembling in his arms.

"Joe, please," I cried, overwhelmed by the extreme flood of emotions. "Wait."

He straightened up and let me go. One hand settled on top of my head and pushed down, taking me to my knees as he unbuttoned his jeans. "You agreed I could use you any way I wanted. If you're not ready for me, I'll use your mouth."

He pulled his jeans open and shoved them down past his hips. His cock sprang free, hard and full, directly in front of me. His hand gently cupped under my jaw, he pulled me forward until my lips touched the swollen head. I pulled his hand away from my jaw and eagerly opened my mouth. I breathed deeply, and inhaled the musky scent of him before I stuck out my tongue and licked slowly up the underside of his cock. When I reached the top I wrapped my lips around the head and swirled my tongue around it. Sucking gently,

I slid my mouth down again, enjoying the saltiness of his pre-come and the sound of his throaty groan.

With deliberate slowness I took him deeper. When he hit the back of my throat I relaxed my muscles and moved in another inch, swallowing him completely for a brief second before pulling back.

The taste of him, the feel of his hot and hard maleness in my mouth, made all rational thought disappear. I was overcome by the pure joy of being able to please him and make him groan. I ran my hands over his thighs and behind him to cup his ass cheeks as I started a slow and steady rhythm. Taking him in and pulling back while sucking gently.

His fingers skimmed across my head and I felt him pull the elastic from my hair. When it was loose he wrapped his hands in it and cupped my head. Light pressure from him had me speeding up my rhythm, my tongue pressing firmly against the throbbing underside of his cock with each stroke.

His ass flexed under my hands and his hips jerked forward, thrusting him deeper and making me strain to keep my jaw and throat relaxed. The muscles of his thighs trembled beneath my hands and the sound of his sighs and groans went straight to my pussy. I squirmed a little and reached between my own legs. Shoving my thong aside, I thrust two fingers into my hungry sex.

"That's it, slut," he encouraged. "Play with yourself for me. Sucking my cock really turns you on, doesn't it?"

I hummed my response to him and felt another shudder rip through him. Liking the power of that, I moaned around his cock, and heard him groan. A hand cupped my jaw once again, this time more firmly, and the other held my head still as his hips began to pump faster.

"I can feel my cock in your mouth, feel your tongue working me over." His hand tapped me lightly under the chin. "It feels so good, to use my little slut like this. You like it, too, don't you?"

He was completely in control now, fucking my mouth swift and steady. I fought for breath as he hit the back of my throat repeatedly. Saliva and pre-come spilled out of my mouth and dribbled down my chin, my eyes tearing up at the rough use.

A whimper worked its way up my throat and echoed in the room, surprising me because it was one of pleasure, not pain. I frigged my clit faster, an orgasm just beyond my reach. My other hand reached between his thighs to cup his balls briefly before burrowing in further, and pressing firmly against the tight skin behind them.

"Ahhh . . ." With a guttural cry, he pulled back and shot his load all over my naked chest.

I watched in awe, fingers frozen within my cunt, while he threw back his head and stroked his cock, squeezing the last drops out. When his strokes slowed I couldn't stop myself from leaning forward and gently licking him clean.

Firm hands gripped my shoulders and he lifted me to my feet again. Placing a gentle finger under my chin, he lifted my head until our gazes met.

"This is just the beginning, angel. You said you were mine, and I'm holding you to it." He placed a loving kiss on my lips and stepped back to button his jeans. When he reached for his leather jacket I came out of my lustful trance with a bang.

"Where are you going?"

"Home."

He headed for the door and my jaw dropped. What the hell? I was standing in the middle of my living room floor, naked from the waist up with come cooling on my tits and my pussy clenching hungrily.

"That's it? What about me?"

"You made me worry and wait tonight; now it's your turn to wait." He stopped at the door and turned to smile at me. "And I'm not giving you permission to make yourself come tonight. From now on, you come only with my permission."

And he was gone.

Bastard!

I stomped into my bedroom and searched through my panty drawer. When my fingertips landed on the smooth surface of my favorite toy I pulled it out and slammed the drawer shut. The super-powerful little silver egg was attached to a remote with five speeds, and five settings. It was the Häagen-Dazs of sex toys. I've been able to achieve body-racking orgasms in less than three minutes with that baby.

Tell me I wasn't allowed to come until he said. Right. I came when I wanted, not when he wanted. Sure, I was willing to submit to him when he was there, but to leave me in a state was just plain mean.

I stripped off my clothes and crawled between the sheets. Flat on my back I thumbed the button on the remote and the egg hummed to life. Spreading my thighs I set the little toy between them so that the egg lay against my clit, and closed my legs. I set the remote on pulse and let the hum work on me while I ran my hands over my body.

Fingertips scraped across my neck, my breasts, my nipples. I closed my eyes and saw a naked Joe Carson in front of me, large hand wrapped firmly around his cock, stroking himself, just for me. The knot of arousal returned to my belly again, my hips moved, thrusting against the toy.

My legs parted, my knees bent, and I reached down with one hand to hold the toy against my clit. In my mind Joe got on the bed and knelt between my spread thighs. I watched him jerk off while he watched me tease myself. My thumb bumped the speed of the pulsing up a notch and a low moan eased from my throat. I envisioned Joe shifting closer still. His hands gripped my hips and pulled my hips up on his thighs, so the head of his cock brushed against my slick opening while he stroked himself. My hips jerked and the vibrations stopped.

Nothing.

Without opening my eyes or losing the fantasy, I reached for the control and turned the toy on again. A strong pleasant thrum beat against my clit. I moaned and the toy stopped.

Damn it! The batteries were dying. "Please. Not now. Please," I prayed.

I shook the toy, hit the on button and felt it jump against my juicy clit. The minute I took my finger off the button it died. Then it wouldn't even start! Tears of frustration started to fill my eyes.

I threw the toy on the floor and dipped my fingers between my thighs, going straight to my swollen clit. The image of Joe in my fantasy morphed from a daring and eager lover to a dominant, erotic, commanding master that dared me to come when he'd said I was not to.

Rebellion surged through me and I frigged myself faster. The knot in my belly tightened and I teetered on the verge of orgasm, but nothing could set me off. I slid a finger into my entrance and pressed the palm of my hand against my clit. My other hand pinched and pulled at my sensitive nipples, but nothing worked.

"Damn you!" I smacked my fists against the mattress and cursed the mental image of a satisfied Joe.

As much as I didn't want to obey him, my body did.

6

"Arghhhh!"

I threw myself back in my office chair, hands covering my face while I shouted out my frustrations. I'd been cheated out of a monster orgasm the night before, and it was making me grumpy as hell.

"Is it safe to come in?"

My hands dropped to my side, and I turned my head. Sara, one of the night-shift supervisors, peeked around the corner of the door into the cash cage, suppressed laughter clear in her expression.

"Come on in." I waved her in and straightened up again. Her appearance was a good thing. It meant my shift was almost over. After a completely shit day, I was ready to go home.

"Problems?" she asked.

"I can't get the freakin' safe to balance!"

"How much are you out by?"

"Three hundred."

Sara snorted. "Katie, I know you're Ms. Perfect and everything, but that's not that bad. Leave it alone and the bank will figure out where it is."

"I'm far from perfect, Sara." I tried to bite my tongue, but a bit of snark slipped into my reply. "But it *is* our job to balance the money. I like to know I earned my paycheck. Besides that, I know that we're allowed a bit of leeway, but it was only out fifty bucks when I came on shift, so I know the money is here somewhere."

The bank is a small room in the basement of the casino where the big money is kept. The women that work down there double-check our deposits, chits, balance sheets, and take care of all the money that goes in and out of the place. I had a good relationship with them because on my shift, the cash cage vault almost always balanced within fifty dollars.

They didn't panic unless it was off by a couple hundred. Then the ladies went looking for who screwed up. It had only been me once, and I didn't plan on being the person who screwed up again.

"Okay, let me grab a fresh cup of coffee, then we can give this another shot. I'm probably just not seeing something."

Sara leaned back in her chair, clipboard on her lap. "Go for it. I'll wait for you."

I made a quick run to the lounge and grabbed a new cup of coffee. I hadn't gotten much sleep the night before. I'd tossed and turned only to have such erotic dreams when I did finally fall asleep that I woke up with my pillow clenched between my legs and the feeling that I'd just missed out on a fantastic orgasm. When I got back to the office Sara was right where I'd left her. I stepped over to the small vault and starting calling out what was inside for her. When I was done with the coin, I called the cash, and balance sheet totals out as well.

And I still came up three hundred bucks short.

"Think, Katie. Think."

"Does talking to yourself really help?"

Heat crawled up my neck, and I threw an embarrassed glance at Sara.

"Quarters. It's got to be the quarters."

"Huh?"

"It was short by fifty bucks when I came on shift, it's off three hundred now. A bag of quarters is worth two fifty. It's got to be the quarters."

I went over to the vault and started pulling out the bags of coin. "Aha!"

There, buried in the back, under the bottom shelf was the missing bag. I showed it to Sara, we changed the count on the sheet, and both signed off on the paperwork.

Sara giggled and gave me a playful push towards the office door. "I guess talking to yourself really does help, doesn't it?"

"Ha, ha," I said. "What helps is a determination to get the job done so I can get out of here and have a drink! Have a good night."

I waved to the cashiers on duty and headed for the parking lot. Julie was working in the lounge, but I didn't stop to talk. I did want a drink, but I wasn't eager for company or small talk.

No one stopped me on my way out, and I was unlocking my car when a distinctive shiny black Dodge Charger eased into the lot. I knew that car, and I knew who drove it.

My heart pounded, my nipples stiffened, and saliva started to pool in my mouth. To distract myself, I reminded myself I was still pissed at him for his desertion the night before. I settled into my car, started it up, and to give off a calm cool image, fiddled with the radio while Joe parked next to me.

Out of the corner of my eye I saw him climb out of his car and I casually tossed my hair back, glancing over at him. Our gazes locked and he gave a brief nod. It looked like he was going to walk away from me and I felt my face tighten and my eyes narrow. But when he took his next step it was toward me. He bent down and leaned on the open window of my car door.

"How was your day, Katie?"

"It could've been better."

He cocked his head to the side and took off his sunglasses. There was real interest in his intense gaze and my frustration started to melt away. "How so?"

I took a deep breath. It was easy to pretend with most people. I could pretend to be happy when I wasn't, I could pretend to be the good girl when really all I wanted to do was tell everyone to fuck off and leave me alone. But with Joe, when his attention was focused on me, pretending never even entered my mind.

"I had a shit day. The cashiers were in and out of the office all day, we had an upset customer who said he'd been ripped off when he cashed in his coins, the vault wouldn't balance, and I'm not sure how I feel about last night."

"Was the customer right?"

"Huh?"

"Was the customer right? Did one of the girls shortchange him?"

Obviously the security guard in him came before everything else. "No. We pulled the till and it balanced. I think he was just trying to scam us. But then the vault wouldn't balance. It was weird."

"How much is the vault short?"

"It's not short now. I found a missing bag of quarters, so it's all good. But it was a weird day."

He nodded and reached a hand into the car. He cupped the back of my neck and stroked a thumb over the sensitive skin beneath my ear. "And you didn't like last night?"

Warmth crept up my neck and I looked at my clasped hands in my lap. Should I tell him I'd tried to get off after he left? How was I supposed to explain how I felt when I didn't even know?

"I wouldn't say I didn't like it," I said softly. "I just didn't like you leaving like that."

UGH! How whiny did that sound?

"I'll remember that next time." He tugged my head closer and pressed his lips to mine. When his tongue probed, I let him in with a sigh. His flavor filled me and I reached up to pull him tighter to me, only to have him pull away. He looked at me, eyes shuttered for a second, before pressing a fast and hard kiss to my lips again and walking away.

I fought the urge to bang my head on the steering wheel and tried to focus on the fact that there were cold ciders in my fridge at home. The frustration left over from last night's session with Joe was at least partly to blame for the crappy day I'd had. And while I felt slightly better about it now, I still wasn't sure what exactly was going on between us.

Pushing Joe to the back of my thought, I cemented the image in my mind of a cold frosty drink on my deck, and turned the car toward home. I'd made it all the way to the stairwell of my apartment building before I got waylaid.

"Katie, I've been wanting to talk to you for days now, but you're such a busy girl."

Mrs. Beets's door swung open just as I hit the last flight of steps to the third floor. What? Had the woman been watching at the window for me? My God, I knew she was nosy, but really, if I'd wanted to answer to anyone I'd still be living with my mom.

Yeah, right. I never had to answer to my mom. I was the more adult out of the two of us, which is why I really didn't want to live with her.

"Mrs. Beets, what can I do for you?"

I injected as much sugar into my tone as I could manage.

"I'm going to visit my son and his wife this weekend, I was hoping you'd look after Pepper for me."

Pepper was Mrs. Beets's cat. I hated cats. Dogs I loved, but cats were beyond me. But I couldn't bring myself to say no.

"Sure, I can do that. Just drop your key off for me, and I'll check on her every afternoon."

"Oh no, dear. That won't do."

I was two steps up when her words registered. Turning on the step I tried not to look impatient.

"Excuse me?"

"Pepper is a sensitive cat. I can't leave her in the apartment alone for more than a few hours. I'll just bring her and her goodies up to your place and that'll make everything all right. I'd ask you to stay in my apartment, but I don't want to inconvenience you. Cats really aren't that good with change, but I've been walking Pepper in the hallway of your floor so she should be fine."

I bit my lip to keep my jaw from hitting the floor.

"You're such a good girl, Katie. I knew I could count on you." Before I could utter a protest Mrs. Beets backed into her apartment and closed the door.

"Don't want to inconvenience me? Yeah, having the cat and all its paraphernalia in my own apartment will be so much more convenient that just giving me your keys." The muttered dialogue continued for my ears only as I stomped up the stairs. Dropping my purse on the floor of my apartment, I headed straight to the fridge and pulled out a chilled green bottle.

I twisted off the top and was taking a long pull of the cold crisp pear cider when the phone rang. Tension snapped back into my shoulders and I groaned. I knew that ring. Don't ask me how, but I knew my mother was on the other end of the phone.

Ignoring the shrill summons, I headed for my bedroom and stripped off my work clothes. I'd just grabbed my bikini bottom from the dresser drawer when my mom's voice echoed through the apartment.

"Katie, dear. Aren't you home from work yet? I don't know why you insist on working at that horrid place. The hours are just terrible. Audra is hiring, you know. You'd have a better chance of meeting a nice young man working at the library than that . . . place. Anyway, I was calling because there's a movie on tomorrow night that I'd like to see. But tomorrow is Thursday, and Thursday is bowling night. You know I can't miss my bowling, so I'd like you to come over and set the machine for me so it will tape the movie. Thanks, sweetheart!"

Click.

"Jesus! Can I not have any peace?" And where did my patience go? I never really relished the good girl image I'd somehow gotten, but I wasn't so sure I liked the bitchy side of myself that was becoming harder and harder to suppress.

I pulled on my bikini bottoms and went straight for the patio. Stretched out on a blanket and pillow from the sofa, I basked in the late afternoon sun. My mind was whirling with people asking me to do favors, the funky money stuff at work, and the puzzle that was my relationship with Joe.

Even though I'd never met one before, there was no doubt in my mind that Joe was a *dom*. I thought about the erotica novels I'd read, and how my fantasies had gotten darker since Joe came to town. I thought about all the single men in town that had asked me out since I broke up with Brad, and how none had appealed to me. Even Brad hadn't really appealed to me when we were together. It had been more a do-what's-expected of me thing than a do-what-I-enjoyed thing.

Joe had taken complete charge as soon as I made it clear to him that I wanted him, and I'd loved it. I'd even loved it when he'd had his hands tangled in my hair and his cock was hitting the back of my throat so hard and fast tears had come to my eyes. He'd taken all control and responsibility away from me, and it had been thrilling. Even though I never got to come, I did feel a sense of pride when I remembered the way his knees had quaked when he did. I'd given up part of myself, and I was pretty sure he had, too.

The sun's rays started to seep through my skin, into my muscles, and my body started to loosen up. After relaxing in the sun for a bit, my thought process slowed and expanded.

It was clear to me that Joe wanted me. But it was equally clear he didn't really *want* to want me. Maybe it was because we worked together, or maybe it was my perceived innocence. No, it couldn't be that. Joe had looked into my eyes and seen my soul. I think I got a peek at his, too, before the walls dropped back into place, and I figured the fact that my body was more innocent than my mind was a turn-on for him.

The more I thought about it, the more I figured his emotional distance was a protective thing. It gave me a bit of comfort that he might feel just a bit out of control, when I felt so completely undone by him. I didn't know what it was that was holding him back. All I knew for sure was that despite his callous treatment the night before, I'd seen some tenderness in him at times. I'd heard it in his voice, if not his words, and I'd felt it in his touch. Deep down I trusted that he would never hurt me, or use me in any way, if I seriously said no.

Even if the head games with Joe weren't so much fun, the sex games were enough to make up for it. I just needed to have a bit of fun in my life while I worked towards getting out of town.

Pushing Joe and everything else to the back of my mind, I concentrated on breathing evenly. Soon, I was drifting on a mental cloud.

The sun was warm and my steps were light and carefree. It was early evening in my mind and things hadn't really started to get going, but there were plenty of people around. I was in the city. People were passing alongside me in each direction, some sat at little metal tables in front of coffee shops. There were a couple of buskers playing some music, guitar cases in front of them to collect tips. No one gave me a second look, no one asked me how I was or what I was doing, where I was off to, or how my mom was. I was just one of a crowd.

It was complete anonymity, and I loved it.

Just then I spotted a man coming toward me. Tall, well-built, with a particularly sensual stride. My body started to stir, arousal unfurling in my belly. I smiled and gazed into his intense blue eyes and—

What the hell?

I jerked up straight, swinging my head around trying to get oriented. Another strident ring broke the silence, and with a slap on the forehead I lay back down.

It was a dream. I wanted so bad to get out of this town, to go someplace where nobody knew my name that I'd dreamt of the anonymous streets of Vancouver. Only this time, Joe was there, too.

My answering machine kicked in and I reached for my cider, waiting to see what was next.

"What's this I hear about you and a new boyfriend? A security guard at that place you work at?" my mom asked. "Roberta called me to say he was at your place for a long time the other night. If you don't have plans on Saturday night, why don't you bring him over for dinner? Please call me back and let me know if you can make dinner."

I slumped back on the deck and threw my arm over my eyes. How did my life get so suddenly complex?

All I'd wanted was a little action with a hot guy, but I should've known when he spent the night that word would get around. There were no secrets in a small town.

How Joe managed to impact my longtime dream of getting out of this town so easily, I had no idea. Sure I'd fantasized about him before, the same way I dreamt of getting out of town. The fact that the two dreams were blending now wasn't a good sign.

I thought of my mom, and the way she set everything and anything aside, including me, when a new man came into her life, and a frisson of fear shot through me. If I wasn't careful, it wouldn't be long before I gave up on my own dreams to stay here with him.

It was past time to stop pussyfooting around.

The next phone call I made was to Brandon. I needed to bank some more money fast and he could help me do it.

7

I'd taped my mother's TV show for her and dropped it off on Saturday afternoon after work. Listening to her lecturing me for fifteen minutes on the fact that men and women can't be "just friends," I was tempted to tell her she was right, Joe wasn't a friend, he was a fuck. The reason he was at my place was because he was unclogging a pipe. *My* pipe!

My patience was at an all-time low point, so I used baby-sitting Pepper as an excuse not to stay for supper.

Before I could get home, my cell phone rang. Lillian's car was in the shop. Could I take Julie grocery shopping?

I swung by Julie's apartment, figuring I could whine to her about my mom while we shopped. But then Lillian jumped in the car, too, and I couldn't help but feel a bit . . . displaced. The two of them laughed and talked about what they needed, planning their meals for the week like any couple would, and I had to swallow my jealousy. I'd wanted to live alone. I wanted to be able to take off and go when my bank account hit the right number. I had no right to feel jealous and territorial over Julie just because we'd been best friends from grade school.

But I did.

By the time I dropped them off, I was more than ready to escape from my everyday responsibilities. I unlocked and pushed open my apartment door and stepped inside. My foot hit something soft. A screech filled the room and my heart dropped to my stomach. I stumbled, barely avoiding a face plant on the carpet.

"Pepper?"

I set my own grocery bag and a case of pear ciders on the kitchen table and looked around the small apartment. A few feet away, in the middle of the living room, sat a big fluffy orange tabby with a hurt look on its face.

"Are you OK, baby?" I walked over to make sure she wasn't hurt by the near-miss. A quick scratch behind her ears had her purring and I was reassured. I may not be a fan of cats, but I wasn't completely heartless.

After I changed out of my work clothes and into some comfy yoga pants I tripped over Pepper *again*.

"I'm sorry, baby," I crooned to the glowering feline. "I'm just not used to someone being at my feet all the time."

By the time I put the groceries away and made a turkey sandwich, I was fed up with the cat. When I tripped over her on the way to the couch with my sandwich, her injured screech filled the room once more, and I snapped. "For pity's sake Pepper! When my feet are moving, get out of the way!"

I sat down, opened my newest paperback, and munched my dinner. Curled up on the couch, engrossed in the adventures of the undead vampire queen with a shoe addiction, I forgot about the world around me. Until an orange ball of fur jumped over me to the back of the sofa, then dashed away, scaring the crap out of me. I watched as Pepper ran from one end of the room to the other like a demented patient in a rubber room. Her claws ripped into the carpet before she'd take off and land on the sofa or the chair. I yelled at her when she jumped on the curtains and laughed at her when she went skittering across the coffee table. After ten minutes of the madness her energy was gone and she jumped on my lap, curled into a ball, and started purring.

We stayed that way until just before dawn. I finished my novel and took strange comfort from the warm living thing in my lap.

"Life would be so much better if only someone would open a real coffee shop in this town."

It was Sunday morning and three days had gone by with no further contact from Joe. Pepper had shot me a gloating look from the foot of my bed as I got ready for work that morning. My eyes were full of morning grit and my mind was a tad lethargic as I drove past the Main Street Diner. It was the only place open for coffee at 8 A.M. on a Sunday morning, besides 7-Eleven, but their coffee was more like mud than anything.

Some people are just not morning people, no matter what. I'm one of them. After two months of day shifts only, I still couldn't make my brain wake up early enough to make coffee or eat breakfast before running out the door.

I pulled into the casino parking lot, saw the distinctive black muscle car parked by the staff entrance, and my body started to wake up, fast. In that moment, I was thankful that I was in the habit of picking out my outfits for work before I went to bed, and that I'd perfected the art of putting on makeup with my eyes closed.

OK, they weren't *closed*, but they certainly weren't wide open.

My armor today was a straight black skirt that looked almost businesslike, if a bit short, and the button-down white pinstripe blouse gave me a crisp professional look. I'd pinned my hair up with a clip and had even-toned neutral makeup on. I was a woman in charge and I was not going to let some security guard make me feel like anything other than that.

I strolled through the empty casino, straight for the lounge. The place didn't open until eleven, but I knew Jimmy the day bartender would be there, stocking and getting the bar ready for business. And he'd have the coffee on by now. A nice steaming pot of the gourmet coffee he stocked for personal use.

"Hey, Jimmy. How are you today?"

He had to be in his late forties, and he'd been working at Black's for ten years. He used to live in Vancouver and work on the movie sets. It gave him a lot of stories to tell anyone who took the time to listen.

He lifted his head from the lemons he was slicing. "Hey, Katie. Doing good, and you?"

"Good," I replied while pouring a cup of coffee. "What's today's affirmation?"

"Success doesn't come to you . . . you go to it." He pulled a carton of French Vanilla creamer from the cooler to set on the bar for me and winked at me. "Go after what you want, girl. Whatever it is."

My body might've stirred awake at the sight of Joe's car, but my mind had waited until then to kick into gear. Jimmy was right, as usual. Nobody was going to look after me and my interests, but me.

Cradling the steaming mug in one hand, I threw my shoulders back and strode towards the cash office.

For security reasons the casino insisted a security guard be there when the small vault was opened, and the cash was counted every morning. It wasn't necessary the rest of the day because there was always more than one person in the cage. But now that some caffeine was hitting my veins, it occurred to me that Joe might be my morning escort.

Every step of the way, my blood heated a degree in anticipation.

It was that damn one night of full-on, down and dirty sex. It had flicked a switch inside me that turned on my libido, and all I wanted was *more*. My body didn't seem to care that he'd got it all revved the next night and then walked away. It was just getting frustrated as hell that there hadn't been any action since.

Enjoying the flutter in my stomach I turned the corner . . . and saw Tom leaning against the dummy door to the cage.

Well, shit.

The deflated feeling in my chest was relief, not disappointment. Honest.

I greeted Tom and unlocked the first door, then waited while he keyed in his code to unlatch the inside door. There was no lock on that one. You needed a numbered code, or you had to be buzzed in by someone already inside the cash cage.

Once through the second door, we passed the four windows where the cashiers sit to change in people's winnings and over to the third door. This one I had a key for.

Inside the office Tom dropped into the seat next to the door, and I strolled over to the desk, slid my purse beneath it, and checked the logbook to see if Sara had left me any notes. All this was done in the comfortable silence born of routine.

"May I?"

I glanced at Tom and saw him wave at the CD player on the filing cabinet. "Go for it."

The music wasn't allowed to be played when we were open because we needed to be able to hear what going on with the cashiers and on the security radio. It was there for mornings like this. Only Tom knew that on some mornings, like when I was hungover, music was not a good thing. The sound of Aerosmith filled the room, and I opened the safe to start counting.

The morning passed uneventfully, an average Sunday. Just before noon, I checked on the two cashiers, made sure they had enough cash in their drawers, and headed to the lounge area for lunch. Julie started her shift at one every Sunday, and we had a standing lunch date.

"You're looking a little rough," I commented when I joined her at a small table. We were seated to the side of the lounge, away from the slots and the Keno screen.

She gave me a pissy look. "Just tired. I haven't had my coffee yet."

I glanced around the deserted lounge. "Who's working?"

"Renee."

Enough said.

Renee had been a pain in the ass ever since we first met her. That was in the fourth grade. She'd moved to Chadwick from somewhere in Saskatchewan and had done nothing but whine her first months here about the way the town was built on the side of a mountain.

If that wasn't enough, in fifth grade she'd made the mistake of calling Julie a dirty Indian in front of me. Normally, I had no problem with my temper. Until then. I hadn't even known that I *had* a temper. But when my fist connected with her face before anyone, including me, knew what was happening, it had become clear that I did. Renee's first two weeks of that school year were spent with a black eye and I'd realized that my role as the "good girl" could be used to my advantage.

All in all, punching Renee had not only been satisfying, but also a learning experience.

The grudge between us continued all through school and after-wards, when she tried to steal my boyfriend several times. The real shit thing was she hadn't wanted Brad because he was good-looking, or even because he was mine. Those were just bonus features. She'd wanted him because his family was one of the more wealthy ones in town, and she was a pretentious bitch.

Now she worked in the casino and was a pretentious slut who partied with whoever was winning that night.

I wanted money, but I didn't want it as bad as Renee did. Scanning the lounge I didn't see her anywhere, so I eyed Julie for a second, then blurted out the plan I'd come up with over the weekend. "I want to go to Hemlock Lake next weekend."

"What for?"

"To play poker." Hemlock Lake was another small town, less than a mile from Chadwick. There was a casino on the reservation land there that I could play at, since as an employee at Black's I wasn't allowed to gamble there.

Her eyebrows rose and she looked a little more awake. "You're not happy taking my and Lil's money?"

I grinned.

"Of course I'm happy to take it. But I need more, fast." I leaned forward, intent on convincing her how serious I was. "This town is killing me, Jules. I want to be out of here at the end of the summer. I just need another couple thousand and I'm set to move to the city."

"You're really going to do it, huh?" She fiddled with the saltshaker on the table, not looking directly at me.

I reached out and put my hand over hers. "I am. But you know I'll always have room for you whenever you want to visit."

She heaved a big sigh and straightened up. With a weak smile, she started planning. "Okay, so you want to hit another casino, and test your card skills? You do know that you might actually lose money with this plan, don't you?"

"Yeah, I know. And it's not just a casino. Remember what I said about Brandon? He called here this morning to tell me that next weekend would be the last chance for me to get into their tournament. He said if I go to Hemlock and play at Greg's table on Saturday night, and I win, then I can get in on the private game with three other winners."

Julie's eyebrows crawled up her forehead. "You actually think you can win in a tournament?"

"It's not a real tournament, and why can't I win? I've been studying all the poker manuals, and I even played on-line at the cafe the other day. I did well, Julie. I think I can win."

"Okay. And you know, uhmm . . . if you really want to win some extra money, there's a wet T-shirt contest at Moe's in Travers every Tuesday night. First prize is two hundred fifty dollars and a chance at a grand at the end of the summer."

A sharp bark of laughter escaped me. "You've got to be kidding!"

"Not at all, Travers is only a two-hour drive and full of tourists. It's not like we'll see anyone we know. It's a safer investment than gambling."

I glanced down at my modest B-cup breasts. "I don't exactly have what it takes to win something like that."

"Phfft!" Julie waved her hand through the air. "You have a great body, and it's just as much about how you work the crowd as it is anything else. Size doesn't matter."

Our eyes met and we both cracked up. "Size *does* matter!"

"Are you guys going to sit here and be idiots all day, or are you ready to order?"

Wiping tears of laughter from my cheek I glanced up at Renee. "Laughter is good for the soul, Renee, but I'm not surprised you don't know that."

She glared at me, and Julie placed her order before Renee could think of a comeback. When she was done I ordered and we watched Renee walk away.

"What a bitch," Julie said.

"Yeah, I bet the only size that matters to her is the size of a guy's bank account, not his dick."

8

I didn't expect to see Joe, not after he wasn't there when I opened. I knew that as head of security there was more to his job than walking the casino floor, or watching the cameras. So it surprised me when he showed up to help me bring the day's take down to the vault.

At first I wasn't sure how to act with him. I knew what we had was strictly sexual. That was how I wanted it; how we both wanted it. Joe was a hot man that could help me forget the fact that I had responsibilities. That was it. If he couldn't find the time to let me know what was going in the past couple of days, I wasn't going to let him know how much his absence bothered me.

Success didn't come to me; I went to it. And right now, that meant focusing on the job, saving money, and getting out of town. A bit of erotic fun on the sidelines was OK, I told myself, as long as it stayed on the sidelines.

By the time the elevator came for us I was mentally where I needed to be. Almost.

I stepped into the lift first, pushing the cart with the cash in it, and Joe followed me in.

"Hey guys!" A few feet away Renee waved for us to hold the doors as she strode toward us, a flirtatious smile on her face for Joe. Satisfaction wafted over me when he just shook his head at her and let the doors close.

Joe had let the doors close on her because nobody was allowed in when we had a cash delivery. I knew that, but I told myself it was also because he had no interest in her. Why would he when he could have me any time he wanted? Speaking of which . . . "It wasn't very nice of you to leave me like that the other night."

The elevator jerked to a start, and Joe turned to meet my gaze. His eyes were shuttered and a small chill ran through me. "Who said I was nice?"

"Nobody actually." I glared at him. "My mistake."

His lips lifted in a half smile and I got the distinct feeling he was laughing at me.

Fine, let him laugh. What he thought didn't really matter.

My eyes strayed to where his hand stroked the baton on his hip and my insides clenched. I fought the blush creeping up my neck as his large hand deliberately caressed the hard wood. Why had I told him the sight of that phallic thing on his hips turned me on?

The elevator pinged and the doors slid open. He stepped into the hall and I followed, pushing the trolley. Neither of us said another word as we moved down the corridor, but the tension between us was undeniable. I tried my damndest to keep my eyes from his tight ass, and the handcuffs there, but when we passed the surveillance room I couldn't help it. Memories of those cuffs restraining my wrists as Joe filled me from behind flashed vividly through my head and my sex moistened.

Damn it!

We arrived at the bank room. Joe greeted Fran, the woman working there today. He acknowledged the guard at the door to the vault room before we entered it, and waited in silence for the timer to release. At exactly three forty-five the red light would change to green and signal we could then enter the combination to the vault itself.

I couldn't help myself any longer.

"So, Joe, what's going on here? I mean between us, because I'm a bit lost with what's happening since you've left me hanging for almost a week now." There was a bit of a belligerent edge to my voice.

"I told you I'd take care of you when I saw you again."

I didn't want to be a typical clingy, needy female. I had plans. I had goals that didn't include him. But I needed to know what *he* had planned. Sex had never been a huge priority before, but somehow, because of Joe, it had become much more important.

"Uh-huh," I said. The light on the vault changed and I stepped forward to open it, my back to him.

"Are you horny, Katie?"

"Are you surprised, Joe?" I snapped back.

"Not really, but I am pleased." His chuckle echoed in the hollow vault and I glared at him over my shoulder, trying to ignore the warmth creeping about inside me at his words.

"I'm so happy for you," I muttered.

The silence built as we worked to unload the rest of the cash bags. When the cart was empty, we closed the vault back up. Joe reached for the door and I bit my tongue to keep from questioning him some more.

We passed through the bank and headed back down the hallway. I knew what would happen next. Joe would step into the surveillance room, and the guards would rotate. He'd be in that room alone. Just like when I'd teased him so wickedly only seven days earlier. I tried to convince myself that the urge to taunt and tease him, or to please him, was gone.

Joe grabbed my elbow and slowed us as we approached the surveillance room door. The guard there deliberately looked the other way, and Joe lifted my chin with a gentle finger. "I hadn't planned to make you wait this long, but it is nice to see the real you instead of the polite princess you pretend to be. I'll make it up to you for the wait, Katie. I promise."

He planted a quick kiss on my forehead, and was gone, leaving me weak-kneed and eager in the middle of the hall.

The niggling at the back of my neck as I drove home after work had me turning off Main Street in the middle of town, and heading for my mom's house.

When I'd dropped off the videotape with her TV show on it on Friday after work, she'd been real disappointed I couldn't stick around and help her get ready for her date. Mrs. Beets and Pepper had come in pretty handy as an excuse then. But now, the good old Mom guilt radar was humming and my hands automatically steered me home.

I rang the doorbell and walked right in. There was no immediate response to my greeting, so I followed the sound of canned music, and was surprised to find my mom doing a step aerobics video in the living room.

"Katie dear!" she called out when she saw me. "What a nice surprise. I'm almost done here. Will you stay?"

She talked as she stepped up and down, up and down, raising her knee, kicking her leg out, her arms swinging energetically the whole time. As silly as I thought step aerobics were, I had to admit she looked pretty good. Not just good for her age, but good for any age.

Her body was slim and trim, with only a bit of jiggle at her arms and her boobs. Shit, I wish my boobs jiggled like that even in a bra.

Anyway, her skin was glowing and her honey blond hair still looked perfect. She was obviously a woman who perspired, not one who sweated.

"Sure I'll wait." I dropped into the overstuffed sofa and took a deep breath. She was actually pretty graceful, too. I'd tried to do aerobics once. It took way too much coordination for me. When I felt the urge to exercise, which was never, I'd put my sneakers on and go for a walk around the block.

Sometimes I'd put my hiking boots on and drive to the edge of town to the trails. The solitude of nature was great, and the fresh air always made me feel good. I'd hike with Jules, or by myself. It had been a long time since I'd done either.

Watching my mom was making me feel real lazy, so I got up and headed for the kitchen. I pulled a can of Diet Coke from the fridge and popped the top. I heard the television go off, and a second later Mom walked into the room, a pink towel over her shoulders while she patted her face dry.

"What brings you home? Will you stay for dinner?"

I did a mental inventory of my fridge at home. I had food, but I was sure Mom had more to offer than a sandwich or macaroni and cheese. "Sure, what are we having?"

"There's some chicken in the fridge—why don't you pull it out while I change?"

And she was gone, leaving me to cook. Not what I'd had in mind, but at least she had a dishwasher. I enjoyed cooking, but I hated cleaning up afterwards. In point of fact, since I was at Mom's, I knew I wouldn't have to clean up the dishes at all.

I pulled out the thawed chicken breasts, slapped them on a cookie sheet, sprinkled lemon pepper on them before sliding them into the oven, and sat down again.

Fifteen minutes later Lydia Long strolled into the kitchen looking fresh and energetic.

"There's something wrong with my bathroom sink. It won't drain properly." She paused across the table from me and just stood there with a grin from ear to ear. "Sunday night dinner with my girl. This is so nice. How was your weekend, Katie? I hear you're baby-sitting Pepper for Laverne Beets. You're such a good girl."

The memory of Joe stroking my cheek and telling me I was a good girl brought a flush to my skin. Somehow, it sounded more like a curse when my mom said it.

"Yes, I mentioned that when I dropped off the video yesterday, remember?"

"Oh, yes." She giggled. "I forgot about that."

Oh, lord. She was falling for the new boyfriend. When Mom had a new man, anything not connected with him went in one ear and out the other.

"The cat's OK," I commented. "I stepped on her a couple times last night, but other than that we're doing OK."

"You should think about getting a cat for yourself dear. Someone to keep you company since you're still single." She reached into the fridge and pulled out some lettuce and vegetables.

"I enjoy living alone, Mom. A cat would be a responsibility."

"You enjoy living alone? That will change when you fall in love."

Time to change the topic. Or at least change its direction. "Look at you, all aglow and in love. I take it things with the new man are going well?"

"They are." She giggled again. "He's a sweetheart, Katie. A true gentleman who treats me like a queen!"

"That's good, Mom. I'm glad you've finally found a man that will treat you right."

"He is a bit younger than me, but you know, age doesn't really matter when you both want the same things out of life, right?"

She avoided my gaze as she tossed the salad.

"I think younger is great, Mom. Look at you! You look great, and if Demi Moore can do it, why can't you?"

"I'm so glad it doesn't bother you, Katie. I was so worried." A huge grin split across her face and she beamed at me. "If things go good with him this weekend, I'd like you to have dinner with us. So you can, uhmm, get comfortable with him being in my life."

Since she was in such an optimistic mood, and so sure of this new guy, it seemed like as good a time as any to tell her my plan.

"Why would it bother me? I almost have enough money to move to Vancouver. I'm planning to leave in September. I'm thrilled to know that you'll have a good man around to take care of you when I'm gone."

A small pucker formed between her brows. "What will you do out there?"

"I want to take that tax preparation course, remember? I've always been good with numbers and the first class starts last week in September. It's only a week long, and if I do good I can work for H&R Block at tax time. I'd still have to have another job, but it's a start. The opportunities in a city that size are endless, Mom. It's not like Chadwick."

"But I'll miss you," she said.

I looked at her big doe eyes and felt my heart started to sink a bit. Jumping from my chair I went and wrapped my arms around her in a big hug. "I'll miss you, too, Mom. But I'll visit often. I promise."

The timer on the oven went off, and we pulled apart.

"Now, let's eat, and then I'll fix the plugged sink for you before I leave."

9

Mrs. Beets knocked on my door just after seven o'clock that night, back from visiting her kids. I made a pot of tea and we sat in the kitchen for an hour while she told me about her visit.

"My son is starting his own business in his garage, some sort of computer repair thing. I think it's silly to spend his free time in there tinkering with things when he has a perfectly good job with the government. But he insists that a home-based business will help his family be more stable for the future."

"He's right, Mrs. Beets. A home-based business will really help his family out at tax time. Plus, if he's happy, it's all good, right?" I put a bowl of tortilla chips in front of her. "I don't have any cookies in the house, sorry."

"That's all right, dear." She reached for a chip and nibbled on it delicately. "So you think the boy is doing a good thing?"

"Yes, I do."

"Well, he has always been a smart one."

When the pot of tea was finished, Mrs. Beets reached into her massive purse and pulled out a little box of maple fudge. "This is just a little thank-you for looking after my baby while I was gone. She wasn't too much trouble for you, was she?"

I glanced at the ball of orange fur sitting contentedly in her lap and remembered the comfort I'd felt when that little warm body had curled up with me. "No, she was great company. You let me know whenever you need a baby-sitter."

She left after that, taking Pepper with her, and my apartment was blissfully quiet and still. After slipping a movie into the DVD player I curled up on my couch.

I must've dozed off because I woke up to the buzzer of my door sounding.

I pressed the button and asked, "Who is it?"

"Me."

Just that. One word. And I knew who it was.

I pressed the door lock release to let Joe in, and stepped to the side to look in the mirror. Ugh! I did not look my best. A vivid red crease ran across my check from the pillow I'd been sleeping on, my hair was mussed, and my eyes were sort of glittering with excitement.

"Oh, please woman," I told myself. "He's just a man, and you just want an orgasm. It's nothing special at all."

There was light knock on my door and it slid open.

"Hey," I greeted him.

"Hey."

He closed the door behind him and twisted the lock. He'd

changed after work and was dressed in jeans and a navy fitted T-shirt. He tossed the leather jacket he was carrying on the chair by the door and stepped up close to me.

"You need some attention, don't you?" He stroked a thumb across the crease on my cheek. His intense eyes skimmed over my features and down my body, heating me wherever they touched.

"You could say that."

His hand crept from my cheek to the back of my head. Long fingers massaged my scalp for a minute, then tightened, pulling my hair briefly before loosening up. Everything inside of me softened, and a small sigh escaped. I pressed against his hand. It had felt good and I wanted more. His fingers moved again, tilting my head back to give his lips easy access to my neck.

"My little slut is in need of attention because I've been too busy to take care of her properly." The crude words were spoken almost lovingly as his teeth nipped at my ear. His hand tightened again, and he pulled my head back smartly.

My knees went weak and I could feel myself fading into a puddle of eager flesh, his for the taking.

"Yes, I am." The words were barely above a whisper.

What happened to the woman who was pissed off?

Who knew? *Who cared?*

His other hand slid around my waist and he pulled my body tight to his and everything faded away except the way I felt in that moment.

"You are what?"

"Horny . . . and yours."

"That's my girl," he stroked his hand down my back. Then he gripped my waist and spun me around. His lips worked on my neck, his hands roved freely over my front. He pulled me tight, my back to his chest, my butt cradling the hardness of his erection through our clothes. He cupped my breasts in both hands, lifting them, squeezing them, tweaking the nipples. A shiver whipped through me and I sighed, arching into his hands.

Rusty chuckles vibrated against my skin and he focused on my nipple. He wrapped a thumb and forefinger around each one and squeezed. I moaned in pleasure.

Joe steadily increased the pressure, coaching more passion sounds from me, and sending needles of lust through my body and straight to my sex.

He squeezed a bit too hard and the pain outdid the pleasure, causing me to squeal a bit and jerk back. He immediately let go, hands frozen above my breasts, and whispered in my ear.

"Too much?"

Aware of the flood of cream that now soaked my panties, I shook my head and whispered, "I'm okay."

His hands covered my breasts and cradled them for a brief minute before traveling over my ribs to slide under the edge of my T-shirt. I leaned back against him, pressing my hips against his hardness, rubbing against him. A small moan eased from my lips. It felt so good to have his hands on me again.

Nothing else in the world mattered when he was working his magic. The building could go up in flames and I'd think the heat was coming from his touch.

"You are primed aren't you?" he whispered, nipping at the sensitive flesh between my neck and my shoulder. One hot hand slid up my rib cage to cup a naked breast while the other went under the elastic waist of my cotton shorts and searched between my thighs. "Oh yeah, you're so wet already."

He pulled his hands away and pushed me forward. "Step up."

He guided me toward the sofa, stopping only when my hips were pressed against the back of it. With a firm hand he pressed me forward, until my hands were braced on the cushions below.

"Stay."

Joe stripped off my shorts and panties and planted my feet wide apart.

"I'm gonna take care of my little slut so she isn't so bitchy anymore." His hands ran over my naked legs. Up over one calf, to tickle the back of my knee.

"Ohh," I gasped and locked my knees.

Hot breath floated over the sensitive skin a brief second before his lips touched down. He kissed me there, his lips moving, lightly sucking and then gave a sharp nip with his teeth before he moved up my thigh.

"Oh God," I mumbled, biting my lip.

His breath was floating over the soft skin of my inner thigh and I trembled, waiting for the magic of those lips to touch me again. Fingers dug in as he kneaded my butt cheeks, lifting me and pressing me into the sofa some more. I stretched up, only my toes touching the floor.

"Open up for me, baby." His words landed on my ears a second before his tongue snaked between my swollen pussy lips. I whimpered and tried to push back. His light touch was teasing, and I wanted so much more.

"Please, Joe," I begged.

In reply, his hands shifted, and he spread my lips crudely with his thumbs. I heard him inhale deeply, and then his tongue was on me. Firm and agile, he licked the length of my slit and circled my clit. I squirmed some more, and he thrust his tongue inside me. It didn't go deep, but the stabbing motion hit the right spot. Soon a finger replaced his tongue, and his tongue swept back to my clit.

My sighs and whimpers filled the room as he ate at my pussy. His finger thrust deep and wiggled around inside me, his tongue circled my clit and his hot breath warmed my core completely.

A light pressure started to tease around my asshole and I pushed back. "Yes," I hissed, surprised at the arousing tingles sweeping over me.

"Such a dirty girl," Joe whispered, pulling his mouth away. He shifted a bit and a firm finger landed on my clit. My hips jerked and another finger slid into my rear entrance.

"Oh!" I froze.

He frigged my clit faster and wiggled the finger in my ass.

"Oh, Oh! I'm going to come."

My toes curled and my body jerked as pleasure exploded in my sex and spread outward. Before I could come down to earth again hands latched onto my hips and Joe thrust his cock into my still spasming cunt.

"Ohh God, you feel so good," he chanted as he pumped into me fast and hard.

The wet sounds of belly slapping ass mingled with my moans as my feet came off the floor and I leaned farther forward on the sofa.

"Oh, yeah," he muttered. His hands gripped my suspended legs and slid down to my ankles. He bent them back so my feet touched my ass and my knees spread wide, and he slammed his cock home.

My body slid forward, my elbows now on the sofa cushions. The angle was perfect. Joe's cock hit the magic spot inside me with every thrust, over and over. With every thrust my body shifted forward a bit more and my clit brushed the coarse material of the sofa. A scream leapt from my lips and I shoved my face against the cushions as another orgasm ripped through me. My body shook and my insides clutched hungrily at Joe, setting him off. He grunted, his hips grinding against me as hot come spurted inside me.

I lay in that awkward position for a few minutes, struggling to catch my breath. Joe curled over me, his chest to my back, his arms sneaking under my torso and cuddling me close.

Too soon he was pulling back.

Instead of standing again I just pulled my body over the sofa and curled up with a pillow. My body was sated, and my brain was dead. I watched Joe as he did up his pants and walked around the sofa.

He knelt by the couch, his eyes shuttered, his expression unreadable.

"Don't be scared to talk to me. To tell me what you need, OK?" One hand reached out and he gently brushed aside a lock of my hair.

I couldn't suppress a smile. "You don't exactly come off as approachable, you know?"

His lips twitched. "I know. That's why I'm telling you this."

I nodded. "Okay. But I warn you now, I think you've truly turned me into a sex maniac."

That made him smile for real, and it lit up his face. God, he was gorgeous.

"I'm strangely okay with that." He gave a small laugh, then leaned forward and kissed me softly before leaving.

10

On Tuesday night, there was a small debate about who would drive to Travers. I love driving, especially highway driving heading *out* of Chadwick. But since we agreed that a few drinks would be needed before I jumped onstage and flashed my breasts through a wet T-shirt, we figured it was best for Lillian to drive.

We piled into Lillian's old VW van just after seven and headed out. Julie sat in the back with me, ready to do my makeup as the three of us laughed and sang along to our favorite eighties songs. What was it about that era of music that made the music so much fun?

"Did you hear about Renee and Joe?" Julie asked, reaching for her makeup bag.

"Excuse me?" Renee and Joe? What the hell did I miss?

"Close your mouth," she said, tapping my chin with the cosmetic sponge. Julie's foundation was much darker than my own, so she applied hers instead of mine. "Renee accused a customer of sexually assaulting her and Joe had to escort him out of the casino earlier today."

"Joe escorts people out all the time. No big deal. Although, I must admit, I'm surprised Renee complained about a guy hitting on her."

My relief was short-lived.

"True, but not everyone tries to thank Joe with oral sex."

"What? No fucking way!"

"I swear," Julie held up her hand. "I heard her myself."

It was wrong for me to get angry. Joe wouldn't take her up on it, not when he had me willing to play the slut for him. Unless I wasn't doing a good enough job of it.

I waved Julie's hand away from my face. "He didn't take her up on it, did he?"

"God, no!" Julie laughed. "He didn't even blink. It was funny, actually, because Renee wanted to actually charge the guy, and Joe was cool with that, until Jimmy told him that Renee had been all over him when he was winning earlier and tipping her big. All the guy had done was slap her on the ass, and he'd been doing the same thing every time he sent her for another drink. Apparently, the last time, though, he'd just finished losing all his money and had asked Renee to give back the money he'd tipped her. When she said no way, he grabbed her ass and asked for her to pay him back with a blow job."

I rolled my eyes. "He should've asked for that when he was winning."

She leaned forward and went to work on my eye makeup, doing the lids with dark smoky shades and lining them heavily. "True. He probably would've gotten it then. Anyway, when Joe came back after escorting the guy out the side door, Renee was all over him. When she told him she'd happily pay him with the favor, he just gave her that same small smile he gives everyone, said, 'No, thank you.' And walked away."

There was nothing I could do to stop my face from breaking into a super grin. Julie laughed and nudged my knee. "You think maybe it's because he knows where he can get one anytime?"

I fought a blush. "Maybe."

She giggled and rolled her eyes at me. I snatched the lip liner from her and used it and the compact mirror to make my lips seem fuller—and avoid her gaze. Joe wasn't something I was ready to talk about. Pulling a tube of colored hair gel from my bag, I waved it at her. "Let's do the hair now."

Doing my whole head was out of the question. The stuff was a vivid red, and as a gel it would be gross all over. So Julie did some chunky highlights around my skull, and we did a solid layer of it underneath. I prayed that after it dried, and I used the brush on my hair, I would look somewhat like a hottie, and not a little girl playing dress-up.

When it was dry, I ran the brush through my hair and was told it looked funky and cool. Nothing like my normal self.

"Meaning I normally look like a geek?"

"No, not a geek, just a Goody Two-shoes."

Great. That was just what I needed to hear to boost my confidence on the way to a wet T-shirt contest.

"Go ahead, Jules," I said, throwing my hands up. "Make me look hot."

With a wicked grin Julie reached into her tote bag and pulled out a top. "Put this on."

"Take the bra off," she said when I was about to pull the new shirt on. With a shrug I unsnapped my bra, and pulled on the tight tank top. It had a built-in bra, and I felt squished in it. "Ugh!"

"Here." Julie slid forward on her knees and reached for me.

She pulled the top down from the hem with one hand and reached into my top with the other. She cupped one breast and lifted, then the next. Her touch lingered a bit on the last one and I looked away from her eyes. My libido was on fire and I didn't want her to know that her touch had actually aroused me. When she removed her hands my nipples were hard, and my breasts were almost bulging out the top of the shirt.

"Holy Mother! Who knew I had this kind of cleavage?"

Laughter filled the van.

"Use this." Julie handed me a fluffy blush brush.

"Why? The makeup looks good."

"Just put it on her yourself, Jules. She can't see what you see."

I gritted my teeth at Lillian's use of my own personal nickname for Julie.

"Chin up," Julie ordered as she reached out with the blush brush.

"What about you and Joe? Anything new and exciting happening there?" Lillian called out from the front seat. I guess she didn't get the hint earlier that I didn't want to talk about him.

"Not really." Once again I avoided Julie's gaze, tilting my head back. The blush brush whispered over my throat and collarbone, then over the tops of my breasts. "I've seen him at work, but that's it."

"There! We can't have your face dark and body the color of a fish's underbelly," Julie declared.

She leaned back and gave me the critical once-over. "Forget about Joe for now. You'll need to work the room a bit before the contest if you want to win. Flirt, tease the guys that will be cheering. Usually the winner is whoever gets the loudest cheers, so it won't hurt to be nice to as many of the *judges* as you can. That button-up blouse you were wearing will not get the men clapping for you, but this will."

"Got it. Flirt, tease, and basically play the slut before I even get up on stage." I grimaced. "You're sure we're not going to run into anyone from Chadwick there?"

Worry niggled in the back of my brain. I didn't need rumors of this escapade reaching my mom. I could just hear her now. "How will you ever find a man now that half the country has seen your breasts? This was all that Julie's idea wasn't it? She's always been such a troublemaker."

If it weren't for the conscience she'd raised me to have, I'd be tempted to try skimming some extra money from the casino, too.

Lillian spoke up from the driver's seat. "Travers is two hours from home. It's Tuesday night, not Friday night, and even on a Friday, I doubt many people from Chadwick would be here. It'll be mostly summer people and kids home from university. Plus, you don't exactly look like yourself."

That was true. Excitement started to seep through me. This could be a lot of fun.

Moe's was a small red brick building on the edge of town. The yellow neon sign simply reading MOE'S PLACE could be seen from the highway.

Lillian made good time on the road, and we arrived just before nine o'clock. There were a lot of pick-up trucks, a few SUVs, and almost a dozen motorbikes in the lot; big monster Harley's and such with shiny chrome and metallic colors. Anticipation awakened my senses as the possibilities of the night ahead stretched before me.

We stepped into the bar as a threesome, and a few heads turned. Julie was wearing a short leather skirt and tight tank top similar to the one she'd had me put on. Only she had a lot more plump flesh spilling over the edge. Lillian's red hair and exotic looks drew many eyes to her. The flowing camisole dress that skimmed her curves kept them there.

Julie had rolled up the waistband of my skirt when we'd stepped out of the van, and my legs got a bit of attention. My funky look didn't stand out, but I wasn't being ignored either.

"Look at him," Julie said, eyeing the bartender.

He wore black jeans and black button-up shirt, completely undone to show off the colorful artwork splashed across his hairless chest and belly. I was checking out the way a dragon's tail disappeared into the waist of his jeans, pointing me the way to a decent-size bulge when Julie nudged me in the ribs. I glanced up and saw one eyelid dip in a flirtatious wink.

"What can I get you ladies to drink?" he asked.

Hoping that the dark foundation I wore hid my blush, I ordered a round of tequila shots, including one for him.

"Let's get started, girls."

The small shaker of salt was passed around, my gaze locking with the bartender's just as my tongue darted out and swept across the inside of my wrist. I felt so . . . awake. Erotically charged. Every touch made my blood heat more. From the touch of Julie's hand dressing me, to the rasp of my own tongue across my skin.

"A toast," Julie said, holding up her shot glass. She flashed a naughty grin at the group and spoke loud and clear. "To letting the inner bad girl out to play."

"I'll definitely drink to that!" The stud behind the bar said and tossed his shot back with the rest of us.

The tequila caused a sharp burn in my chest, which eased to a pleasant warmth when I bit into the lime slice and the juice squirted down my throat.

"So what's your name, darlin'?"

Julie and Lillian shifted down the bar a little, leaning against each other and making it obvious they were a couple. I smiled at the hot guy behind the bar. Making friends with the bartender was always a smart move, no matter what bar you went into.

"I'm Caitlyn." The fake name came easily to my lips.

"Well, Caitlyn. I think we need another drink. How about you?"

He set up two more shot glasses and filled them with amber liquid. I smiled. Ohhh, I was going to have fun. I could feel it in my bones. And every other part of my body.

"Sure. What's your name, Mr. Bartender?" I leaned against the bar, using the edge of it to plump up my cleavage a bit more.

He, of course, noticed, and made no effort to hide the way his eyes lingered on my pushed-up boobs when he spoke. "Rick. You need anything tonight, you come see me, OK?"

We clicked our glasses together and another ounce of tequila slid down my throat.

The second shot went down much smoother than the first one did, and the warmth in my chest was spreading fast. Julie grabbed my elbow and pulled me over to them. Leaning close she whispered in my ear. "Cute as he is, *Caitlyn*. You need to flirt with more than him to win this contest."

"No problem," I assured her, scanning the crowd.

"You have an hour before the contest. There's a bunch of guys back at the pool tables, let's start there."

She waved at Rick and we headed to the back of the room where a group of college-looking guys surrounded one table, and a few bikers surrounded the other.

Lillian put a coin on one table and Julie a coin on the other. Which ever came up first, we'd play on.

We leaned against the waist-high rail that portioned off the pool tables from the rest of the bar. From there we let guys at both tables watch us, as we watched them play.

The human mating ritual had begun.

Soon a college boy approached Lillian and she stood regally while he tried to chat her up. If she gave Julie the signal, Julie would chase him away, but one of the best things about going out with them was that they did their best not to exclude me by being too much of couple.

The waitress came over and handed us three more shots of tequila.

"From Rick," she said.

I smiled and waved at him, and Julie slipped her a five-dollar bill. "Thanks, but tell him no more for a while, OK?"

The waitress smiled and eased away.

Lillian looked at the shot and shook her head, still talking to the clean-cut college boy. When she mimed her hands on the steering wheel, Julie and I grinned at each other. Oh, boy. Trouble was brewing.

Sure enough, as soon as we'd downed those shots, two more appeared. This time in the hands of one of the biker guys.

"You girls look like you're out to have a good time. I thought you might need a hand."

I gave him a small smile and looked him over while he made eyes at Julie. He wasn't bad-looking. A bit older, maybe in his early thirties. Dark hair and a bit of a beard. The scar that cut across his eyebrow gave him a dangerous look, but the way he looked at Julie was actually sorta sweet.

Go figure.

"We are . . . and we always like a guy who knows how to party."

He introduced himself as Mark and gestured to the shots he'd placed on the partition's top rail. Jules reached for a shot, handed one to me, and we all tossed them back. I shifted away from them a bit and watched the pool game some more, while Julie flirted with him.

Normally, I had a pretty strong resistance to alcohol, but tequila was the one thing that knocked me for a loop every time. I've heard people say it's more of a high than a drunk, maybe that was why. I didn't know, and I didn't care, because right then I welcomed the floating feeling that was edging its way into my head.

As I watched, my eyes kept straying to one guy in particular. Tall, slim, with dirty blond curls. He'd look almost angelic if it weren't for the wicked tattoo on his neck. The mix of leather and denim he wore took a bit away from the saintly look, too. But it did increase his sex appeal.

He threw back his head and laughed at something one of the others said, and I noticed that while he wasn't gorgeous, there was something about him that was very attention-grabbing. He must've sensed my staring, because he turned his head and our gazes locked. A fission of arousal zipped through me, straight to my sex.

He closed one eye in a slow lazy wink and my breath caught in my throat. An arm wrapped around my waist, distracting me, and I was pulled close to a warm soft body.

"We're here because Caitlyn is going to win the wet T-shirt contest," Julie was telling Mark.

Mark's eyes slid over me and I fought the urge to stick out my newly developed cleavage.

"I am. You'll cheer for me, right?" Sticking out my bottom lip in an exaggerated pout, I placed a hand on his arm. The universal move of a woman flirting, the casual touch.

"We'll all cheer for you, pretty girl." He waved his hand at the group behind him.

"Cheer for you? What are we cheering for?" The sexy blond stepped up beside Mark, his lips lifted in a lazy smile.

"Girls, this is my buddy Karl."

Karl's chocolate-colored eyes roamed my body. My nipples puckered in reaction, and I forgot about the contest. He reminded me of a lion. The blond curls, the lazy sensuous aura; very laid-back and mellow. But in his eyes . . . in his eyes I could see an intensity that didn't show in his body language. An intensity that reached down between my legs and stroked my pussy.

A sharp elbow nudged my ribs and I started.

"Oh! I'm going to enter the wet T-shirt contest," I told him.

"Since the winner is picked by crowd reaction, I need as many of you to cheer for me as possible so I can win.

He stepped closer, between me and the others. With his back to them, he cut us off and built a sense of privacy. "You're going to have to put on a bit of show."

"I plan to."

His smile changed from lazy to downright amused. "Ohh, the little kitten has some claws."

"Kitten?"

"Yeah, you look like a kitten to me. You know, one that will purr real nice when petted properly."

Cheesy as his line was, I felt it. The fire hidden behind the playful spark in his gaze said this guy knew how to make a girl purr, maybe even scream.

But he didn't need to know I felt it.

"You think you can make me purr?" I turned away from him slightly, scanning the room. Making it clear I was checking out the other men in the club.

Hot breath brushed against my ear. "I know I can," he whispered.

And walked away.

Well, crap. I'd wanted to intrigue him, not dismiss him. What was it about me that made men turn me on, then walk away?

An hour and a half later my head was a bit higher in the clouds, and my body was throbbing to the beat of the music. The crowd was loud, and big, and I was on the stage at the front of the bar with four other women.

A couple of them had fantastic breasts. Obviously fake, but wow! Did they look good in the skimpy cropped white T-shirts we all had on. They looked so much better than my average B-cups that I wanted to crawl under the stage and sneak out the back door. Except then I'd have to listen to Jules and Lil rag on me for the full two-hour drive home.

"Deep breaths. It's okay, you can do this."

The girl next to me gave me a funny look, but I just smiled. So I talked to myself? So what?

I stood back and watched as the first three girls stepped forward in turns and had jugs of water poured over their chests, trying not to hyperventilate the whole time

Then it was my turn.

I stepped forward. Right to the edge of the stage like Julie had said and smiled big. My gasp of shock wasn't fake when the ice-cold water hit my chest. My nipples instantly pebbled to the point of pain, and I slapped my hands over them automatically. Only when the crowd cheered did I realize what I'd done.

I stepped back and let the last girl move into the spotlight. But while I was back there, my knees started to tremble and my chest got tight. What the hell was I doing? A wet T-shirt contest? My God, putting on a show for a security camera was one thing, flashing a bar full of strangers was another.

Strangers.

My eyes scanned the crowd while the first girl stepped forward for judging. All eyes were on her. Even Julie and Lillian were huddled together watching her and not me.

Number One stepped back, and Number Two stepped up to be judged.

Julie and Lillian were the only people there I knew. Chances of me even seeing anyone else again were slim to none.

Number Two stepped back, Number Three stepped up. With the makeup and colored hair, even if I did see someone, they'd have a hard time recognizing me.

The weight in my chest lifted and my heart started to pound. I was practically anonymous. I was free.

"Contestant Number Four! Who thinks Caitlyn's got the best set on her tonight?"

My lips split into a wide grin as I stepped forward with more strut than I ever thought possible, and the crowd roared. People were yelling and cheering, eyes shining and egging me on. I spotted Rick behind the bar, whistling and clapping, and the sexy blond biker Mr. Purr at the back of the crowd, hooting and cheering.

I ran my hand up over my belly and shimmied my hips; my fingertips flirted with the edge of my wet shirt, lifting it, teasing him. Teasing the crowd.

The cheers got louder, and I trailed my fingertips around each nipple, flashed a wink at the cheering crowd and with a flip of my hair, went back to my spot.

I stood there, adrenaline pumping through me, juices flowing and realized that not only did I feel free. I was turned on. A lot!

"All right everyone, the crowd has spoken. Caitlyn, baby, you are the winner of this week's Best Boobs contest! Step forward and flash the crowd!"

"Whooo-hoooo!" I strode forward and danced around the stage, being completely uninhibited in my joy. Two hundred and fifty bucks! All for letting a crowd of strangers ogle my tits through a wet T-shirt.

Wet T-shirt contest down. Next up, high-stakes poker!

I let out another whoop and accepted the cash from the MC before stepping off the stage and getting tackled by Julie and Lillian.

———

Flying high on the win and the freedom of anonymity, I joined the girls by the pool tables after changing back into the tight cleavage top. They greeted me with another shot of tequila and a fresh frosty cider.

As I was taking a long drink from the bottle and Julie was salting her hand in preparation for another shot, Lillian spoke up. "Okay, we got what we came here for, but we all have to work in the morning, so let's head out soon."

I opened my mouth to disagree, but snapped it shut when Julie nudged me and shook her head. It had been a good night so far, but for whatever reason, Jules was okay with cutting it short, too, so I decided to just enjoy my final drink and keep my mouth shut.

Between the adrenaline and the steady flow of tequila, I was feeling no pain. So when I slammed down the empty shot glass and turned to see Mr. I-Can-Make-You-Purr leaning on a stool, arms crossed over his chest, eyes eating me up . . . my brain shut down. He gave me that lazy wink again and I didn't hesitate.

My feet carried me right to him. I stepped between his widespread thighs, reached behind his head, and tugged his face down to mine. His lips parted and let me in, but he didn't try to take over. Our tongues rubbed and slid against each other as I rubbed against his lean frame like a cat in heat. All thoughts of anything but feeling good were gone.

Hoots from the surrounding watchers penetrated my lust, and I brought the kiss to an end.

I pulled back and he grinned at me.

"Thank you," he said.

"Thank *you*," I replied. Then walked away, twitching my tail as I went.

God, it felt good to have my chance to walk away from a man. There was no denying how sexy Karl was, and the fact that he was a stranger that I'd never see again would normally make him a front-runner in my search for a good time, but the kiss had proven something to me. Something I hadn't really wanted to face before. Joe was getting to me.

He was special.

And he made me feel special, too.

The way he was cool and aloof, mysterious and even harsh at times was what caught my attention. Even more so than his good looks. But it was the seductive softness in his eyes when he called me his "little slut" and touched me tenderly after using my body that made me crave him. It had become clear to me that while I might find others attractive, even sexy, Joe Carson was the only man that brought forth the completely seductive eagerness to please from within me. He was the only man I wanted to have complete and full access to my body.

Julie and Lillian were leaning against the rail when I reached them. Lillian flashed me a grin, and Julie gave me a high five followed by a big hug. "Look at you go, woman! Get all the hot men panting after you!"

Man, I loved my best friend. She was always ready to encourage that bit of bad girl inside me.

Since we all had to work the next morning and I'd gotten what we came for, it was time to leave. As we were settling our tab with the waitress, I felt distant vibrations in my pocket. I pulled out my phone and looked at the number. I didn't recognize it but answered anyway.

"Where are you?"

"Excuse me?"

"I'm at your apartment, you're not here. Where are you?" His tone of voice was light, and my heart jumped.

"Uhmm, I won't be home for a couple hours still."

"Where are you?"

A masculine arm came around my waist and warm lips pressed against my neck, causing a shiver to whip through me. I turned my head and saw Mr. Purr's hot dark eyes looking down my top. His hard body pressed against my back, and I felt a decent bulge pressing against my butt.

"Let's go for a walk," he murmured and bent his head to nibble at my unoccupied ear.

"Katie?" Had he heard Mr. Purr?

"I'm in Travers with the girls. We wanted a girls' night out . . . where nobody knows us."

"Come on, baby." The body pressed against mine some more, and I couldn't help but push my butt back and tease him.

"Who's the guy?" The light tone was gone and Joe's voice developed an edge, making me worry that what little closeness we'd managed to accomplish was fading fast. I quickly disengaged myself from Karl's arms and stepped down the hallway to the restrooms. "No one, just a guy that we were playing pool with. He wants us to stay for one more drink, but we're leaving."

"I was hoping I'd get to see you tonight."

Despite the arrogant edge to his voice, my current state of arousal kicked up in high gear. If I thought I was hot before, it was nothing compared to hearing him say he wanted me. And I was two hours away!

"I should be home in about two hours. Less, actually, because Lillian doesn't like to pay attention to the speed limit."

"It's nice to hear the eagerness in your voice, angel. It pleases me. You're not going to let anyone else near my cunt, are you?"

"No, sir." The words slipped from my lips with ease.

"Good girl," he said warmly. "I have a surprise for you, one I'm sure you'll like. You have a good night with the girls and I'll give it to you tomorrow."

"A surprise? Really?"

"Good night, Katie."

———————————

We piled into the van and I reclined on the back seat. "You're OK to drive, right, Lil?"

"Only one drink all night, girls! The rest was just Coke."

I glanced at the clock on my cell phone, just after eleven. It would be at least one o'clock by the time I got home. Damn! My body protested at the fact that I'd missed out on a session with Joe. I wondered what his surprise might be. Could it be another all-night session?

Just the thought of having him in my bed all night again was enough to make my panties damp. Mind you, they were already damp.

We hit the highway and I could hear Julie and Lil chatting quietly up front. Between the thought of an all-nighter with Joe, and tonight's flirting with Mr. Purr, I was ready for action.

Karl was pretty hot. And he was from Vancouver. A one-night stand with an out-of-towner that I'd never see again certainly had its appeal. If it weren't for Joe, I probably would've done something really stupid with him. When I'd admitted as much to him before we left the bar, he'd grabbed my cell phone and programmed his own phone number into it.

"I travel a lot on my bike. Call me sometime," he said when he handed the phone back to me. "You never know what might happen."

I wondered what it would be like to have them both.

Lord, to be sandwiched between the lazy seductiveness of Karl and the dark intensity of Joe. Hands would be everywhere, all over me, stroking, teasing, pinching. Karl behind me, his mouth on my neck, teeth nipping at my ear as he whispered with that purring voice of his. Joe in front of me, spearing me with his eyes while his hand got busy between my thighs. Joe pushing me to my knees, having me take his cock in my mouth while he commanded Karl to lick my pussy until I came.

"Katie." A firm hand rubbed my knee. "Katie! Wake up. You're home."

I dragged myself back to consciousness, leaving Joe and Karl behind. With a limp smile I gathered my purse and clothes from the van seat. With a final wave at Julie and Lillian I plodded into my apartment, to my warm bed where I could rejoin the men of my dreams.

12

When I arrived at the cash cage the next morning Tom was waiting for me again. And this time he had a small package for me. "Joe said to give it to you."

The rest of the opening routine was normal. We kept the music low, and I tried to pretend I didn't have a hangover. When the first cashier showed up and Tom left the office, I opened the brown paper bag he'd given me. Inside was a note, and another smaller paper bag. I pulled out the note.

"Do not open the bag until I call you. It will be today."

Joe's name was at the bottom.

Curiosity whipped through me. I took the second package out

and played my fingers over the surface. It was something small and bumpy, dropped into the bag and then the bag was folded over at least three times, creating a thick wrapping. It felt like a chain.

An image of me on my knees, wearing a collar in front of Joe filled my head and my belly tightened. I'd read a story where a woman had been completely submissive to her man and he made her wear a collar whenever he wanted to remind her who was the master. At the time that I read the book, the sexual submission scenes had turned me on, but the thought of ever calling a man "master" had made my skin crawl.

I didn't think I could bring myself to call Joe "master." But the thought of being on my knees in front of him, wearing a collar, maybe with a tag on it that bore his name . . . that was hot.

"Katie, they need another bag of loonies for the floor."

Susan's call from the front cage dragged me back to reality and I put the small package in the side drawer. Hope's hopper jammed and I went to work on the coin counting machine, while Susan handed off the bag of coins to the floor supervisor.

The floor supervisors were the ones that refilled all the slot machines with coin, so that when people won, there was actual coin coming out of the slot. They collected the coins from us, after we collected them from the customers, and we'd re-bag them. With coin, it was all about recycling them in a casino.

"Hurry up, would ya?"

I looked up from the innards of the coin machine and saw a disheveled guy shifting restlessly from foot to foot on the other side of the Plexiglas.

"It'll just be a minute or two, sir," I said before going back to work on the stuck quarter.

"I don't have a minute. I told the stupid bitch it was a hundred bucks. Why can't she just pay me?"

I straightened from the machine and leaned forward so he could hear me clearly. "If you'd like these coins cashed in, you won't talk like that to the cashiers. *And* you have to wait until they're counted."

"I'll talk to the bitch any way I want to. Now give me my money."

With a glance at Hope I closed the hopper up, tossed the rebel quarter back into the plastic bucket with the rest, and asked her if that was all he'd given her. She nodded and I slid the bucket of quarters back through the window to the punk on the other side.

"There's your money back, sir. Now I'm going to ask you to leave the casino and not come back until you can be civil."

"Fuck that!" He slammed his fist down on the counter and ignored the bucket of coins. "I don't want no fuck'n quarters! I want paper money."

A line had formed behind him, as well as at Susan's window and everyone was watching now. A lot of the watchers were regulars, and they knew as well as I did what was coming next.

"You have to leave now, sir."

"I'll leave when I get my money, bitch!"

Without taking my eyes from the pissed-off jerk I snatched the walkie-talkie off the counter where I'd put it to work on the hopper and depressed the button. "Security to the cash cage, please. I have a gentleman that needs to be escorted out."

"You can't make me leave!" Hope and I just watched as he waved his arms around, hopping from one foot to the other as he ranted.

Joe turned the corner, and I ignored the kick of lust I got at the sight of his confident form. He stepped up close behind and to the left of the agitated customer and nodded to me.

When the guy slowed down to breathe, I leaned forward and spoke calmly.

"I warned you. You can't verbally abuse the staff. We don't allow

that here and you need to leave. You can take your money with you."
I edged the plastic bucket forward with my fingers.

The guy's face turned red and he gave the bucket a shove back at
me, almost knocking it over. "Shut up and do your job—"

"Excuse me." Joe interrupted his tirade with a firm grip on his
arm, just above the elbow. "It's time for you to leave, sir."

"Hey, man!" He tried to turn to Joe, but the way Joe held him kept
him from facing him completely. "All I wanted was to cash in my coins
for bills and these sluts couldn't even do that! Why is it my fault?"

Pain pinched the asshole's face, his left shoulder dropped and he
leaned into Joe.

"You need to apologize to these lovely ladies if you want to be
able to use this arm anytime soon." Anger laced Joe's voice and his
eyes glittered as he looked down at the man in front of him.

"I . . . I'm sorry," he whispered.

Joe gave him a small shake and his eye's widened perceptibly.
"Louder."

"I'm sorry!"

"If you want the money, pick it up with your right hand, and you
can take it with you. You're leaving now."

A whimper came from the much-calmer man as he reached for
his bucket of coin and cradled it to his right side. Joe pulled him out
of the line and toward the back door of the casino. Two steps away he
turned and winked at me over his shoulder and my knees just about
buckled.

The waiting customers clapped and chuckled. Most of the regulars had seen versions of this before. They knew that if they wanted to
gamble at Black's, everyone got treated with respect.

"He is so hot." Susan sighed. Hope agreed and we all gazed at
Joe's retreating form for a minute.

"Ahem." I cleared my throat and gave them a stern look. "Hopper's fixed, now let's get rid of this line-up."

The rest of the morning I kept busy, but thoughts of Joe's bag were always present in the back of my mind.

What if it was a collar? What did it mean? Was it a gift to make up for his making me wait so long? Or was it just another way to remind me of the promises I made? Would I wear it? Would I actually wear a collar for this guy and let him treat me like I was his pet?

My body loved the idea. My nipples were so hard that I had to keep my blazer on over my tank top. Butterflies had taken up permanent residence in my belly, and my thought process was completely scattered.

The phone rang in the office as soon as I walked in after my lunch break. I snatched it up and set my purse on the floor by the desk. "Cash office, Katie here."

"You haven't peeked at my gift, have you?"

My heart pounded and warmth flooded my body.

"No." Before I could ease into the chair behind the desk he spoke again. "Go close the door to the office."

I glanced at the security camera in the corner and knew he was watching me. I did as he asked, arousal blossoming inside me at the thought of giving him another show.

"Good girl. Now, where's your gift?"

"In my desk drawer."

"Take it out and open it up."

I reached into the drawer and started to rip at the paper bag wrapping. My fingers were trembling with my excitement. When I saw the silver metal links of a lightweight chain my sex heated, and I knew I'd wear it for him.

Then I got the rest of the paper torn away and noticed it wasn't a collar. It looked like two rubber-tipped roach clips chained together.

"Lift up your shirt, angel." He voice was tender and soft. Cajoling, but with steel beneath the words.

I glanced at the security camera again. "You're the only one watching me, right?"

"I'm not one to share what's mine. Something you should know by now . . . and remember. Now do as you're told."

I lifted the hem of my shirt to my chin and tried to control my breathing.

"Pull your bra down, and play with your nipples. Make them nice and hard."

I balanced the phone between my shoulder and my ear, so I could listen and play with myself at the same time. A sigh eased from my throat and pleasure shot from nipple to groin. Why did this feel so much better when he was watching?

"Enough," he said. His voice was a bit gruff and I interrupted him.

"Are you hard, Joe? Does watching me do this turn you on?"

"Everything you do turns me on."

My heart pounded and I ignored it, concentrating on his instructions. "I want you to pick up the clamps and put one on each nipple."

That's what they were! I picked them up and pressed the end of one, opening it up and fitting the rubber tipped ends over a rigid nipple. I held my breath, let it close, and watched it slip right off.

"Tighten it with the screw and try again." Joe's voice was firm, guiding me.

I tried again, and gasped at the sharp pain. "Don't take it off!" Joe's command stopped my hand where it was, hovering over the pinched nipple. "Breathe, angel. It'll ease."

He was right. Within five seconds the initial shock was over and the pain had eased to include pleasure. I did the other one and sat there, panting at the sensations ripping through my body.

A small whimper escaped and Joe's husky chuckle echoed through the phone line. "I knew you'd like those."

"Oh, yes, I do." I sat back in my chair and started to slide a hand under my skirt.

"Uh uh," Joe chastised me. "No playing with yourself, I want to make you come. So pull down your shirt, Katie, and keep those on until I come to remove them."

And he hung up.

With my eyes on the security camera, I straightened up, adjusted my bra over the clamps, and pulled my shirt down. I tugged at the lapels of my blazer and went to open the door and get back to work.

The next fifteen minutes passed in agonizing slowness. Every nerve in my body was awake and begging for attention. Heightened sensations made even the rubbing of my thighs together seem erotic.

I was just filing the last of the balance sheets in the metal cabinet when I heard the buzzer signal someone entering the cash cage. Unconcerned because it was close to the shift change for the cashiers, I kept working and didn't look up until I heard his husky voice.

"I need you to come with me, Katie," Joe said from the doorway.

Adrenaline pumped through me, and I fought to remain calm. I stepped out of the office and into the cage where Jane was chatting with Susan and Hope before her shift started. I made sure they were OK for cash for a few minutes, locked the office door and told them I'd be back before it was time for Susan to cash out.

Then I was following Joe once again.

Instead of going to the elevators and heading for the security office, he headed down the long hallway toward the staff exit with me keeping pace beside him.

"How do you feel?" he asked softly as we walked.

I looked straight ahead and debated how to answer that. I decided blunt was the way to go with a man like Joe.

"I'm a bit hungover, a bit confused, and horny as hell."

He slowed his steps and turned to me.

"Horny is good, hungover isn't so good, confused . . ." He stepped closer, invading my personal space. Gripping my shoulders he urged me backwards into the ladies washroom. "Why are you confused?"

Once through the doorway he reached behind him without looking and turned the lock. The sound of the lock clicking into place echoed loudly in the small room and made my heart pound in my chest.

He leaned against the door and looked at me with those intense eyes that seemed to see deep into my soul. I couldn't hold back.

"I'm confused because sex was never that big a deal for me before." I'd waved my hands in the air and the movement had my pinched nipples rubbing against my lace bra. Fire licked at the sensitive tips and my sex clenched in response. "But now it's a constant craving. And I realized last night that it isn't just sex with anyone I'm craving . . . it's *you*! Those days last week when I was waiting for you? I tried to get myself off, but I couldn't. Even though I didn't want to listen to you, my body did!"

With one large step Joe had me pinned me to the wall with his body. Blue heat flared in his eyes seconds before his lips covered mine, and we went up in flames together.

His work-roughened hands circled my wrists and brought them over my head. The sides of my blazer fanned out and he tugged my shirt up with one hand, while the other kept my wrists pinned. His knuckles dragged across my clamps as he shoved my bra aside, sending bolts of pleasure/pain to my groin. As cool air landed on my aching nipples, his hand lifted my skirt.

I lifted a leg and wrapped it around his hips, bringing the hard bulge in his pants into direct contact with my aching clit. He thrust against me, his whole body pressing me higher up against the wall.

His chest brushed against mine, as he slid his lips across my cheek to nip and bite at my neck and earlobe. My whimpers echoed in the hollow room, turning to actual cries. Soon his hand was in my panties, fingers playing with my slick opening.

"Please, Joe." I tugged at my hands, thrust myself against him, and tossed my head from side to side. So many sensations, so many feelings, I was going to explode. I wanted to explode.

He groaned and I felt his chest reverberate against mine. "You're so wet. So hot, baby. I love the way you want me. You need this don't you?"

A firm finger circled my clit and my hips bucked.

"I need you . . . inside me . . . fuck . . . me!"

A low groan filled the room before he spoke, his hot breath filling my ear. "I want to please you. This is for you, babe, not me."

"I want you!" I pulled back as far as I could and made him look into my eyes. "If this is for me, then I want your cock. I want it deep inside me when I come."

"Shit," he muttered. His hand left me to unzip his pants and pull out his impressive cock. Then my wrists were free and he was gripping my ass cheeks, lifting me off the floor and pinning me to the wall with my legs wrapped around his waist. I sank my finger into his thick hair and held on tight. Lifting his head he stared into my eyes and I felt him probe my entrance. "I was willing to just see to you, but I'm not saying no again."

With a quick jerk of his hips, he was inside me, stretching me, filling me.

His fingers dug into my ass, his chest brushed against my chest with every thrust and one of the clamps came off. A rush of heat shot through me and I came.

Every muscle in my body tensed and I bit down on his neck to muffle my cries. He continued to fuck me hard and fast, pumping in and out, until he buried his face in my neck to muffle his own guttural cry and his cock twitched inside me.

After a moment, he braced his hands on the wall and pulled away so I could stand up again. My knees were so weak I had to hold him close for another minute while I caught my breath. When I could walk, I stepped into one of the stalls and cleaned myself up a bit. My panties were history. My own juices dampened them all morning and Joe then had actually ripped one side to get access.

When I came out of the stall Joe was standing by the door, his cock hidden away inside his uniform once again. The only sign of what had just happened was the devilish glint in his eye.

I smiled at him and let my eyes roam over his six-foot frame, my gaze lingering on the handcuffs and nightstick attached to his waist.

Seeing where my gaze lingered, his lips curved up on one side and he winked at me. "Feel better now?"

I could feel my cheeks flush, but I met his gaze head on. "Yes, I do."

"Good." And he exited the room.

I was washing my hands a second after the door swung shut behind him, when I heard some muttered curses and shuffling sounds, and one of the stall doors swung open behind me.

13

"Good thing I have half an hour for lunch, or I would've had to interrupt you two!"

My jaw dropped and my mind went blank. Julie was here. In the bathroom. In a stall.

"You were in there the whole time?" I squeaked.

Laughter filled the room as she nodded, her hands smoothing her uniform. "You bet your ass I was! And you owe me for staying in that stall. It was damn uncomfortable to sit still and stay hidden."

"Ahhh." My hands covered my face and prayed for the floor to open up and swallow me whole.

"Hey," Julie said. "Don't worry about it, Katie. It was just me. It's not like I didn't know you and he were fucking around, and it's not like I was offended by what I heard. Shit, you should be thankful I didn't try to join in!" She laughed.

"I can't believe I didn't even think to check and see if anyone was in here. How stupid is that?" I slumped against the sink. "I can't believe *he* didn't think to check!"

"At least it was me. It could've been worse."

"True." It could've been Renee.

Neither of us spoke for a minute until I lifted my eye and finally met her gaze. Then we both burst into giggles.

"Shit, girl. From what I heard, you were due, and that man gave you a great payoff!"

"Oh Jules, you don't know the half of it." I thought of the blow job and him walking out, of the futile attempts to get myself off, of the silver clamps in the pocket of my blazer. "I don't know what it is, but I can't say no to him."

"Seems like that's not such a bad thing when yes includes things like a quickie at work."

"Yeah . . ."

"What?"

I knew I could tell Jules everything, the whole submissive thing that seemed to be happening, and she wouldn't judge me. But it was too private to share. Even with her.

"Nothing." I shrugged, and the movement reminded me of how sensitive my nipples still were. "I guess I just surprised myself."

"You surprised me, too!" She flashed me a wicked grin and pulled me toward the door. "But I'm proud of you."

A helpless laugh bubbled out of me. "You would be!"

"Hey!" she said as we made our way down the hall. "You need to have some fun, Katie. Then maybe you'll realize that life in Chadwick still holds some surprises for you."

———— ■ ————

We walked into the Starlight Casino that Saturday night in Hemlock just after 8 P.M., the air-conditioning enveloping us and drying the sweat on our skin. Jules and I didn't speak, there was no need. We went straight to the bar and ordered a couple of margaritas. Big fishbowl-sized slushy ones.

Summer had hit with a vengeance the last couple of days and my car didn't have any air-conditioning. Having the windows unrolled on the drive had created a bit of a wind, but because the temperatures had been so high for the last three days, the wind was a warm one. The hour stuck in the car had been hell.

The bartender placed the frozen drinks in front of us and I handed him a twenty. He made change and I left a hefty tip on the bar.

"Which table is Greg's?" Julie asked when half her margarita was gone.

"Not sure," I replied. "Brandon said he had dark hair and wore a name tag so I should be able to find him."

We took our fishbowls in hand and started to walk to casino floor, our body temperatures slowly lowering to a tolerable level. When we finally found Greg's table Julie shook her head at me. "You're nuts."

I hid my own grimace. "No, I'm determined."

"It's a fifty-dollar table, Katie! You could lose a lot of money!"

I grabbed her elbow and pulled her back from the table.

"I can win a lot, too! If I thought I was going to lose it all I wouldn't here." I dug around in my purse and pulled out one thousand dollars. "I can double, maybe even triple this, Jules. Think about it! I have a chance to make enough money that I won't need to panic about finding a job and paying my rent for a couple of months.

Please, just support me in this okay? I won't be able to concentrate if I know you're sitting behind me cursing me."

Her eyes cleared and her lips lifted. She gave me two thumbs up. "You got it. I'm here to be your cheerleader."

I gave her a one-armed hug and joined the couple already seated at the table. They were pretty clean cut and stylish in their matching khaki shorts and cotton T-shirts. Obviously tourists. Greg was a tall, slim guy in his mid-twenties, with dark curls surrounding a friendly but average face. He gave me a welcoming smile when I put some money on the table. He cashed it in for chips, and I settled in for a long night.

The game was five-card draw, like most casinos played, and I was glad. Before the Texas Hold'em craze had kicked in, this was the game I'd played every week with the girls. It was the game where I'd learned to play the cards, not the players.

After an hour of play, the couple had left the table and it was down to the dealer and me. I smiled at Greg.

"So why exactly am I playing at your table?"

"Excuse me?"

"I'm Katie. Brandon told me to come play at your table until you told me I was good to go. So what are you looking for?"

His dealer façade cracked and he gave me a big grin.

"Brandon is my man. He sucks at poker himself, though, so he asks me to screen the players for him."

"He sucks at poker?"

Greg chuckled. "He does. He loves the game, and he does OK with draw poker, but I've played with him at his poker nights, and he sucks at Hold'em."

"Then why does he do it? Why does he play Hold'em at the poker nights?"

"He loves to watch the way people play. The risks they take, the way they bet. That's where I come in. I'm a good judge of character. He pays me to help him create an entertaining dynamic in the games."

"Hmm, thanks Greg." Interesting. So we, the players, were basically pawns for his entertainment. "So, am I in?"

The knots in my stomach tightened and, despite the air-conditioning, a fine sweat broke out on the back of my neck while I waited for his answer. Finally, he nodded, a devilish grin on his face. "Oh yeah, you're in, and I know just who to put you against."

Elation lifted me up. "Thank you!" I jumped from the chair and leaned over the table to give him a quick hug. "When and where?"

He chuckled and shook his head, "Where . . . the Hartman Hotel. When . . . Brandon will contact you when he gets the game organized."

I turned to Julie, who had been sitting at the slot machines several feet away. "I made it, Jules!"

"Good luck!" Greg called out as I walked away.

"That's it?" she said as we exited the casino. "You know you're going to be entertainment for this guy and you're okay with that?"

"You heard that, eh? Well, Jules, to be honest, this could be my ticket out. If Brandon or Greg or whoever is going to give me a shot at it because I'm a blond female who can possibly make the 'game dynamic' interesting, I'm not going to turn it down." I met her gaze. "It's not the first time someone's underestimated me."

"Cooking a big meal tonight, Katie?"

I looked down at my already half-full basket. Lettuce, vegetables, potatoes. Now I was standing in the meat section being questioned by the butcher. The joy of a small town: people look at my groceries and know something unusual is happening.

"Yeah, it's been a while since I cooked, but the urge has struck." I reached for the pork chops Dave the butcher held out to me. With a smile and small wave I stepped away before he could ask anything else.

A week had gone by since Julie and I had returned from Hemlock. There'd been no word from Brandon, and no more sessions with Joe since the bathroom incident. It wasn't for lack of trying. Our schedules just weren't matching up at all and I was feeling like a cat in heat.

Joe was better at being attentive, in a weird way. He talked to me more at work, shared telling looks with me. He'd dropped by my place for another sex session just three nights ago, but I was still craving more.

Not just more as in more often, but more as in dirtier, rougher sex.

Maybe rougher wasn't the right word. I didn't know exactly what it was I wanted. I just knew that Joe could give it to me, if only I'd ask him.

So, instead of telling him what I wanted sexually I asked him over for dinner. I figured I'd cook him a meal, and have a few drinks, and hopefully he would just read my mind and give me what it was I wanted, without me having to figure out what that was myself.

"Oh, cooking a big dinner tonight aren't you? It's not often you get more than salad or popcorn."

This time it was Joyce, the cashier, who was curious.

"Yup, just craving some meat."

As soon as the words were out of my mouth a hot blush crept up my cheeks. I didn't think Joyce caught the double entendre. How could she? But in my mind, the meat I was craving wasn't the meat I was going to be cooking.

I paid for the groceries and started to walk the three blocks home. It was dinnertime for most families and the streets were quiet, so I got to enjoy the early evening warmth and sun. When I turned off Main Street and headed up James Avenue toward my building, the sounds of nature became more apparent.

I watched a rabbit dash out from under the hedge of one yard and into the trees across the street and smiled.

Chadwick really was a beautiful place, small enough to feel like a small town, but big enough to legally be a city. And spread out over the lush mountainside. The trees were green and full of singing birds, the grass was plentiful and rabbits and squirrels were common visitors in every family's yard. The occasional bear or coyote would be seen, but mostly on the outskirts of the city.

I was just starting to break a sweat when I reached my building. The fresh air, warm sun, and uphill walk with the grocery bags had been slightly invigorating. The sight of Joe leaning against his car in my parking lot was downright exhilarating.

He was early. But really, when he looked so damn good, I didn't care, better early than late. Without a word he joined me at the door to the building and took hold of the grocery bags. Once up the stairs and inside my apartment I turned to him, nervous for the first time. This was almost a date, not just a sex session.

"You're early." I started to take the food from the plastic bags.

He leaned against the counter, placed his arms across his chest and gave me a half smile. "You want me to leave and come back?"

"Nope. I want to put you to work." With a laugh I tossed the potatoes at him. "You can start by peeling a few of those."

Surprisingly, we worked well together. We kept things light, joking a bit as I chopped vegetables and tore up the lettuce while he made quick work of the potatoes. It was almost scary how good he was with the knife.

"Joe, can I ask you something?"

"Sure, I told you to never be scared to talk to me." He met my eyes, his hands still working the knife over the last potato.

I set down the spice bottle I'd just finished sprinkling the meat with. He *had* said that.

"Why did you move to Chadwick?"

He cubed the last potato, and put it in the pot I'd given him earlier. Then he reached into the fridge, pulled out a beer for him and a cider for me.

"Well, I'm not sure if I'm here to stay or not. But basically, Charles Fiddler is a friend of a friend. When he heard I was looking for a change, he offered me a job."

I nodded and thought for a minute. Charles was the general manager of the casino. It was a simple answer, a good one. We both knew there was more to it than that though. Our gazes locked. His eyes were patient, yet guarded, while he waited to see if I was going to ask for more from him.

"Do you like it here?"

He nodded. "I do. The hotel's on the highway, with a few trails around it. It's . . . peaceful."

A strange look came over his face, and pain flashed in his eyes. He took a drink from his beer, and when he looked at me again I wondered if I'd imagined it.

"The mountains are good for peace and quiet." I put the salad in the fridge and started to clean up the countertop. "I used to hike a lot, but now I work too much."

"You shouldn't work so hard, Katie. You're young and you need to enjoy life." Joe's voice was sure when he spoke, but soft. As if he was surprised to be giving me clichéd advice.

Neither of us spoke for a few minutes. We cleaned up the countertop and set the potatoes to boil. Then Joe turned to me and raised his hands. "What else?"

It was a chance to ask more questions, or get on with the night. I got the impression that he would answer any of my questions, but I wasn't sure if I really wanted to know much more than I already did. I was leaving town soon, and I needed to remember that.

I smiled at him and took a step back. "Nothing really, just the meat. If you can handle that, I'll go jump in the shower."

A hungry gleam sparked to life in the blueness of his eyes, and I felt an answering pull in my sex. My breath quickened and my nipples poked rudely through my shirt when his gaze ran down my form.

"Shoo," he waved me away. "I can handle it."

I stripped in my bedroom and headed for the bathroom. After letting the shower run for a minute I stepped under the steamy spray and went about my business. I ran my soapy hands over my body and ignored the tingles that spiked every time I touched a sensitive spot. Although I did wash my breasts a bit more than they needed.

Using a new razor I shaved my underarms and my legs, and did a quick check on the bikini line. All was well so after a quick rinse, I turned the water off and swept aside the curtain to grab a towel. And saw Joe leaning against the doorjamb.

I froze, and the beast inside me that had been craving more from Joe woke up and roared inside me.

"Uhmm, hi," I said.

He snapped out the towel I'd left on the counter. "Come on. I'll dry you off."

Oh, lord.

My heart pounded and butterflies took flight in my tummy. He opened his arms and I walked into them.

"Lift your arms," he instructed. Then he patted me down all over. He even took my hair in the folds of the towel and squeezed it dry. When he was done he reached for the hairbrush on the counter.

"Do you have a new razor?"

When I nodded, he asked for it and my hairbrush. Without a clue what he was going to do, I retrieved both items from the cupboard under the sink.

"Take a seat." He pointed to the straight-back chair he'd placed in the middle of my bedroom.

"Dinner?" I gave him an uncertain look.

"It's under the broiler, we have time. Now do as I say."

I walked over to the chair and sat down on the padded seat. Joe stepped behind me and started to comb my hair. He ran the bristle brush over it with smooth sure strokes. As confident in doing a woman's hair as he was in everything else. I closed my eyes and reveled in the luxurious treatment.

When Joe was done, my fine hair was tangle free, and his fingers ran through it smoothly. He put his hands on my bare shoulders and leaned forward. "I'm going to see all of you tonight," he whispered in my ear.

He went to the bathroom and I heard the tap running. When he came out he stopped just in front of me. My breath hitched in my throat when I saw what was in his hands. The small pink razor I'd given him was in one hand, a towel and aerosol can in the other.

He knelt down in front of me. His two hands cupped my knees and pressed them apart. He hooked my legs over the arms of the chair and instructed me to hold them there. I was just as exposed as if I were in the stirrups at the doctor's office. Except my pussy didn't weep with joy when I was there.

"I want to see every inch of you, nice and clean." He gave the aerosol can a good shake a sprayed a fluffy pile of shaving cream into his hands. With quick, sure fingers he spread the cream evenly over my trimmed pussy and I let my head fall back. I wanted to watch him, but at the same time, being so exposed and taken care of so intimately was more than I could handle.

As if sensing this, Joe called my name. "I want you watch this. I want you to watch me shave my pussy. Because this is my pussy, right? I can do whatever I want to it, right?"

"Yes." I met his intense gaze. I knew this wasn't about the neatness of my pubic hairs. I waxed and trimmed them consistently. This was about control and possession; just what I was craving. "Whatever you want."

Saying those words to him, and meaning them, lifted everything from my shoulders. The stress of dealing with my mom, of being in a place I didn't want to be. They made me forget about everything around me, until the world shrunk down to only the two of us and nothing else. And I could hide nothing from him. I didn't need to pretend that I was happy, or that life was completely perfect. He stripped it all away and replaced it with pleasure.

Using one hand Joe pushed lightly against my lower belly and ran the razor down the edge of my blond bush. He quickly shaved the front of my groin area, using the towel that he'd wet with hot water to wipe both me and the razor off. I watched his every move, my heart pounding, and tamped down any embarrassment at my arousal.

"Closer to the edge," he said and urged me forward a bit more. I was sitting on my tailbone, my ass over the edge of the seat, and my body on the edge of an orgasm.

"Don't move, angel." The whisper of his words floated across my damp labia and I suppressed a shiver. I watched as he pulled the loose skin taut, and quickly and efficiently, he shaved me completely bald. The feather-light touch of the razor across my most sensitive skin pulled a whimper from me. I wasn't scared he would cut me. He had my trust completely. The beast inside me was craving a firmer touch, and my hips pressed forward.

"Careful," he warned. "Did I say you could move?"

I sighed and bit my bottom lip.

He ran deft fingers over the smooth skin, over the crease between thigh and groin, and between my swollen pussy lips. When he was satisfied all was smooth and bare, he pulled back. After one last wipe with the damp towel to get rid of any lingering shaving cream, Joe leaned forward and planted a soft kiss on my newly bare skin.

"Let's go have dinner now." He stood up and held out a hand.

Weak kneed, and a bit disappointed, I accepted the hand and was pulled to my feet. I headed for my closet.

"What are you doing?"

I glanced at Joe over my shoulder. "I'm getting dressed."

"Did I tell you to get dressed?"

"You said let's go eat." I raised an eyebrow at him. "I assumed we were done here."

"We are done here." He smirked a little and the beast inside me purred. "But I want to see all of you while we eat, so you stay like that."

14

Heat flooded my cheeks as his meaning sunk in. He wanted me to walk around with no clothes on. He wanted me to sit and eat with him while completely naked!

A shiver danced down my spine and I bit back a smile. He was so bad.

Without even a glance at the clothes in my closet, I pushed the chair back against the wall and followed Joe to the kitchen. It felt a bit weird, walking around my apartment completely naked when someone else was there. But the heat in Joe's eyes as he watched me move about the kitchen, setting the table, made it all good.

Cool air rushed over my overheated body and goose bumps popped up on my skin when I pulled the salad from the fridge. The timer went off, and wearing nothing but oven mitts, I pulled the pan with the pork chops from the oven. The silence in the room was comfortable, and I prepared two plates for us at the counter. When I brought them over to the table, I set one in front of Joe and then moved to sit across from him.

"No," he said, his hand encircling my arm before I was out of reach. "I want you to sit on my lap."

Our eyes met and I blushed. I set my plate next to his and sat across his thighs. He wrapped one arm around my waist and instructed me to feed him.

This sorta fell into the area of complete domination that I'd always thought would never appeal to me. Yet, sitting naked on Joe's lap, cutting his meat and feeding him dinner felt good. It seemed right.

His hand roamed leisurely over my back and my thighs while I fed him. He kept my arousal alive through nothing more than a casual touch. He made sure I ate, too. Sometimes picking pieces of meat off my plate with his fingers and feeding them to me. At one point some mashed potatoes slipped from my fork and landed on my leg. Joe swiped a firm finger across my thigh, scooped it up, and licked it from his fingers.

I'd never thought of mashed potatoes as sexy before, but the erotic image of him doing that will forever be burned into my brain.

"Yummm." He hummed his pleasure. "Nice dinner, angel. I think you deserve a special treat for dessert."

The slow throb of arousal in my groin kicked up a notch. The famous fridge scene form *9 1/2 Weeks* flashed through my mind and I pressed my thighs together.

Joe stood, shifting me in his arms so his hands slid down my back and cupped my butt. I wrapped my legs around his waist, my arms around his shoulders, and curled into him as he walked to the bedroom.

Once inside the room, he went to the empty space at the end of my bed and set me on the floor. He stepped back and began to undress.

"On your knees," he told me.

My insides trembled with excitement and blood roared in my ears. I stood naked for a moment, briefly unsure, but when he just arched an eyebrow at me, my knees bent and I was on them.

It was a bit awkward. Kneeling naked in front of him. I didn't know what to do with my hands. I wanted to reach out and help him undress. But he'd already taken off his shoes, socks, and shirt. His jeans were still on, but I could see the bulge there, and it made my mouth water.

In the dim room, his scars were highlighted by the moonlight creeping in the window. He looked dark and dangerous and another shiver went through me.

He walked over and placed a warm finger under my chin. He tilted my head up and gave me a small smile. There was that hint of tenderness again.

"Always keep your eyes on me. I need to see into them, to know how you're feeling. You are mine and I intend to use you well, but I don't ever want to hurt you. You understand?"

I nodded, too turned on to speak.

He stroked my hair and ran his hands over my shoulders as he walked around me. With a firm hand he pushed me forward. "On your hands and knees."

His hands stroked over my back and buttocks, down the back of my thigh and up the inside. His fingers brushed across my pouting pussy lips but didn't really touch them, and a whimper leapt from my throat. My back bowed and I tried to press myself against his fingers, but he chuckled softly and pulled his hands away.

"Not yet, angel. Straighten up again."

I did as he said and lifted my eyes to him. He leaned down and cupped both my breasts in his hands.

He fondled them and ran his thumbs over the nipples, tweaking them a bit. Then he circled each nipple with a thumb and forefinger . . . and pinched. Slowly and steadily, until my head dropped back and my eyes slid shut.

"Open your eyes," he commanded.

Another moan slid from my lips.

He released my nipples and stroked them. "You like that?"

I nodded.

His fingers tightened on my nipples again, and he pulled upwards. "Stand up."

I scrambled to my feet and gasped when he cupped my breasts again, holding one up as he lowered his head to suckle at the tender tip.

"Ohhh." I couldn't suppress the long low moan that came from inside me. My hands reached up and I sank my finger into his soft thick hair, holding him close as he loved one rigid tip, then the other.

I shifted my body forward, enjoying the rough denim of his jeans brushing against my body.

He shoved a leg between mine and lifted so that I was riding his thigh. His lips nibbled their way up to my neck as his hands reached back and grabbed my ass, holding me against him roughly.

One hand urged me to ride the hard thigh he shoved between me, while the other reached up and tangled in my hair again. He lifted his head away.

"Look at me."

I lifted heavy eyelids and looked into his intense blue eyes, seeing lust—and . . . pride?—shining in his gaze.

He lowered his head and took my mouth. His tongue thrust between my lips and ravaged the inside. Tasting and touching every part of me as I writhed against him. I scraped my nails across his chest and flat stomach, working my hands between our bodies so I could cup his hardness through the denim.

The thick length of his cock was pushing against the button fly, eager to come out and play. In seconds I had both hands on his waist-band, struggling to undo the belt buckle, but he gripped my shoulders and thrust me away.

"Stop! Hands off."

I stifled a curse at the loss of contact and started to rebel, but obeyed when I saw that he was undoing his jeans. "Bend over, hands on the bed. I want a good view of all that's mine."

When my hands were on the bed he stepped up behind me, gripped my hips and kicked my feet wider apart. His hot naked cock brushed against my ass for second before he slipped it between my thighs. He slapped it against my hungry pussy, running the head all over the labia, teasing me.

I arched my back, leaned back into him, and tried to subtly shift so he'd slip inside me.

"Poor baby," he crooned. "You want this, don't you?"

"Yessss." The word came out in a hiss.

"Did you enjoy being my serving wench tonight?"

"Yes," I answered softly.

"Did you enjoy knowing that I could bend you over like this, and fuck you at any time? I enjoyed it. I enjoyed knowing that the whole time you were squirming on my lap, rubbing your thighs together and trying to act like a lady, that really, you just wanted to be fucked." The thick head of his cock breached my entrance and stilled. "Didn't you?"

"Yes." My answer was louder, firmer this time. "Please, Joe."

"I love to hear you beg, baby. Here you go." He gripped my hips with both hands and thrust deep and true, filling me up.

He didn't hesitate, he pumped his hips fast and hard and fucked me fiercely. My body was slick with welcome and the sound of skin slapping against skin filled the room. I dropped to my elbows, my fingers curling into the comforter.

"Oh, God, that feels so good."

Joe's pace slowed to a torturous rate at my words. "Very good," he growled. "But I want more."

His hands spread across my butt cheeks and pulled them apart. "I want this ass."

I stilled. His gruff words were straight out of my fantasies, but . . . "I've never done that."

A fingertip swept across my puckered hole and electric tingles shocked my insides.

"Are you telling me I have a virgin ass in front of me?"

"Only you've ever touched me there. The other day." I bit my lip.

Our panting dialogue was more than I could handle. I shifted my weight and started to thrust back against Joe. Riding his cock.

"Oh, angel, you just made my night." His fingers dug into my hips and he helped me move. "You liked it, though, didn't you? Your cunt clamped down on me like a vise that time."

His cock twitched deep inside me as he pressed his hips against my butt. My fingers curled, clenching around the comforter for leverage. He wasn't fucking me anymore, just staying put deep inside while I rocked back and forth, picking up speed again. "Tell me you liked it, Katie."

"I did," I panted. "I liked it."

He snaked his hand around my waist and tweaked my clit. My body went slack, my forehead dropped to the bed, and he played with me. His fingers rubbed around my clit, then lower, stroking all over my sex, playing where we were connected. My insides clenched around him and he moaned.

"Oh baby, you're so wet! You feel so good. You were made for my cock, weren't you?"

"Yes!" My body slammed back against him, my insides were knotting and I could feel my orgasm coming . . . coming . . . there . . .

"Yesss!"

My pleasure cry echoed through the apartment at an embarrassing volume.

Joe pulled out of me slowly and I fell forward onto my belly. He crawled up next to me and silently pulled my backside to his front, spoon style. We lay there for a few minutes, the rough denim of his jeans brushing against the back of my thighs, his erection sandwiched between our bodies.

When my breathing had steadied again, I turned my head and looked over my shoulder at him. He winked at me, climbed from the bed, and left the room. When he came back he tossed his handcuffs and a bottle of olive oil on the comforter next to me, then went to my dresser.

He opened the top drawer—does everyone in the world use the top drawer as their underwear drawer?—and sifted through my panties.

"What are you looking for?"

He ignored my question and pulled out a pair of pantyhose.

15

The sight of Joe, naked and hard, at the foot of my bed with a wicked gleam in his eyes and a pair of black nylon pantyhose stretched between his hands had my heart pounding and my pussy weeping with eagerness.

He continued to sift around in the drawer for a few seconds. When he was done, he had the nylons in one hand and an old bandana in the other. I tried to speak, but my lips parted and no words came out. The urge to ask what he had planned was strong, but not as strong as the thrill of not knowing.

"Sit on the edge of the bed."

I got out of his way, and Joe moved to the side of the bed. He weaved the nylons through the headboard in a way that the legs were dangling down the middle, like a rope would hang from a roof.

When he was done with that, he moved in front of me. He knelt down until our faces were level.

"Hands," he commanded, holding out his own. I placed my hands in his, and he gave them a quick squeeze. Our gazes broke when he began to wrap the old bandana around one wrist, then the other. My brow puckered and I wondered if he thought that would hold me. Then he snapped his handcuffs on over the cotton, and I realized he'd done it to protect me from the hard metal of his service issue cuffs.

My heart pounded and my recently sated body began a low-level hum of anticipation. I licked my lips and waited for what was next.

"Ready?" Joe asked.

"Oh, yes." I didn't know for what. But I felt ready for anything.

"Lie on the bed, on your back. Hands above your head." His voice deepened. It still had a touch of tenderness in it, but the commanding tone was there in full force.

I stretched out in the middle of the bed, arms lifted so my hands were above my head. My eyes were glued to Joe as he leaned forward, his muscles flexing under taut skin, while he wrapped the nylon around the chain between the cuffs and pulled it back to the headboard to secure it.

"My personal playground," he said. He'd stepped back to survey my nakedness with a satisfied gaze. "What to do with you now?"

Arousal was swimming through my veins, heating me up, making me pliant, yet tense at the same time. Joe ran a lazy hand over his belly and down to his groin, where he took hold of his semihard cock and started to stroke it. A sigh of longing escaped before my throat closed up tight with lust and saliva pooled in my mouth.

"You like that?" he asked. "You like to see me jerk off?"

I nodded, my eyes glued to his sure movements.

"Tell me."

My eyes flew to his. A shyness I hadn't felt with him since our first night together swamped me, and I licked my lips. I pleaded with my eyes.

"You need to say the words. You need to ask for what you want, angel, or you might not get it."

I hesitated a second too long and his movements stopped, his hand dropping to his side.

"I want to watch you," I whispered.

"Too late."

"Please."

"No." He climbed onto the bed next to me. "You didn't speak up when you had the chance. Now I get to do what I want. What you want doesn't matter."

His words brought a rush of fluid to my core. When Joe spread my legs and knelt between them, there was no hiding my reaction. He gave me that half smirk, half smile of his and made a show of inhaling my scent.

"Umm, horny, slut scent. I love it."

The flush that heated my neck and cheeks was a combination of embarrassment and pleasure. My eagerness embarrassed me, but it pleased Joe so much, and really, all I wanted was to please him.

"What are you going to do?" I couldn't help myself.

"Whatever I want." He ran his big warm hands over my body. He started at my ankles and ran them up my legs, over my hipbones, skimming my ribs, tweaking my nipples as he passed my breasts. He braced himself on the bed with one hand and continued his journey with the other. Over my shoulder, under my arm, he tickled the inside of my elbow and my arms jerked in reaction, making the restraints snap tight.

"Oh, look at that. You can't pull away." He braced both hands on the mattress and kept his body above mine. His skin just barely skimming against mine. I sucked in a breath and whimpered. Arching my back and pressing myself up against him.

His breath drifted hotly over the skin of my neck. He leaned closer and nipped at my earlobe. "I love the sounds you make when you're all submissive and horny."

That drew another whimper from me. Joe buried his head in my shoulder and licked the side of my neck. He nipped at my earlobe and found the hot spot behind my ear. His mouth pressed against me, and he sucked.

"Ahh," I panted.

He sucked harder and my body jerked. Goose bumps popped up all over me, and I tried to pull away, the sensation too intense. He eased back and chuckled. "Poor baby. That really gets you going, doesn't it?"

Lifting my legs and wrapping them around his waist, he smirked and pressed me into the mattress. The weight of his body was a comfort. Until he shifted lower, his mouth trailing over my collarbone to my breasts; he nipped at the rigid tip atop my breast and his belly scraped across my pouting clit.

"Ohh." My legs tightened around him, and I closed my eyes as he suckled and teased first one nipple, then the other. My insides clenched and I felt myself creeping farther from the edge of reason. Just when the knot in my lower belly was starting to thrum, to signal an orgasm about to burst, he moved.

And he knew what he was doing, too, because he glanced up at me and chuckled. "Not yet, babe."

My lips pursed and I glared at him with my eyes, not willing to voice my objection to his teasing for fear he would make me wait even longer.

Ignoring me, he shifted lower still, until his shoulders had my legs spread wide and his breath teased over my newly shaved and superpensitive mound.

"So pretty," he murmured. Fingers touched me, sliding up and down my slit, spreading me wide, exploring me. "So pink and wet and luscious."

His tongue darted out and he licked the soft skin at the crease of my thigh, up one, then down the other. Then his mouth was on me. His tongue snaking inside me, his lips closing around the sensitive nub of my clit, applying suction that made me press my heels into the mattress and thrust my hips against him.

A finger slid in my entrance, then two, and my hips kept thrusting, it felt good but I wanted more. He wiggled those digits inside me, and my belly fluttered in response. "Ohh," I said. "Yes, Joe, there. Like that."

I wasn't taking a chance on him stopping when I was so close. "Don't stop."

He wiggled his digits again and sucked on the small nub of nerves, and I was off.

"Yesss!" The word hissed out, and I raised my hips off the mattress as an orgasm rippled through me. The waves of pleasure eased and my body crashed back to the bed, slack.

Joe gripped my hips and flipped me over like a rag doll. The nylon twisted and my hands remained stretched out in front of me.

"On your knees, slut."

The rough handling, the rough language, and the command in his tone almost had me coming again. In the blink of an eye, my hands were flat on the mattress in front of my face, my weight resting on my elbows and knees. The bed shifted, and Joe grabbed the forgotten bottle of oil. He poured some in his hands, recapped it, and set it back on the bed a foot away.

Slick fingers gripped my butt cheeks and spread them wide. I held my breath, thinking he was going to try and slide right into me. Instead, he bent over and blew gently on my puckered hole.

"You're going to lose your virginity tonight, angel."

I put my forehead to the mattress and wiggled my ass in the air. "It's yours."

"I'll take care of you." His finger whispered over my exposed entrance. Once, twice, then it settled there. He spread oil over and around my rear entrance.

"Don't tighten up, baby," he murmured, pushing against me. "I know you like the finger."

I looked back over my shoulder and our eyes met. His were bright and glowing with lust. A small smile played about his full lips and he raised an eyebrow at me. I nodded, licking my lips. My answer to his silent query. I wanted this. I wanted him to play with every inch of my body, to do whatever he wanted.

It was then that I realized it wasn't just the physical sensation of him playing with my ass that had me so excited I was trembling. It was the mental thing. It was as if everything else we'd done up until now had been just playacting, but by letting him do this to me, by letting him touch me and use me in a way that I'd never let anyone else do or even imagined letting them do, I was really committing to being his.

"Stay still now for me," he coached me in a gruff voice. "Tell me if it gets to be too much."

I nodded, then let my head fall down again. He pushed forward, and I felt myself stretch to let his finger in. I sucked in a deep breath. Relax, I told myself. I let the breath out slowly and pushed against the intruder. It slipped in deeper, and I moaned.

Joe wiggled his fingertip and sensations ripped through me. It felt like he was directly petting the tight ball of nerves low in my belly. He wiggled a bit more, sliding in deeper and the knot grew.

"That's it."

He pulled out a bit, and thrust forward again, slowly and gently, but this time, he was stretching me more. There was more than one finger there. I knew it. A whimper escaped, and I shoved away the mental image of what he was doing and concentrated on the fact that I was pleasing him.

"Good girl," he crooned. "My little slut is being such a good girl tonight."

He leaned forward and I felt his lips on my back. His other hand ran up and down my back, petting me, soothing me. I sighed and arched my back, pressing against his hand. He took the hint and started to thrust his hand back and forth, finger-fucking my ass. His other hand reached underneath to stroke my pussy, and a moan jumped from my lips.

"That's it, baby."

His hands left my body and I practically growled at the desertion. Then I felt his thighs behind mine and the head of his cock hot against my skin. One hand gripped my hip and he pressed forward. A low moan rumbled from my throat at the pain/pleasure of his cock sliding into my ass. He slid in slow and steady, all the way.

Then he leaned forward, covering me completely with his body, and he wrapped his arms around my torso in a hug. He pressed kisses to my neck and whispered in my ear. "Okay, baby?"

I let out the breath I'd been holding and nodded. "Yes."

"You're sure?"

"Yes," I said more firmly. "It feels . . . different. Full. It hurts a bit, but it's a good hurt . . . You know?"

I turned my head and our eyes met. Joe leaned forward and covered my mouth with his. Our lips parted and our tongues touched in a slow sensual kiss that stole my breath.

He pulled back and straightened up. Firm hands cupped my hips and he started to move. I felt every inch of his cock as he pulled out and pushed back in again. Slow and easy was the pace, and I relaxed. Then I started to enjoy it. Not just for the fact that I could feel the erotic tension in the air, or hear Joe's excitement in the harsh breathing that echoed through the room. I started to actually enjoy the physical sensations.

Soon I was rocking on the bed in time with his strokes. I kept trying to pull my hands underneath me, so I could push back, but the restraints didn't reach that far and I was helpless to shift position. The orgasm building up inside me was stronger than anything I'd ever felt. Every stroke brought intense new sensations. Joe picked up a bit more speed with his hips, and I couldn't stop the sighs and moans that escaped, making me sound like a porn star.

"That's it, baby," Joe chanted and he got a bit rougher. The beast that had been riding me for days, demanding more was crouched low in my belly, purring, getting ready to roar. My hands clutched the bed sheets and I rocked back into Joe.

"More," I moaned. "Faster . . . harder."

Joe grunted and slammed into me one last time. His cock twitched inside me and I was flooded with warmth that set me off. Every muscle in my body tightened as my orgasm washed over me. Joe folded himself over my back, and we stretched out on the bed together. Limp and exhausted, but satisfied.

Joe lay next to me on the bed, silent and still. I shifted restlessly on the mattress, only to be stopped by the lack of give in my still restrained arms.

Before I could say anything Joe's warm hand swept over my skin and he shifted. "Sorry, angel. I just needed a minute to catch my breath."

He reached over the side of the bed and came back with the key for the handcuffs. He quickly released my wrists and brought them down between us, rubbing my arms and wrists to restore the circulation. "Okay?"

I nodded tiredly and curled closer to him before drifting off on a cloud.

————————————

When I woke up the next morning, Joe was gone. I stumbled to the bathroom, brushed my teeth, and tried to pry my eyes open.

The night before had been amazing. Beyond anything I'd read or fantasized about. Yet, my mind screamed at me, "Stop seeing Joe *now*."

Things were getting to the point where more than just my mind and body were engaged in the relationship. When I'd read my first erotica novel that had domination in it, it had turned me on unbelievably. But it was just a scene in a book. A fantasy. The intense emotion brought forth when Joe touched me, roughly or gently, was starting to feel like more than just sex.

I stepped into the shower and began to wash. Not everything had been a physical turn-on for me, but the knowledge that what I'd done, or let him do to me, was pleasing Joe, brought me pleasure.

The image of my mom doing everything and anything to please a man went through my head, and I twisted off the water taps. I'm nothing like her, I reminded myself as I dried off.

This thing with Joe was sexual. That was it. I wouldn't be lost if he left me, and despite the fact that I'd served him dinner naked, there was no way in hell I'd let him tell me how to run my life. The naked serving thing had been an indulgence, a tantalizing thrill for us both, not a mandatory requirement.

Joe had done a great job dominating me from the minute I stepped out of the shower to find him waiting for me. But he'd been firm and demanding, never demeaning. He'd been downright tender at times, too. Not once had I ever feared that he would hurt me, or that he wouldn't stop if I'd asked him to.

I stopped dead in front of my closet. He hadn't given me a safe word. In all the books I'd read a "safe word" had been mentioned, a word for the submissive person to say when they wanted to call a stop to things. Joe hadn't given me one.

Maybe he doesn't know as much about all this as I thought? I dressed quickly and headed for the door only to stall as I passed the kitchen.

It was clean. Joe had cleared all the plates and washed them. They were stacked in the drying rack next to the sink. He'd made the kitchen sparkle and I hadn't even woken up.

Something fluttered in my chest.

"No time for that now," I muttered. No time to stop and think too much. I jogged down the stairs and out to my car. There was a convenience store on the way to work, and I'd stop for a Diet Coke. Cold caffeine was better than the sludge they called coffee and I needed to wake myself up.

I needed to remember what my priorities were.

When Joe had shown up in town, the scenes from books had become scenes in my dreams, with him in the starring role. But really, we'd never talked about a relationship. Shit, we'd never talked about the whole domination/submission thing either. It had all seemed to just come naturally to him. The same way my desire to be used by him and to please him had come naturally to me.

"It's just a sex thing. Good chemistry," I told myself as I drove. "There's nothing special, and I can walk away from it any time."

I had to.

Because Joe had just settled in Chadwick, and I was determined to leave.

16

"Katie!"

I glanced over at the tables and saw Brandon wave at me. A quick peek at my watch told me I had ten minutes left on my lunch break so I strolled over to greet him.

He looked great, as usual. Short blond hair cut close to his head and spiked up a bit on top. Eyes so light they were almost freaky with his tanned skin and a square jaw made him so good-looking I wondered how I hadn't noticed him sitting there right away.

"How are you doing today, Brandon?"

"Good, good," he nodded. "Much better now that I've gotten a look at your beautiful face."

Not many guys could deliver a line like that in exactly that tone and have it not sound completely cheesy. But he was smooth.

"Thank you."

He shook his head and tossed his cards in the middle of the table. "Fold."

He stood up, put a hand on my elbow, and steered me away from the tables. "I'm hosting another poker night at Hemlock Lake this Friday. You think you can make it?"

Disappointment filled me after I did a quick mental search of my schedule. "I don't think I can do it this time, Brandon. I have to open the casino on Saturday and Hemlock's a ways away."

He shoved his hands into the pockets of his pressed khakis and gave me a sly look. "The potential for a lot of money is here, Katie. More than enough to make it worthwhile to miss a day of work."

I spotted Joe entering the casino over Brandon's shoulder, and a shiver skipped through me. He had on black jeans and a black T-shirt that molded to his body, and even at a distance, my fingers itched to touch him. Brandon might be movie star good-looking and slick with the charm, but he didn't heat my blood with a glance the way Joe could. "I admit I'd like to give it a try. The most I make with the girls is a couple hundred dollars. But money isn't everything."

"You're right. And sitting at the table with my colleagues and me offers a lot more than money, Katie. Didn't you tell me you were moving to Vancouver soon?"

"I'm going to try, yes."

"Do you have a job lined up already? No, eh?" He smiled, the perfect whiteness of his teeth almost blinding in the dim light of the casino. "One of the guys at the table owns a restaurant out there. It might be good for you to meet him. You know, a chance to line up possible employment in the city."

That had my attention. I'd been working and skimping to save, so that I would have time to find a job when I got there. Not only did the poker game give me a good shot at a windfall, but a job hookup. The lure of ditching work pulled at me. "I can't, Brandon. Believe me I wish I could, but I can't just dump a shift." I chewed at the inside of my cheek and made a decision. "I'll try to get my shift covered, but I have a responsibility, so I'm not making any promises."

"All right. But you're missing out."

"I know. Just give me more notice next time, OK? I really want to do this."

He reached into his pocket and pulled out a small notebook. I could feel Joe's eyes on us as Brandon wrote something on a page in the book and tore it off. He held the slip of paper out for me. "My cell number. Call me if you change your mind."

I nodded and took it. "I will. Thanks, Brandon."

———————————

There wasn't much to do in Chadwick for entertainment. I guess that's why the casino did such good business. The three pubs and two bars were fun if you were with a big group celebrating something, but that was about it. I didn't like to go to them often because whatever happened there was fodder for the gossip mill the next day. That meant no fun.

The apartment felt too small and I needed to get out. I picked up the phone and called Julie at work.

"What time is your shift over?"

"Eight. What's up?"

"I'm going a little stir crazy. Want to go to a movie?"

"Sure. You'll pick me up?"

Just before eight, I strolled into the casino and headed to the lounge. The bartender was a new guy so I introduced myself and climbed onto a barstool.

He poured me a coffee and I waved at Jules.

It was pretty busy in the lounge, especially for a Monday night, so

I was left alone with my thoughts while I waited. Not the best thing when I was already feeling restless.

Another phone call from my mom earlier that evening was the main reason for the restlessness. I was sure of it. She'd called every evening for the last four nights. Each time leaving a message with an invitation for dinner. It was time for me to meet the new man.

Part of me was glad things were progressing enough that she wanted me to meet him. It could mean that she would have a man around when I left town. For a while anyway.

Tired of dodging her calls, I'd answered when she'd called earlier. I'd asked, but she wouldn't tell me anything about him over the phone. She insisted I meet him in person first and that *they* would be happy to answer any questions I had after.

Typical Lydia. Now that she had a man in her life, she wouldn't do anything without him.

A movement in the mirror behind the bar caught my attention, and I spun around on my chair to watch Joe. He prowled the perimeter of the lounge area, eyes scanning the patrons and staff alike. He was dressed in the same uniform as the other security guards and carried the same gadgets on his utility belt. Yet something set him apart.

You could tell just by looking at him that he wasn't your typical security guard.

There'd been a chance I could've found out more about him when we were working in the kitchen together the other night. But some instinct had held me back. Now, my blood heated as I watched him come closer, and I wished I hadn't been such a chicken-shit.

"Hey," he said when he reached my stool. He stood next to me, still watching the crowd, not looking at me.

"Hey," I replied. "Having a good night?"

"Not really."

That surprised me. Not that he wasn't having a good night, but that he would admit it to me.

"What's up?" I put a hand on his arm, trying to get him to look at me.

"Why are you here, Katie?"

Joe glanced at me, expression blank and eyes shuttered. He was even harder to read than before I'd seen him naked.

My spine stiffened. "I'm picking up Julie. We're going to a movie."

He didn't say anything to that, but I sensed some of the tension leave him. "Is that OK with you?"

"Yes."

"I was being sarcastic."

"I know." He leaned forward and planted a light kiss next to my ear. "Have fun."

Then he walked away.

"Did he just kiss you?" Julie dropped her tote bag on the bar stool next to me.

"Katie?" She snapped her fingers in front of my eyes. "Hellooo?"

I turned my head and met her dancing eyes. "Yeah, he just kissed me."

What the hell was going on?

Movies didn't hit the theaters in Chadwick until at least a month after their release date. So, on the drive from the casino to downtown, I kept Jules from bugging me about Joe by making her check the paper for the listings. We grabbed tickets for a big dumb action flick full of hot men, and hit the concession. Loaded down with hot buttered popcorn and huge cups of diet soda, we settled on seats in the middle of the theater.

The place wasn't exactly busy, so we had plenty of empty seats on every side, and a few minutes to kill before the show started.

"So tell me, Katie. What's going on with you and Bad Boy Joe?"

Julie slouched back in her seat, popcorn bucket in her lap, and gave me a steady stare.

"What do you mean? You know we're . . . screwing around."

"Uh-uh." She shook her head. "A guy that was interested in just sex wouldn't be sneaking you tender little kisses when he thinks no one is watching. There's more to it than a casual fuck. Give."

I munched some popcorn and sipped from my drink. How much did I want to tell her?

"It's still just sex, but the sex is pretty intense. That's all."

"Intense." She turned her head against the seat, and I felt the strength of her stare. "Intense, how?"

I met her gaze and felt my resolve crumble. "He can be a bit rough at times." I couldn't help it. I had to tell someone.

Her brows drew down sharply and she stiffened. I quickly put up a hand when she opened her mouth. "Not in a bad way. I like it."

"What do you mean not in a bad way? How can someone rough be good?"

"It's different. Like a little bit of domination and submission play. When I'm with him, I don't have to think. Chadwick, the casino, my mom . . . everything that I feel the need to control in my life fades away, and I give it up to him." A small, satisfied smile pulled at my lips. "It's simple. He tells me what he likes, and I do it. Or I let him do it to me."

"What about what *you* like? Doesn't he care about what you like?"

"That's just it. I like pleasing him."

She snorted and shook her head. Suddenly, it was important to me that she understand. "None of this was his idea, Jules. I started it that first day. I told him I wanted to do whatever he wanted, and he took me literally."

"You are such a control freak. I just can't imagine you telling a guy, any guy that he could do whatever he wanted."

"Yeah, well, you couldn't imagine me making a move on Joe in the first place either, could you?"

We stared at each other in silence for a minute.

"Just because I give him control doesn't mean he doesn't take care of me." Except for that first week. "Trust me on that. I never even knew there was such a thing as the extreme pleasure that man can give me."

"So give me an example of how he dominates you. That whole D/S thing isn't something I've ever had a yen to try. Give me details."

"You just want the dirty bits for your diary, don't you?" I threw a handful of popcorn at her. "You're such a pervert."

She laughed. "Yeah, so what? Give me details!"

We both settled back in our seats and I leaned over, talking in an almost whisper. I'd never share even the smallest of details with anyone except her. Julie was my best friend since childhood, and I trusted her.

"Okay, okay. Take last night as an example. Before he came over, he called me and told me to get a few things ready."

"Like what?" she interrupted.

"Well, I had to light some candles, and . . ." I felt a blush creeping up my neck.

"And what?"

"And when he got there I was to be waiting in the bedroom for him with nothing on but nipple clamps and a blindfold."

"Ohhh."

"Yeah. He spent a lot of time just touching me. Teasing me until I was almost ready to beg. Then he had me suck him for a while. When he was close to coming, he laid me on the bed and teased me some more. When I finally did beg, he gave me several mind-blowing orgasms."

It was a pretty simplistic description of what had happened, but best friend or not, I wasn't ready to share more with her.

Hell, I wasn't sure I was ready to know more.

17

After last night's phone call, I agreed to go to my mom's for dinner.

When I'd dropped Julie off after the movie, I'd told her I couldn't make our poker night and explained why. I hated to give up the poker practice, never mind the coin I could make off the girls, but Julie told me I was doing the right thing.

There was a pain between my shoulder blades, and I could feel a tension headache coming on strong when I stopped at the bakery on the way to Mom's. I was scared this guy would turn out to be just another loser. A man that Mom would get all wrapped up in, and then, when he was sure she was in love, he'd leave.

If that happened, how was I going get out of Chadwick with a clear conscience? It was time to meet him and decide if I could trust him with my mom.

When I arrived, I parked on the street because I didn't want to get blocked in when her man showed up. I walked up the drive and took a good look around. The yard looked good.

Mom's flower bushes were blooming and the grass was neat and manicured. Someone was taking care of the chores.

After ringing the bell, I stepped into the house and was greeted by the mouthwatering scent of a garlic roast. Yummy. My mom cooked a fantastic garlic rump roast.

The stereo in the living room was on and I could hear Mom in the kitchen singing along with Faith Hill. I turned the corner and saw that she was dancing, too. When she spun around and saw me, she jumped a foot in the air and dropped the ladle she'd been holding.

"Katie! You scared me to death!"

A laugh bubbled up and I couldn't stop it. "Sorry, Mom. I called out but you didn't hear me over Faith. I brought cheesecake for dessert."

I slid the package on the counter and hugged her. "You look great."

"Thank you." She hugged me back. Tight. "I love you, Katie. You know that, right?"

I pulled back and looked at her. "Of course I know that, Mom."

"And you know I would never do anything to deliberately hurt you right, baby?"

"Yeah." The hairs on the back of my neck stood up.

"Good." She patted me on the shoulder and turned back to her pot roast.

"Uhmm, Mom?"

"Yes, dear?"

"What was that all about?"

"I just want you to always remember that I love you."

The doorbell rang as she spoke, and she set down the baster, closed the oven door, and set the pot holders on the counter. "That's him. You stay here, dear. Pour yourself a glass of wine, and I'll be right back."

I watched as she hustled out of the kitchen, undoing her apron as he went. Something really strange was going on, and I didn't know what. Muffled voices echoed through the house as I dug through the drawer for a corkscrew and opened the bottle of red wine that was on the counter.

I'd just taken a sip from the glass when Mom walked into the kitchen holding hands with Brad.

Brad Marks.

My Brad.

If it weren't for the mixture of guilt and happiness on their faces, and the fact that they were holding hands, I might not have clued in as fast I did.

A younger man. A hard worker. The hardware store. The well-maintained yard, the front porch railing being fixed.

UGH!

I fought the urge to smack myself in the forehead. How could I have missed it?

I missed it because they deliberately hid it from me.

"Katie?" My mom's voice trembled.

"How long?"

"Katie—" Brad stepped forward and I put my hand up to stop him.

"I can't believe I didn't clue into this," I said.

"Katie—"

"Stop!" I commanded. I took a deep breath and met my mom's eyes.

"I think I need to leave now. I'll talk to you later."

I needed to get out of there. Fast. Before I said something or did something that I could never take back.

My whole body was hot. It felt like my stomach was a volcano, and it was spewing red-hot lava through my system. I needed to escape before it spewed right out my mouth in the form of vile accusations.

Staring straight ahead and shaking my head, I brushed past them and out the door. It took two tries to get the key in the ignition of my car because my fingers were trembling so badly.

What the hell had just happened? My mom had introduced my ex boyfriend, the guy who took my virginity, as her new boyfriend.

I dropped my head on the steering wheel and closed my eyes. A slow ten count and I felt slightly more in control, so I put the clutch to the floor and pulled away from the curb. At the end of the street, I had to fight the urge to hit the highway and go to the roadside hotel where I knew Joe was still living.

So many things were swimming in my mind. The clues about her and Brad that I'd missed. If they'd had sex yet—Yuck! What a thought! If they were serious, how could they possibly be serious? How did this all start? Was it for real? Maybe it was all a joke.

I swung by the liquor store on my way home and grabbed a bottle of tequila. Cider was not going to cut it this time. I thought about going over to Julie's, but it didn't feel right. I needed time to think.

When I got home, Mrs. Beets was searching the parking lot, looking for Pepper, who'd gotten out. I wanted so bad to just walk away and not care, but when she looked at me with watery eyes and her hands fluttered about, I told her I'd help her. It only took me a couple of minutes to see Pepper hiding behind a wild fern on the edge of the lot.

Without calling out to Mrs. Beets, who'd probably rush over and scare the poor cat up a tree, I set down my purse and brown paper bag. With slow baby steps, I walked over to the cat.

Pepper's pink nose twitched and she gave me the unblinking cross-eyed cat stare, but didn't move. I reached beneath the plant fronds and grabbed her by the scruff the neck. Once I knew she couldn't run, and I realized she didn't want to run, I reached in with my other hand and picked her up. Sharp claws dug into my arm and Pepper looked up at me and meowed.

She was shivering a bit and I realized she was scared. "Mrs. Beets," I called out. "Over here."

Mrs. Beets hustled over and cuddled the animal to her.

"Thank you, thank you, Katie," she warbled.

"No problem." I went and picked up my stuff off the pavement and headed to the door.

Once inside, I dropped my purse on the floor and went straight to the fridge, a glass, some ice cubes, a few ounces of tequila, and the fog in my head started to shift.

I needed to think logically.

Brad was a good guy. And he did really want the same things my mom wanted. To settle down in Chadwick and build a family. What would they do about a family? Brad had always said he wanted kids, but Mom was too old to have another child. My heart started to pound and little lights danced in front of my eyes.

Breathe. Count to ten. Breathe.

Okay. No one said anything about getting married. Maybe I was jumping the gun.

I tried to take another drink and realized my glass was empty. The phone rang and I debated answering it. The machine clicked on and Joe's heavenly voice filled my ears.

"Katie, I know you had plans for dinner. But if you—"

I snatched up the receiver.

"I'm here."

"Dinner ended early?" he asked.

"I left before dinner was served. What are you up to?"

"Just got out of the shower. I know I just saw you last night, but you said whenever I wanted."

"Yes, I did. Come now."

There was a brief loaded silence. "Are you OK? You sound odd."

I reached for the bottle of tequila and poured myself another drink. "Just come over."

By the time Joe buzzed my apartment, there was only half a bottle of tequila left. I looked at the clock and saw that only twenty minutes had gone by. When I stood up to let him in, the room spun a bit and it felt like my head was floating three inches above my neck.

I unlocked the door and sat on the sofa. Joe strode into the room, closed the door behind him, and leaned against it.

"What happened?" he asked.

"My mom's boyfriend is my high school sweetheart."

His eyebrows jumped and something like relief crossed his face. He pulled away from the door, crossed the room, and dropped on the sofa next to me. Without a word, he wrapped an arm around my shoulders and cuddled me close.

Suddenly, I was crying. Tears were rolling down my cheeks, my empty glass dropped to the floor, and I covered my face with my hands. I didn't know why I was crying.

Nobody died, I wasn't hurt, and everything was OK.

Yet the tears wouldn't stop. I shifted, turning into Joe and buried my face in his shoulder.

When my sobs subsided I became aware of his hand rubbing slow circles on my back.

"Better now?"

I nodded.

"Want to tell me about it?"

I thought about that. Joe and I were in a sexual relationship. At least that's how it started. I really didn't plan to let anything grow from that. He seemed to like Chadwick, and I really wanted to get out of there. But our relationship was shifting, growing. I trusted him. I liked him.

But I didn't want to think anymore.

I shifted my weight and straddled him on the sofa. "No, I don't want to talk."

With no hesitation I leaned forward and kissed him. Our lips touched, tongues tangled, and heartbeats merged.

Large hands cupped my shoulders and pulled me close. For a minute we just kissed. Joe's hands were gentle as they slid down my back to my hips and settled there.

But gentleness wasn't what I wanted from him. I wanted to forget everything that had happened. I wanted to get lost in the taste of him. The scent of him, the feel of him beneath me.

The need to be immersed in him took over, and I raked my hands through his hair. I nudged his jaw with my head and angled in so I could lick and suck at his neck. His fingers dug into my hips, and he dropped his head back against the sofa, leaving himself exposed.

I heard his breath rasp next to my ear and felt his cock harden beneath me. Then, without hesitation, he stood from the sofa, with me in his arms and strode to the bedroom. He tossed me on the bed and started to strip.

No words were spoken. None were needed. I got on my knees in the middle of the bed and whipped off my own clothes. I threw my bra on the floor just in time to see Joe step out of his jeans and put a knee on the mattress. I welcomed him with open arms and fell back on the bed, with him stretched out on top of me. Chest to chest, belly to belly, groin to groin.

Our mouths met hungrily, our hearts pounding in time, as hands caressed known pleasure zones. My nails scraped against his skin, delighting in the way the muscles flexed beneath them. My legs wrapped around his waist, and I rubbed against him, searching for the friction I needed. A low growl rumbled from my throat and I arched my back, rolling us over so I was on top. Joe's hands lifted me up and settled me directly on his cock. I sat up. With a roll of my hips I had him right where I wanted him. Where I needed him.

Neither of us moved for a minute. We stayed there, motionless, looking into each other's eyes and enjoying the connection. He was so deep inside me that I swear he was touching my heart.

Joe's hands rested on my thighs and I rolled my hips again. I leaned forward, balancing myself by placing my hands on his solid chest, and withdrew my hips. Then I slid back down the full length of him. Slowly I rotated my hips, up and down. Just enjoying the feel of him filling me up again and again. Drowning in the emotion in his eyes, as he watched me take my pleasure.

Soon, it wasn't enough. I planted my hands on the mattress next to his head and really began to ride him. I rocked back and forth. Using him to forget everything but the knot of pleasure building in my sex.

Our panting filled the air, erotic music in the utter silence between us. His hands skimmed over my rib cage to my swaying breasts. He cupped them, tugging at the nipples until I lowered myself enough so that he could clamp his lips around one of the rigid tips. He suckled briefly and then nipped it sharply with his teeth. I ground down hard on him, seeing stars at the same time he dug his heels into the mattress and thrust up, lodging himself deep and shooting hot fluid into me, filling all the emptiness inside.

I closed my eyes and collapsed on top of him. Our bodies slick with sweat and still connected. I could feel his heart pounding against his chest. And the rhythm was in tune with mine.

18

The obnoxious scream of my alarm clock woke me up the next morning. After slamming my hand on the snooze button three times, I dragged my ass from the bed to the bathroom and propped myself under the shower for a few minutes.

When the pounding in my skull dulled from a hard pounding to a steady throb, I was able to peel my eyes open and wash. The foul taste in my mouth was probably due to the tequila, but I was pretty sure the headache was from the emotional upheaval of the night before.

Joe was gone, as usual, and I was glad for it. I didn't think I was ready to face anyone, let alone him. Despite the obvious increase in the comfort level between us, last night pushed this thing over the line of just a sexual relationship. I couldn't lie to myself anymore. I was falling for him. And that was a complication I did not need.

I reached for my makeup bag and went to work on hiding the bags under my eyes. Last night, Joe's behavior had shown me a new side to him. A sensitive side that had only been hinted at before. He'd been there for me in a way I hadn't anticipated.

It was as if he had known that I'd needed *him* more than anything, that the connection was important, not just the sex. And to be honest, the whole idea of the growing closeness between us was just another tie to Chadwick I didn't want.

"Fuck!" I'd stabbed myself in the eye with my mascara wand. Just what I needed to start the day off right.

"You OK?"

I jumped a foot in the air and clamped a hand to my chest, as if to calm my racing heart.

"You scared the crap out of me!" I glared at Joe's reflection in my bathroom mirror. He looked tired. He still had on his clothes from last night. He hadn't shaved and his hair was just a bit mussed. And he was still here. "I thought you were gone."

He held up a bakery bag and a steaming plastic coffee cup. "I figured you'd need a little 'pick me up' this morning."

He set the cup on the counter and turned away. "I'll be in the kitchen."

I gave up on the mascara and got dressed. Thank God it was summer. I could dress casual in nice shorts and a cotton top for work, and not wear any makeup, and most people wouldn't think anything of it. The second my shift was over, I was heading for home. Sleeping on the couch sounded like a good plan.

Joe was standing out on the balcony. I spotted the bakery bag on the rail next to him and carried my coffee out there to join him.

"Enjoying the early morning sunshine?" I squinted, wishing I'd brought my sunglasses out with me. After pulling a muffin from the paper bag I leaned back against the rail, away from the sun.

"We need to talk," Joe said.

I glanced up at him. His piercing eyes were shadowed, but they met mine in a steady gaze.

Something like panic made my pulse race and I started to babble. "Brad Marks was the first real boyfriend I ever had. He was older than me, he'd been away to college, lived in the city for a few years, and I worshipped him." A hiccup jumped from my throat but I didn't stop.

"I tried to seduce him when I was sixteen, but he turned me down. He waited until I was eighteen, and my first date with him was my high school graduation. A year later I gave him my virginity. When I say I gave it to him, I mean I threw it at him. It was all my idea. Brad wasn't a virgin, but he was pretty damn straight laced. At the time I thought he was just gentlemanly, but it became clear after a few months that his lack of enthusiasm had nothing to do with being a gentleman. He was leaning towards marriage, but I knew it wouldn't happen. We just didn't connect."

"Katie—" He raised a hand, as if to stop the flow of my words.

"No. Let me finish."

After holding my gaze for minute he pressed his lips together and nodded.

"After my father passed away, my mom transferred all her attention to me. Until the next man came along." I took a deep breath and shook my head. "She had a real knack for hooking up with losers and drifters. Somehow, I became responsible for her. Or at least I started to *feel* responsible. She doesn't like to drive around town, she only goes out when someone else drives or she can walk. She can't program her VCR or even record the message on her voice mail without help. Every time I mentioned moving away, or going to the city, some big drama would happen and she'd need me. About six months ago, I realized it was never going to change. She was going to keep manipulating me as long as I let her, and I started making plans. Plans to move to Vancouver."

Joe's eyes narrowed and I gripped my coffee cup.

"I'm leaving Chadwick next month."

"Katie—"

The buzzer to my apartment sounded, interrupting Joe. I gave him a small smile and dashed inside. "Who the hell is here at eight in the morning?"

Holding a hand to my pounding head I pressed the intercom. "Who is it?"

"It's Julie. Let me up."

I pushed the buzzer and let Jules in. She must've ran up the stairs because she was inside my apartment before I could stick my head out the patio door and tell Joe I'd be another minute.

"How was dinner with the mom last night?"

"Not so great," I said. "What are you doing here so early? You're normally dead to the world until at least noon."

She shrugged and strolled toward me. I was standing in the sun that streamed in the open patio door, letting it warm my back. I could hear Joe crumple up the bakery bag out on the patio, but he stayed out there.

"I thought you'd call after you left your mom's last night, and when you didn't, I got a bit worried." Julie stopped in front of me and I could see the concern in her dark gaze.

Something wasn't right. There was an itch at the back of my brain, but the fog in my head was making it hard to think.

Julie shoved her hands deep into the pockets of her denim cutoffs and cocked her head to the side. "What do you think of your mom's new boyfriend?"

The fog parted slowly and I gasped. "You knew! You knew all along who it was!"

Hands on hips, chin jutting forward, I dared her to deny it.

"Yes," she said. "I knew Brad was dating your mom."

She said the words softly as she reached for me. I stepped away and felt Joe at my back. My insides started to tremble and anger at her betrayal surged through me. "How could you not warn me?"

"I didn't know how to." Julie's gaze flicked over my shoulder, and I felt Joe's hand on the small of my back, strong and comforting. "You're always bitching about the losers your mom hooks up with. I thought you'd be happy she found a good guy."

"That's bullshit! If you thought I'd be happy about it, you would've told me."

My chest heaved and my head spun. How could she, my best friend, the person who I thought knew me best, hide such a thing from me?

"You're right," she said. "I knew you'd be pissed to start with, but think about it, Katie! Brad is perfect for her! He's a good guy. He won't hurt her, and he won't leave her. He wants to stay in Chadwick and run the family hardware store. He wants a wife who will cook him dinner and fuss over him. Your mom wants a man who will support her and let her fuss over him. It's perfect!"

"It's Brad and *my mom*!" I threw my hands up and turned away from her. I pulled away from Joe's touch and looked at them both. "I have to go. I'm going to be late for work."

Without another word, I snatched my purse off the floor by the door and left, slamming the door behind me.

———————————————

I kept my mind blank and concentrated on my breathing during the drive to work. I ignored Mrs. Beets as she waved at me from her patio, and I didn't even spare Matt a glance as I drove past the gas station where he still sat watching the world go by.

It took every once of willpower I had to steer the car into the parking lot of Black's and not just keep going down the highway.

"You're overreacting," I muttered to myself. "What's the big deal? It's not as if you were still in love with Brad yourself."

I turned the car off and sat there for a minute. The sun was heating up already, and the birds were singing happily. The world had not come to a complete standstill because my life was falling apart.

Okay, it wasn't *falling apart*. This was just a shock, that's all. A couple of shocks really. One right after the other. I pushed Julie to the back of my mind to deal with later and focused on the first surprise.

I dropped my head back against the seat and closed my eyes. Brad really was a good guy. My mom had made a good choice with him. He wasn't the kind of guy that would use her and then stroll right out of town, even if he didn't want to stay in Chadwick forever.

It wasn't the age thing. Although, when Mom had said she was dating a younger man, I did think ten years younger at the most, not twenty.

So really, what was it that had me the most upset here? The fact that my mom was fucking my ex-boyfriend and might even marry him, or the fact that she hadn't told me before now?

I did a gut check, and confirmed my own suspicions. It didn't bother me that much that it was Brad. What bothered me the most was that she never told me it was him, even though she'd had many opportunities.

Even worse was the fact that Julie had known.

19

"Katie."

"What?" I snapped without thinking. My heavy sigh filled the silence and I looked at Hope in the doorway. "Sorry, Hope. I didn't mean to snap. What do you need?"

"Are you okay?" she asked. "No offense, but you don't look so hot, and you've been out of it all day."

Out of it was putting it mildly. My mind had shut down in self-defense after the third phone call from my mom.

"I'll talk to you in a day or two, Mom. Just give me some time, okay?" I'd said on that final phone call. "Don't call me at work again."

"I'm fine," I told Hope. "Just a bit hungover."

"Ahh. That I understand. My loonie machine is jammed. Can you fix it for me or should I call tech?"

After fixing the hopper, I went back into the office and started to count the cash bags. Joe would be there in ten minutes to escort me down to the bank vault.

When the security door buzzed, I braced myself, and saw Tom walk into the office.

"Hey, Katie, ready to take that down to the bank?"

"Uhmm, yeah. Let's go."

Tom opened the door, and I pushed the cart through. I waved bye to the girls and followed Tom through the security doors, pushing the cart. When we got to the elevator, I glanced over at him. "Where's Joe?"

I couldn't help it.

"He's in some meeting with the boss. He put me on escort duty."

The lift arrived and we entered it. When the doors slid shut he turned to look at me. "You know, if you ever need it, my wife tells me I've a good shoulder to cry on."

Startled, I stared at him with my mouth open.

"You look like you lost your best friend," he said in explanation.

He'd hit the nail on the head there.

"I look that bad, huh?"

The elevator stopped and the door slid open. Tom stepped outside and checked that the hall was empty then put a hand on the cart, blocking my exit. "I know Joe has a lot of walls, Katie, but I've seen the way he looks at you. Almost like you're too good to be true. Just give him some time."

Huh?

"Uhmm, okay. Thanks, Tom."

He gave me a brotherly smile and stepped back, letting me out of the elevator and going down the hallway.

One of the side effects of a small community. If people didn't actually know what was going on in your life, they usually knew enough to *think* they knew what was going on.

———————————— ▬ ————————————

After a shitty day with everyone under the sun asking me if I was okay and trying to give me advice on matters they really didn't know anything about, I was exhausted.

Instead of going home, I followed Main Street straight through town to the other side. After ten minutes on the highway, I pulled off at the roadside restaurant in the middle of nowhere.

The Burger Shack was a small square stand-alone building. It was made out of brick and had survived every forest fire that had swept through the area for the last twenty-five years.

Lots of people in British Columbia, especially in the Kootenays, preferred to live out of town. The mountains were full of lush flora and teeming with wildlife.

The parking lot of the Burger Shack was almost full, but the deck with picnic tables that ran along two sides of the building was empty except for one table. I went inside the shack and stood in the line up. Most people were picking up dinner on their commute home from work, but when it was my turn at the counter, I got my burger, fries, and chocolate milk shake on a tray and went to sit outside.

Aside from the comings and goings of the takeout crowd, it was pretty quiet out there. Peaceful.

Until I saw a shiny blue pickup with a familiar sign on the door pull into the lot. It parked next to my car, and the driver came over to sit at my table.

It didn't surprise me that, if he was looking for me, he'd know to come here. I used to make him drive me out to the Burger Shack at least once a week to sit on the patio, drink milk shakes, and watch the squirrels and rabbits. Occasionally, we even saw deer. I sure as hell wasn't going to talk first.

I munched a french fry and waited for him to speak. A furry little squirrel dashed across the parking lot and up a tree. A bird landed nearby and started to pick at the ground. Finally, I looked over at my companion and met his dark gaze.

"What?"

"Your mom is really upset."

I clenched my jaw and counted to ten. Okay, I only counted to five. "Look, Brad, I talked to her a little while ago. What part of 'give me some time' does she not understand?"

"Don't be a bitch, Katie. It doesn't suit you." He leaned forward; elbows on the table hands clasped in front of him. "What are you so upset about? I knew it would be a bit of a shock, but this reaction seems a bit extreme."

I heaved a sigh. "There's more going on in my life than me finally finding out who my mom is fucking."

He flinched at my harsh words, and I felt a touch of remorse. Brad, like my mom, thought that women should never swear, and he really didn't deserve the brunt of my bad mood. He was a good guy, a nice guy. He was perfect for my mom.

While I was trying not to let my buried temper reemerge, Brad was silent. Then he looked at me calmly and spoke in a soft but firm voice, "There's more to it than that. I'm in love with Lydia."

I sat back, milk shake in hand, and stared at him. His gaze was sincere and I believed him. "What about kids? You always said you wanted kids."

"I don't know. I did want to have kids. But your mom is an amazing woman, and if she doesn't want to have more kids, then that's fine with me. I've started an after-school program out of the hardware store. I deal with a lot of kids there, and I feel like I'm actually being a mentor. I'm helping them to learn and grow, and really, that's enough for me. I have a good woman to go home to."

"Touching."

"Katie." He shook his head at me.

"OK, here's what I think." I leaned forward, arms on the table, face close to his. "I don't really want to think about the two of you in bed together, but strangely, other than that, I can see how perfect you are for each other. Does that mean everything is all right? No. It's not. Because both of you knew this was happening and neither of you told me."

My throat was getting tight, and I could feel emotion starting to swell in my chest, so I stopped, took a deep breath, and continued, "It's not so much that you're together. I can live with that. It's the fact that nobody told me. Even Julie knew, for Christ's sake, and yet nobody could tell me! Did you all think it would break my heart or something?"

"No, it's not that." Brad gave me a small smile. The one that I thought was mysterious and seductive when I was eighteen. Now it just looked lackluster.

"It just sort of happened. I ran into your mom at the Main Street Diner last month and we sat together. I really enjoyed talking to her, so when she mentioned wanting to hire someone to look after the yard, I told her about the after-school program and offered to bring some kids over. Maybe set her up with one of the older ones as a yard boy. The next thing I knew I'd asked her out for dinner and a movie. It just grew, Katie. It wasn't planned." He paused and snitched a french fry from my tray. "We ran into Julie and her girlfriend at Ainsworth one afternoon."

Ainsworth was another small town just over a two-hour drive from Chadwick. The main attraction there was the natural hot springs that were rumored to have healing properties. I didn't know about the healing, but the simmering pools in the side of the mountains were definitely something special. And romantic.

"So, you were on a romantic date at the hot springs, and you ran into my friends, and *none* of you thought to mention it to me?"

"It was still so new to us, and we weren't sure where it was going. Your mom . . ." He paused and looked away. "No matter what I say, Lydia is sure that I broke your heart when we broke up, and that's why you've never had another boyfriend."

I rolled my eyes and Brad chuckled. The tension between us was finally gone.

"You and I both know that you weren't heartbroken. And we both know that us breaking up was for the best. You wanted a bit of adventure and you thought you'd get that with an older man. I wanted a pretty wife. What we had was good, but it would never have lasted." He reached across the table and covered my hand with his. "But I do love you, Katie. You'll always be my friend and I'd never want to hurt you."

"I know."

"So, you're OK with this?"

I nodded. "I am. Just don't expect me to call you Dad."

The look on Brad's face at that was priceless. When he realized I was deliberately trying to shock him, he laughed and shook his head. "I'm going to go grab myself a burger, then you can tell me what else is going on in your life."

I watched him walk away and sighed. I felt a bit better after talking to him, not a hundred percent, but enough that I realized it was time to call my mom.

I'd just snapped my cell phone closed when Brad returned with a tray of food. My mom had been waiting by the phone and had been tearful when I assured her I still loved her and that I was happy for her and Brad. It had all just been a shock, and she'd better not keep secrets like that from me again. It had helped to remind her that I'd soon be in Vancouver and I'd only have phone calls to keep me up to date on how things were, so I expected full disclosure.

"Lydia?" Brad asked when he saw me put the phone away.

"Yup." I settled back with my milk shake.

We enjoyed the comfortable quiet while he ate. I tossed a couple of fries and chunks of my hamburger bun on the ground for the birds. None wanted them, though. I thought about picking it up and was surprised to see a squirrel come dashing out, grab a chunk of bread, and disappear again.

Our eyes met and we laughed. Brad wiped his mouth with a napkin and he searched my expression. "Want to tell me what else is going on?"

Did I?

"I'm just sick of Chadwick. It's the same old, same old. Everyone expects so much. I'm tired of customers who think they can treat us like shit because they've had a bad day at the slot machines. I'm tired of being the good neighbor, the good daughter, and the good friend. I'm tired of everyone thinking they know what's going on in my life, when they have no clue." I blew out a breath. "And it really bothers me that Julie knew about you guys and didn't tell me. That bothers me more than the fact that you guys didn't tell me right away."

"That's a lot to be tired of."

"Yeah. And then there's Joe."

"Joe?"

"Joe Carson. I work with him at the casino."

"Is he your boyfriend?"

"I don't think I'd call him my boyfriend." It was weird, but the urge to tell Brad everything was strong. Okay, not *everything*. But most of it. "Really, I have no idea what to call him. It started out as just sex, but things have gotten sort of complicated."

I looked at Brad, trying to get a read on his thoughts, but he just sat there. Patiently waiting for me to spill my guts. We'd always been able to talk about anything and everything, and I was happy to see that hadn't changed.

"I really like him, but I don't want to."

Brads eyebrows puckered. "Why don't you want to?"

"I'm leaving Chadwick soon, and no offense, but I'm not my mom, I'm not going to let a man keep me here when I want to go."

He nodded. "You need to do what's right for you, Katie. I know you've stayed here this long because of your mom, and I can promise you that I'll be there for her when you leave. As for Joe, only you can decide just how much he's worth to you. You could always try the long distance thing for a while. You'll learn after doing that for a while if Joe is worth moving back here for, or if living in the city is what's important to you. Absence just might make the heart grow fonder."

I shrugged. There was no doubt in my mind that I'd love living in big city, but he was right about one thing. Only I could decide how much Joe was worth to me.

20

The drive home after my little sit down with Brad was an effort. I was tired, emotionally drained, and my head was still aching. I wasn't ready for a showdown with anyone, but when I got to my apartment, I found Julie sitting on the couch watching a movie. Waiting for me.

I ignored her and went straight to my bedroom to change into shorts and a tank top. The summer heat wasn't helping my mood any.

"You ever going to talk to me again?" she asked from the bedroom doorway.

"At some point, I'm sure I will. But not right now."

"You can't run away from me forever, Katie. I won't let you."

I could feel my insides start to heat up again and not in a good way. "I wasn't running away from you, Julie. I went to work, and now I'm tired, hungover, and all I want is to get some sleep."

"Did you call your mom? She's been calling here and leaving messages on your answering machine all day."

"She called me at work. I've talked to her." I strode past her and into the kitchen. With the thought that my head couldn't hurt any worse, I reached into the fridge and pulled out a cold cider. "Don't you have something better to do on your day off than lie in wait at my place?"

"Yes, I do. But even if you don't believe it, I thought you were important, too."

I sighed, my anger draining. I really was tired. "I believe you, Jules. I guess that's why I just don't understand why you wouldn't tell me about Mom and Brad when you found out."

She shrugged. "They asked me not to."

My anger came flooding back. "But I'm your best friend. Not them!"

"You are. But your mom is so sweet, I couldn't say no to her, and sometimes you can be such a . . . a spoiled brat, that I could understand why she wanted to tell you herself."

"Me? A brat?"

"You have everything, Katie. You have a mom who loves you, neighbors who love you, and a good job with a boss who loves you. Everybody fucking loves you! Yet, all you can ever do is complain about this place. About how everyone expects so much from you, and everyone is always sticking their nose in your business. So I kept mine out of your business by doing as your mom asked. And now you're pissed about that, too." She threw her hands up in the air in defeat. "You can't have it both ways, Katie."

Pain knifed through my chest and I struggled to swallow my tears. "I didn't realize you thought so little of me."

"It's not that I think little of you." She stepped closer and reached for my hands, but I pulled away.

I set my drink on the counter and crossed my arms over my chest.

Despite the heat, a chill was creeping through me. "You should've told me."

"Maybe." Her shoulders lifted and fell and she looked at the ground. "But I didn't, and we need to move past that. This is about more than me not telling you about Lydia and Brad. It's about you not seeing what's right in front of you."

"What's that supposed to mean?"

"You need to take the blinders off and see what's around you. My God, Katie! You have everything a person could want right here. And all you ever do is talk about getting away from it." She took a deep breath, like she was bracing herself, then continued in a rush. "I know you think it's a burden to have so many people wanting to be part of your life. But it's a blessing. Some of us . . . all we want is someone to love us. Your mom is like that, and you mock her for it. I'm like that. And I feel blessed that I've got Lillian and you in my life because let's face it, I don't have anyone else. I know where your mom's coming from. But because what we want isn't the same as what you want, you don't even bother trying to understand.

"I don't want to lose you, Katie, but you need to open up your eyes and see what you have before you lose it all."

I stood there, silent, with tears overflowing from my eyes. Jules stepped forward and wrapped her arms around me.

"I love you," she whispered.

I didn't hug her back and I didn't answer. She pulled back and gave me a small smile. Then she turned and walked away.

When the door shut behind her, my knees buckled and my sobs broke free. Why was this all happening? What had I done to deserve being lied to and yelled at? I was the one who'd been wronged. Was I really such a bad person? I tried to be a good person. I truly did.

Why was it so hard to understand that I wanted more from life than to live in a small town where everyone knew my name? I couldn't even go grocery shopping without everyone knowing what I was making for dinner. Was it so wrong to want some privacy?

No. It wasn't.

I sucked in a deep breath and got to my feet. In fact, it was all I wanted. I decided then and there that I was going to call Brandon and go to that poker night. If I had to call in sick the next day, I'd call in sick. But I was going to do whatever I could to bank some more money so I could be out of town by the end of the month.

I needed space from everyone. I wanted to be on my own. And the only way I was going to do that was to move on.

———

Thursday was my day off from work, and I did nothing. I unplugged my phone, turned off my cell phone, and lay on the patio all afternoon. Joe had called the night before when I was sleeping to see if I was OK.

The call had been short and sweet. "Life just sucks sometimes," I told him. "Thanks for caring."

He offered to come over and said we still needed to talk, but I told him I just wanted to spend my day off alone. I'd talk to him on Friday.

It might not have been my best decision. I tried to read, but I couldn't wrap my head around the story, so I just lay around, Brad's words swimming in my head together with Julie's.

They were both right, but they were wrong, too. There was obviously some hidden resentment in Julie that needed to come out. She called me judgmental for not wanting to be like my mom, when she was judging me because I wanted to get away from Chadwick and have a life. Because I wanted something different from her.

It hurt. It really really hurt. Especially since I was one of the few that knew about her and Lillian being lovers, and I'd kept her secret and never judged her for it.

The urge to call Joe was strong. Somehow, in such a short time he'd become my escape from it all. When I was with him, everything else faded away. But as much as I craved the freedom I had when I was with him, I knew calling him before I had my head on straight again would be a bad idea.

I woke up before my alarm went off on Friday morning. I got ready and was at work in time to sit at the bar and enjoy my morning coffee with Jimmy.

"Why did you move to Chadwick, Jimmy?"

He glanced up from the straws he was stocking. "I was tired of not enjoying life."

"What do you mean? From all your stories, you obviously had a full life in Vancouver."

"I saw a lot of things when I lived there. I even did a lot of things, and at the time I thought I was enjoying myself, but when I sobered up, I realized that I was killing myself slowly. And that when I was dead, no one would miss me."

"I'd miss you." It was true, too.

"Why thank you, Katie." He gave me a big smile. "I'm a different man than I was then, and I'm happy to say that I've realized what it is in life that's important to me."

"How did you do that? I mean, you say when you sobered up. Does that mean you had a drinking problem?"

"Drinking, drugs, sex. I've been a bartender my whole life. That's a lot of partying."

"What happened that made you . . ." I paused. "How bad was it?"

"It wasn't bad. I wasn't an addict that had to do a twelve-step program or anything. I just drank every day at work, along with a little drugs here and there. I thought I was living the high life. And to be honest, nothing big and shocking happened to snap me out of it either. I just woke up one morning, in bed with two women whose names I didn't know, and realized that my birthday had passed by a month earlier without anyone noticing. Even me."

I sat at the bar, staring into my coffee for a few minutes. I was trying to see what Jimmy was telling me, but I didn't get it. His epiphany obviously only made sense to him. But that was OK.

"Sometimes, I dream of that. Of being in a place where nobody knows my birthday, or remembers when I was riding around on a tricycle."

"The grass is always greener on the other side of the fence." He looked at me with knowing eyes.

I remembered that I'd decided earlier to try and get into Brandon's poker game that night. If there was a fence separating me from greener grass, it was time to jump it.

"You also told me that 'success doesn't come to you; you go to it.'" I flashed him a smile and slid from my stool. "Thanks, Jimmy."

I was walking past the lounge on the way back from my coffee break, when I saw Julie arguing loudly with one of the regulars. It was only two in the afternoon, and he was drunk already. As I was watching, Joe turned the corner and stopped a few feet away from them to monitor the argument.

If Joe got involved, Louie would be barred for at least a month, and despite the fact that he annoyed everyone there, he was a good guy. So I stepped over to them.

"Hey, guys, what's up?"

"This little girl is s-shlacking off and not doing her job." He slurred and pointed his finger at Julie's chest.

Julie looked at me, anger sparking in her dark eyes. We both knew I had no dominion over lounge business, but Louie didn't know that. We'd played the roles before. "He called me a chimpanzee!"

"I didn't call you one, missy. I said a chimpanzee could do your job better than you were."

I stepped in front of Julie to keep her from taking a swing at the guy. "It seems to me Louie that you've had a bit to drink already."

"A couple of whiskeys is all." His chin jutted out, and I tried not to stare at the dribble of drool trembling on his bottom lip. "What's wrong with that? Drinking and gambling go hand in hand, and I'm gambling."

"The problem with that is that it's against the law for Julie to continue serving you alcohol if she thinks you're intoxicated." He opened his mouth to interrupt, and I stepped closer, putting a hand gently on his bicep and smiling up at him. "And even if you're considered drunk, it's illegal for us to let you keep gambling, too."

"But I'm not drunk." He staunchly defended himself.

I leaned in close and whispered. "There's an inspector from the Gaming Board here today, and we need to be extra careful or we could get a fine. Julie knows this. She's just looking after us."

When he didn't say anything I pressed my point home. "Louie, you would never call Julie names if you weren't drunk, and we both know it. Why don't you apologize, and I'll walk you outside and wait for a cab with you. Okay?"

He looked at his shoes for a second then sucked in his gut and met Julie's glare straight on. "I'm sorry, missy. I didn't mean nothing by it."

"You owe me twenty-five bucks for your tab."

I met Julie's eyes while Louie dug out his wallet. Neither of us said anything. There was nothing to say at that point. Louie paid her, giving her a generous tip, and I walked with him to the exit. There was a cab sitting outside the casino doors, and I waved to Louie as it drove away. When I turned around, Joe was standing there.

"Hey," I said softly.

"You did good with him. You ever consider working security?"

"Not a chance in hell." I laughed. "The only reason I do OK every once in while is because it's *only* every once in a while."

We walked side by side, back to the cash office. I was waiting for him to say something, but he was quiet. The silence wasn't exactly uncomfortable, but it felt a bit heavy.

I should've been embarrassed to see him again. Since I'd cried, babbled like an idiot, and told him my life story in five hundred words or less the last time I saw him. Then there was the fact that I'd stormed out of my apartment, leaving him there with Julie. But I wasn't embarrassed.

Maybe it was because when he'd phoned on Wednesday night he'd only wanted to know that I was OK, and that was it.

When we got the cash office, I reached to punch in the code for the door but he stopped me with a hand on my arm.

"I'm going to come by and see you later tonight."

It wasn't a question.

"Uhmm." I looked at him from under my lashes. "I have plans tonight that might run late."

The brackets around his mouth tightened. "What plans?"

"Just . . . plans."

"You're mine, while you're still here," he growled.

"I know that." At least he wasn't trying to convince me to stay in Chadwick. He'd heard me clearly when I said I was leaving, and he accepted it. "This isn't *that* kind of plans. It's just something I need to do so I can be able to take care of myself when I move. A little something I'm doing to help out my nest egg, no sex involved."

His eyes narrowed and a new tension came into his body.

"We still need to talk. Soon."

"We will." I heard my name being called from inside the cage and I gave him a little smile and leaned closer. "I also need to suck your cock soon."

His sharp intake of breath gave me a satisfying thrill, and I turned to enter the cash cage.

"Tease," he said, and swatted me on the ass. "You'll pay for that."

I opened the door and stepped inside, speaking over my shoulder. "Oooh, I can't wait."

I buzzed at the second door, and Susan let me in. "This fucking hopper is jammed again," she said as soon as the door swung open. Time to concentrate on work.

21

When Joe came up to the office that afternoon to help me take the cash down to the vault, there was instant sexual tension between us. Not just the regular hum of awareness that had become normal whenever we were in the same vicinity, but an intense vibration that arched through the air almost visibly.

He looked so fine in his crisp navy uniform. The shirt hugged his broad shoulders and tightened just a tad over his chest. The pants looked tailored to fit his tight butt and fall smoothly over his thighs. The equipment belt on his hips framed the equipment package under his zipper nicely, making my mouth water.

Neither of us spoke. We went about our normal routine of loading the cash cart and waving to the cashiers. His chest brushed against my bare arm when he reached past me to hit the elevator call button, making me shiver.

When the elevator doors shut behind us and we were alone, Joe turned his head and we just looked at each other. There was an almost magical communication going on as we flirted with each other silently. Anticipation built and arousal unfurled in my belly. A need started to build inside me. The need to get closer to him, to touch him, to taste him. To be claimed by him. To let him know I was still his.

The lift pinged and the doors slid open. Joe stepped outside and I followed him down the hall, the friction of my thighs rubbing together as I walked putting me on edge. We remained silent while we waited for the timer on the vault, while we put the money away, and when we exited the bank. We walked side by side down the hallway again, until Joe stopped at the surveillance room. Our eyes met and said good-bye as I continued on to the elevator.

I stepped back into the cash office upstairs and considered a trip to the ladies room for a quick wank. Just when I'd decided that wasn't what I was craving, the phone on my desk rang. A shiver danced down my spine and I knew it was Joe.

"I need you to come to the surveillance room, Ms. Long," he said when I picked up.

My pulse raced and my sex clenched. The last time I went to the surveillance room, Joe bent me over the counter and fucked me hard. I looked up at the security camera in the corner, and spoke into the phone, "I'll be right there."

Sara was due in any minute because the Friday night shift started early, and the cashiers had enough coin when I checked with them. I locked up the cash office and told them I'd be back in fifteen.

It might be a bit longer than fifteen minutes, but they didn't need to know that right then.

The elevator ride back down made me antsy. I shifted my weight side to side, the motion making the seam of my slacks dig into my slit just a bit. I strode down the hall with poise and a deliberate swing to my hips.

When I entered the surveillance room, Charles Fiddler, the casino's general manager, was in there with Joe. My flirty greeting froze in my throat and my spine snapped straight. "Good afternoon, Mr. Fiddler."

Charles Fiddler was not what one expected when thinking of a general manager. His ink black hair hung in a ponytail down his back, and his mahogany skin was lined from the sun and full of character. He looked like he should be sitting cross-legged in front of an animal skin tepee, smoking a pipe and dispensing wisdom.

"Katie," he said warmly, reaching for my hand, pulling me into the center of the room. "It's so good to see you. How are you?"

"I'm doing well, thank you. And yourself?" I glanced over his shoulder at Joe and he gave me a small nod.

"Life always has its ups and downs, but basically it's good." He released my hand after another small squeeze, and stepped away. "I'm heading out now. Joe, I'll leave everything to you. Have a nice week-end, Katie."

Relief flowed though me when he left the room. For a minute there I thought I'd been called down for a reprimand or something. Not that I'd done anything wrong, but you never know.

Joe and I were left alone and my body temperature started to rise again.

"You teased me," he said and began a slow walk around me. He used *that* tone of voice. The one that told me it was time to play. Time for the freedom of letting go.

"Yes, I did." I clasped my hands together in front of me.

"Why?"

A light touch drifted across my buttocks. "It felt good," I answered.

"And you'll do anything that feels good, won't you, Katie?"

He came to a standstill directly in front of me. I gazed up at him and felt my heart crack at the flicker of uncertainty in his eyes. I'd caught glimpses of it before, and wondered what had happened to put it there. One day, I told myself, I will find out.

"Only with you." I spoke softly and reached for him.

He grabbed my hands before I could touch him. With a dip of his head his lips were on my neck. He kissed the sensitive spot behind my ear, and my insides started to tremble.

"Get on your knees," he whispered, his lips brushing my earlobe.

I remembered the first time I got on my knees for him, and he'd left me aching and frustrated for days afterwards. But my legs bent, lowering me to the floor. When I was on my knees he released my hands and stoked my hair. One hand cupped my chin and lifted, tilting my head back. "Only with me, right?"

I nodded.

"Only for me, right?"

I nodded again.

"Show me," he said. "Undo my zipper and show me how much you love to please me."

The rasp of metal teeth separating echoed through the room, heard clearly over the distant hum of the surveillance monitors five feet away. I reached into the fold of his pants and pulled out his semi-hard cock. Even only half hard he was beautiful.

I could see the shadow of his nest of curls through the flap of his pants when I reached a hand in and cupped his balls. My other hand circled the base of his shaft while I leaned in and breathed. It twitched in my hand at the feel of my breath, and I inhaled the scent of him.

Parting my lips, I slipped him into my mouth and suckled. It was the first time I'd ever had a semihard cock in my mouth, and the feel of it growing as I sucked made my insides hot and my core ache. One hand fondled his balls in their satiny sac while the other squeezed the root of his cock. I slid my mouth along his thickening erection until only the head was inside my mouth.

I sucked at the end and felt the blood rush into his cock. It heated and throbbed in my hand and I pulled my mouth off him. Tipping my head back I looked up to see Joe watching me closely. His large hand curved around the back of my head, his fingers massaging my scalp as he gave me a sweet smile. I watched his face while my tongue darted out and licked him like a lollipop.

"You're such a tease." He shook his head.

I grinned and closed my eyes, lowering my head and concentrating on what I was doing. What I was feeling.

Joe tasted unbelievably good. I pulled my hand away from his balls and braced it on a hard thigh while I leaned into him. I bobbed my head up and down, keeping the suction steady, swirling my tongue around the now-rigid cock in my mouth. Saliva coated him, and things started to get sloppy. Joe groaned, "Oh yeah, angel. That's it."

His praise heated me up and I shifted my knees closer together. With a slight bend forward, my pants rubbed against my swollen clit, and my inner muscles clenched. My mouth was full and I sighed. It was a sigh of pleasure at more than just the physical gratification. There was mental satisfaction as well.

This freedom, this knowledge that I could completely be myself with this man and know that he didn't judge me for it. That he encouraged my inner slut to come out.

The fingers tangled in my hair tightened and I tasted the precious fluid of pre-come. Loving that Joe was letting me control the pace, I eased down the length again. When I reached the flared head, I pressed my tongue on the underside of the ridge and bobbed my head up and down fast. Sucking, just the head, hard and fast. His other hand joined the first on my head. I could feel his tension, the way he wanted to grip my head and thrust in deep, but he teased us both by holding back, letting me keep control.

Another groan echoed through the room and I pulled my lips off him completely. I ran my tongue up and down the shaft, pressing along the throbbing veins and teasing him.

"Katie," he growled.

My satisfied smile was hidden by the act of quickly engulfing his cock in my mouth again. I couldn't fit him in completely, but with my hand matching the rhythm of my mouth he was getting lots of attention. I picked up the pace and added a little twist to the hand movement so it swiveled up his cock and was rewarded when he reached down and cupped my aching breasts through my thin shirt.

He fondled them for a brief minute then slid his hand in under the scoop neck of my top. He pushed aside the cups of my lace bra and his fingers clamped around my stiff nipples.

I hummed my gratification as he pinched and rolled the sensitive tips, bolts of pleasure going from there directly to my sex.

"You like that, don't you, angel?" Joe crooned. "I know all your little hot spots. I bet you can come from this can't you?"

Saliva and a steady flow of pre-come lubricated his cock and the sloppy sound of sucking blended with my hum of agreement. My hips twitched and my clit got friction, bringing another moan forth.

"Faster, baby. Just a bit more."

Joe's thigh was rock hard under my hand, and I could feel a slight tremor run though him. I increased my speed again, sucking harder, running my tongue up the underside and keeping a tight grip with my hand. I used every trick I'd ever read about and gave him my boundless enthusiasm.

His hips thrust forward, his fingers tightened on my nipples, and a long low groan filled the room. His cock throbbed hotly in my hand as liquid warmth spurted down my throat. I pulled back a little and sucked just the tip, swallowing everything he had to give.

When Joe's hands pulled upwards, taking my nipples with them, I stumbled to my feet with a gasp. He wrapped me in his arms and hugged me tight as more small tremors shook him.

After a minute he planted a soft kiss on my lips and spoke softly. "You made my knees week, angel. Thank you."

A pleasant glow warmed my cheeks, but I couldn't help but shift uncomfortably.

"You didn't come, did you?" he asked.

I shook my head. "It's OK, though. I like to please you."

"No, it isn't OK." He took me by the arm and led me to the counter by the security monitors. With a quick spin he had me so that I was facing the camera. My back to his chest. "You watch the monitors now, while I make my good girl come."

He kissed my cheek and then the hollow of my neck. He made quick work of the button on my slacks as he nibbled on my ear. He slipped one hand into my pants, and the other played with my exposed breasts.

A whimper jumped from my throat as his talented finger zeroed in on the hard knot of nerves between my thighs. When my hips started to rotate, jerking against his touch, he dipped in further. With a sure thrust, two fingers slid into my slick entrance. He pumped his finger in and out, the palm of his hand rocking on my clit as I whimpered. His hot breath panted in my ear and his teeth nibbled on the susceptible nub of flesh there.

"Come on, angel," he purred into my ear. "I can feel your muscles tightening. Your hungry pussy wants more doesn't it?"

"Yes," I gasped. "Oh yes, more, Joe. Please. More."

I reached behind me and grabbed his hips, pulling him tight against me as my knees bent, my stance widened and I humped his hand.

"Good girl. Fuck my hand. Make yourself come." His words freed something inside me. When he tightened his grip on a nipple, a sharp bolt of pleasure/pain shot to my sex, and my eyes slid closed, bliss resonating throughout my body.

"You sure you have plans tonight?" Joe asked, his voice husky as he held me close for a few more seconds.

"Yes, I'm sure." I pulled away slowly and straightened my clothes. "Trust me, they're important plans or I'd cancel them for a night with you."

I went up on my tiptoes and gave him a quick kiss. "Tomorrow?"

"We'll see," he said with a tight smile. "You'd better get back to work now."

The walk back to the cash office was a fast one. I got there just in time to start balancing the vault before Sara started her shift.

The drive to Hemlock went fast. Not because I was speeding, but because my mind wasn't on the road that much. I thought about calling Julie for backup. I wasn't sure how smart going out of town to a strange hotel to play cards with men I've never met before was. But, I couldn't bring myself to do it. There was still tension between us, and I didn't know how to deal with it.

When I drove into town, the main street was lit up pretty good, full of tourists and teenagers. Couples were walking hand in hand eating ice cream or carrying gift shop bags, people were lounging on the sidewalk benches, and some kids were attempting stunts with their skateboards on the sidewalk.

I found the hotel at the end of the main drag and parked on the street in front of it. The Hartman Hotel was an old building with a big columned front and cement stairs that led to a grand lobby. Going for the traditional feel, the front desk was dark oak, the carpets a dark flowered pattern, and the staff was dressed in white shirts, black vests, and silk string ties.

Mellow orchestra music floated through the lobby from the restaurant, giving it a real old-time feel. There was a massive curved staircase to the left side of the lobby. That would be the way up. I strode through the loitering people, glancing at my watch. Only ten minutes until the game started.

Once on the third floor, I found room 312 and knocked. Renee opened the door, knocking the wind right out of me.

22

"What are you doing here?" Renee said by way of a greeting.

My spine snapped straight and I gathered myself. Shit, just what I didn't need . . . a distraction. "I was invited. What are you doing here?"

"Brandon," she called over her shoulder. "Come here a minute, baby."

Brandon strolled up behind Renee. He was dressed in casual linen pants and a button-up shirt undone at the throat. A snifter full of amber liquid in his hand completed the look for him. "Katie! You made it. Come in, come in."

I pasted a big smile on my face and brushed past Renee. There was too much at stake for me in that hotel room and I was not going to let her being there get to me. In fact, if I looked at it properly, her being there was sort of a good sign. While she wasn't my best friend,

I did believe that she wouldn't stand by while some strangers robbed me or worse. Her presence in the room made me feel a lot safer about being there with unknown men.

Yeah, I told myself. That's the way to put a positive spin on things.

The room was huge. Heavy drapes kept the sun out, making it seem dark, almost intimate. There was a small sitting area near the window with a love seat and two club chairs. Closer to the door and the bar was a round table with two men at it.

One guy looked in his early thirties and the other in his early fifties. Not my regular crowd for sure. The older guy had the same aura of privilege that surrounded Brandon, but the other was a bit harder to read.

"Gentlemen, this is Katie, the young woman I was telling you about. Katie, that's Ray and the other one is Michael."

He waved his arm at one of the empty seats. "Pull up a chair and get acquainted."

"Hi, gentlemen," I said and sat at the table gingerly. I'd been unsure of how to dress, so I'd gone with a strappy summer dress. Not such a fancy thing, but I'd added heels and makeup, and it put a bit more spark into the outfit. Seems I'd made a good choice, too, because while Ray, the older, sophisticated-looking one was dressed in trousers and a nicely pressed button-up dress shirt, Michael had on jeans and a T-shirt with Bruce Lee on it.

There was a stand up bar in the corner nearest us with a fridge, serving trays, and many, many bottles of liquor behind it. Renee had pulled Brandon over there and they were discussing something rather intently, leaving us to make small talk.

"Brandon says you work in a casino?" Ray said as he spun a rock glass full of ice and very little drink left.

"That's right," I replied.

His lips twisted into a smug, condescending smile. "Well, just because you work in a casino doesn't mean you're good enough to play with the big boys, you know?"

"Uhmm, I'm not a dealer, Ray. I work in the cash office." I glanced at the still-silent Michael and ignored my pounding heart. "Not that it matters where I work. I assure you I'm ready to play with 'the big boys.' "

Ray's cheeks flushed a bit and Michael threw back his head and laughed. "You tell him, Katie."

He reached over and shook my hand. "Don't pay attention to him. This table of big boys is only playing for a few grand tonight."

Brandon had said to bring minimum of three thousand cash, so I brought all I had. Thirty-five hundred dollars. Not high stakes for a lot of people, but it was everything to me. I was gambling with my ticket out of Chadwick.

I watched over Ray's shoulder as I shook his hand, too, and saw Brandon shake his head at Renee and walk toward us. "What would you like to drink, Katie?"

He grabbed me tequila and water, and we were ready. Money was discussed and we decided on a three-thousand-dollar buy in. Cash was traded for chips, cards were dealt and we started. To my relief Renee wasn't actually playing with us, she was just there as Brandon's slave girl. Or should I say hostess?

The small blind was a hundred dollars, the big blind two hundred. That meant everyone had to put a minimum hundred bucks into the pot before the cards were even dealt. The order was Ray, Michael, me, then Brandon.

We all put a hundred in and Ray dealt us two pocket cards each. I had a six of hearts and a three of clubs. I folded. Sure it was like throwing away a hundred bucks, but chances are with those cards if I put more in the pot, I'd be throwing more away. I could be patient. I could wait for the cards.

Plus, I could tell from the way Ray looked at me he thought I was just too chicken to bet. I could use his misconception against him if I played smart.

Brandon folded after the flop was dealt, leaving only Michael, and Ray to play out the hand. Ray won the pot, and he was a bad winner.

"Come to Papa!" he cried out making a big show of collecting the small pile of chips from the middle of the table.

Michael met my gaze and gave a small eye roll as he shuffled the cards. The blind was now two hundred dollars, we each threw in, and Michael dealt the first cards.

Renee walked around the room, primping and fawning until Brandon snapped at her to sit down. After that, she got up and refilled drinks and brought food, but stayed away from the table for the most part. The next couple of hands played out with everyone winning but me. I managed to fold each time without losing too much except for one hand, where I thought I had a chance with a pair of queens but Michael beat me with three eights.

The smallest stack at the table was mine. I was down to sixteen hundred when it was Michael's turn to deal again.

I was first to bet and my pocket cards were a king of spades and a jack of diamonds. "Two hundred." I tossed a couple chips in the middle of the table. The urge to bet higher had been strong, but I didn't want to come on too strong. Ditzy women didn't make big bets.

They each called and the pot was twelve hundred dollars before the flop was even dealt. My chest got tight and I forced myself to take slow, measured breaths. When two kings and a two of hearts were turned over in the flop, my heart stuttered.

Three kings. It was a nice hand. Better than nice. I could bet high; I was pretty confident I had the winning hand. But I wanted the others to keep betting, to build the pot higher so that the prize would be more.

"Two hundred." It was a safe bet. A good way to see how the others dealt with the draw.

Brandon raised two hundred, Ray saw that and Michael folded. I tossed two hundred more in to meet Brandon's raise and the next card was flipped. A ten of spades. Didn't really help me, but my instinct said go hard or go home.

"All in." My voice didn't waver as I pushed all my chips into the middle, and of that, I was proud.

"Whoa, little girl. Are you sure you know what you're doing?" Ray said.

I widened my eyes and gave him a big smile. "Oh yes, I just want to have some fun."

Renee stared at me hard. Brandon smirked and folded. Ray met me all in. It wouldn't break him if he lost, but it would make him the short stack. Michael eyed me, then folded.

I flipped my cards over. Ray flipped his—a king and a ten. My heart stopped, then jumped in my chest and took off at a gallop. We both had three kings. My jack beat his ten, but there was still a chance I could lose it all, then I was out.

Perspiration made my hands slightly clammy, no one spoke while Michael turned over the river card. A seven of diamonds! I won!

Okay. It was only that hand, but it was against Ray, and I knew I had the second highest stack of chips at the table. I sat back and stopped fighting the silly grin that wanted to shine. Ray grumbled, Michael and Brandon grinned back at me, and Renee tilted her head to give me a strange look. Who knew what she was thinking?

It was my turn to deal, so I gathered the cards, along with my composure, and got the next hand started. An hour later Brandon was the first to be out. At the time that he lost, I was once again short stack at the table, with Ray and Michael only a couple thousand dollars apart.

Brandon sat back to watch us play with Renee on his lap. Another hour went by and we took a break. Everyone hitting the bathroom while Renee refreshed drinks and put out sandwiches. I was reaching for a tuna on rye when Renee spoke.

"Why are you here, Katie?"

"To play poker." I put the sandwich on my plate and stepped to the side to sit on the love seat while the men talked over by the bar.

Renee followed me and stood in front of my seat. Feet planted wide, arms crossed over her ample chest. "Are you sure?"

"Why else would I be here?"

"Brandon's mine, you know. It doesn't matter if you can play cards or not, he likes what I can do for him far better than anything you could offer him."

I chewed and swallowed, trying to decide if I should laugh or get mad. There was a sharp pang in my chest and I realized I missed Julie. Swallowing a sigh, I refocused my thoughts. I needed to keep my head in the game and not let Renee distract me. "I'm not after Brandon. I'm here to play some cards and win some money. That's it."

"Just because you got Joe doesn't mean every man wants you. You're a boring little priss and Brandon likes an animal in his bed." She gave me a knowing sneer.

So she knew I was fucking around with Joe. So what? She'd probably seen that little kiss in the lounge the other night, but that was OK, too. It wasn't like we were doing something wrong. The fact that she thought I was a priss in bed didn't bother me. I really didn't want Renee thinking about what I was like in bed. I didn't want anyone but Joe thinking about what I was like in bed.

I finished my sandwich, stood up so that I was face-to-face with her and smiled. "I'm here for money. That's all you need to know."

The guys were back at the table, so I joined them and we started playing again. Ray was the next player to run out of chips and he was a better loser then I thought he'd be. Especially since it was me who knocked him out when he'd called all-in first.

"The luck of the cards," was all he said when he pushed his chair back from the table. He held his empty glass up to Renee. "Get me another scotch would ya, girlie?"

Biting my cheek was the only way to hide my smirk when Renee climbed from Brandon's lap with a frown. Michael saw me and gave a small shake of his head. He shuffled the cards, we both threw in some chips, and he dealt the pocket cards. He won, I won, he won, he won. I won. He won. It went back and forth between us for another thirty minutes, keeping us even.

Then I was dealt a pair of aces. I bet five hundred and he saw me, the flop was dealt and it held the ace of spades, two of spades, and ten of hearts.

I took a deep breath and made my choice. "All in."

The room was unnaturally silent while Michael looked at his cards, looked at me, then his cards again. "You got it, baby. I'm in."

"Whooee! We got ourselves a showdown," Ray crowed and smacked his thigh.

"Let's see 'em." Brandon pushed Renee from his lap and leaned forward, elbows on the table.

With a flick of my wrist I flipped my cards for all to see. Michael grinned and showed us his. The king of hearts and ace of hearts.

I had three aces, and he had two aces and a possible straight flush.

"Look at that," Brandon whistled low. "It's all in the luck of the draw now, people."

"This is gambling," Ray answered.

Michael and I stayed silent. I don't know about him, but I was trying to mentally make the cards in the deck shift to suit my needs. He flipped the fourth card, the turn. A five of clubs.

It didn't help either of us. Michael flipped the last card over quickly, even though it was just a technicality. Nothing he drew could beat my three aces.

All the tension swooshed from my body, my neck turned to rubber and my forehead hit the table. I won. I actually WON!

The ringing in my ears dimmed and I heard the men talking. When I lifted my head and stood, they turned to me, all of them with big shit eating grins on their faces.

"I won," I said.

"Yes, you did." Michael came around the table and gave me a hug. "You won fair and square. Damn good job, Katie."

Ray was next in line. He held out his hand for me to shake. "You did good, little girl." With that he handed me a business card and winked. "If you need a job when you get to Vancouver, you give me a call."

Out of the corner of my eye I saw Ray and Michael shaking hands, then Brandon wrapped me in his arms and lifted me off my feet in a bear hug. "You kicked ass, girl! I'm so proud of you!"

I ignored the glare from Renee who was standing directly behind Brandon. "Thanks, Brandon. You don't know how much this means to me. I swear, I'm never going to gamble again. I think I used up all my luck tonight."

Ray and Michael waved good-bye to me and told Brandon they'd be in the bar downstairs if he wanted to join them for another drink. Brandon walked me over to the bar and pulled a metal lock box out from behind it.

23

For the full hour-drive home, a perma-grin was attached to my face. By the time I saw the WELCOME TO CHADWICK sign on the edge of the highway, my cheeks were aching, right alongside my full bladder.

It was hard to slow my speed when I hit the city limits since I wanted to race home and pee, but there were too many blind corners in a town built on the side of a mountain to try and speed through it.

It was almost one in the morning, and even though it was Friday night in August, there was minimal activity on the streets. Driving past the McDougal Hotel, where the only nightclub in town was, I saw a few people loitering in the parking lot, but that was about it. The urge to turn on Front Street and head to Julie's apartment was strong, but the tightness in my chest kept me from doing it. Julie had known the game was this weekend, and she hadn't called to see if I was still going, or to see if I wanted backup. She hadn't called and tried to make up, and I wasn't ready to try and force the issue either.

In my heart of hearts, deep down, I knew we would make up eventually. Jules was my best friend for as long as I could remember. She was the one that had always been willing to act out my wildest ideas and take the blame for them when we got caught. She was the one that showed me how to kiss with my old doll when I was nine years old, my first practice kiss when I was ten, and witness to my first *real* kiss two days later. She was my spirit sister.

But she'd hurt me. And that was going to take time to get over.

Right then, all I wanted to do was go home, crawl into bed, and count my money. My mind was still whirring with ideas on how to spend it. I now had enough to stay in a hotel until I found a good place to live. I now had enough to get the air-conditioning in my car fixed before I left town. I now had enough to go to school.

And not just the rinky-dink seven-day tax accounting course I'd been looking at. I had enough money to actually enroll in college for business and get an accounting certificate!

I turned right and started up my road, enjoying the breeze of cool mountain air coming in my open window after another hot day.

There was a shiny black Charger in the parking lot when I pulled in, and Joe was leaning against it.

My heart kicked in my chest and I bit the inside of my cheek to keep my grin in check.

"Hey," I said when I got out of my car. "I hope you haven't been waiting long."

"I got here a bit after midnight, so it hasn't been that long." He pushed away from his car and walked to the apartment door with me. "You said you'd be late, but we really need to talk so I thought I'd give waiting a try."

"Guess what?" I said over my shoulder as we walked up the stairs.

I was bursting to tell someone about my windfall. I got to the landing and stopped in front of my door. When I turned to tell him I was instantly aware of how close he was to me, how good he looked, how good he smelled. How good he would taste.

All thought fled my mind, and I licked my lips, my eyes glued to his full lips, only inches from mine. He leaned close, and I could taste his breath mingling with mine as my eyes slid shut.

"Let's go inside," he said softly.

I opened my eyes, a bit confused, to see that he had leaned past me and opened my door. No kisses for me. Something was definitely up.

"Okay," I said. I walked into the apartment and tossed my purse at the couch. Without bothering to see where it landed, I turned to Joe. "What's up?"

He strode across the small space between us, buried his fingers in my hair, and slanted his mouth over mine. His tongue thrust deep into my mouth, staking a claim and switching my brain power to off.

When he pulled back a little, I was leaning against him, boneless, except for the demanding pressure of a full bladder. "Hold that thought," I said to Joe and pulled out of his arms. "I'll be right back."

When I stepped out of the bathroom Joe was sitting on the sofa.

He had his head down, his elbows braced on his knees with hands dangling between them. On the floor at his feet was my purse, and in his hands was a wad of cash. He lifted his head, his expression unreadable.

"This." He waved the money at me. "This is why I didn't want to get involved with you."

"What? What do you mean?" Heat crept through me. "Did you go through my purse?"

"You missed the couch when you tossed it. This fell out when I went to pick it up." He stood and stalked over to me. "It's bulging out of your purse. Where did you get this much cash?"

The look in Joe's eyes wasn't sexy anymore. Instead it was scary. He was mad. His face remained blank except for the tightness around his mouth, but his eyes were fierce. "Don't even think about lying to me, Katie."

My spine snapped straight and I crossed my arms over my chest. "Why would I lie to you? I don't *have* to tell you anything."

"This isn't part of some sex game, Katie. I'm serious. Where did you get this money?" He shook the handful of bills in front of my face.

Instead of noticing the money, all I noticed was the way the muscles bulged in his forearms. Blue veins ran up his arms and my gaze followed them. Over a curved bicep, rounded shoulder, and tight neck to the grim line of his mouth. My nipples tightened, the fire in my blood headed south and pooled in my sex, and I fought the urge to jump on him.

We were in the middle of an argument, and I was getting turned on!

Tightly leashed energy vibrated off him and I wondered what would happen if I pushed him just a little more. "None of your business."

He turned away from me and stalked to the patio window. Silence reigned while he stood with his back to the room, to me, looking out into the night. Joe's posture was rigid, his hands on his hips, one fist still clenching my prize from the bar. Before I could ask what was going on, he turned and stalked over to me. A firm hand gripped my arm and tugged me behind him. "Since you seem to be more honest when we're playing sex games, I guess that's what's needed to find out the truth."

He sat down on the edge of the sofa, and before I knew what was going on, he had me stretched out across his lap, face down, ass up in the air.

A muscled forearm braced across my back kept me pinned there as he lifted my dress and tugged down my panties.

"What the hell are you doing?" I screeched. I wiggled and squirmed, trying to brace my hands on the floor and push myself up.

"I'm getting answers to my questions. Are you ready to tell me where you got all that money, or should I spank your ass?"

I should be angry. I should be degraded. Grown women don't get tossed over their lover's knees because they won't answer a question. Instead, arousal unfurled and my breath hitched in my throat. His hand lay on my naked butt, every inch of every finger burning into my skin, and suddenly I wanted this. I wanted to be punished for . . . for the dirty things I wanted.

"Go ahead. Spank me. I'm not telling you anything." I'd tell him, but not just yet.

A hard hand came down sharply on my naked backside three times in quick succession.

"Ow!" I cried.

Smack! Smack! Smack!

"Where did you get that money?"

My breath was coming in gasps and my ass was on fire. The fire spread to my pussy and I squeezed my thighs together, wiggling around some more. That's when I felt it. The hard ridge of an erection poking against my belly.

"You're enjoying this!"

A reluctant chuckle filled the room. His calloused hand rubbed over my flaming cheeks, distributing sharp tingles of pleasure.

"The sight of your ass always gives me a hard-on, angel. But don't think for a minute that I'm having fun here." He dipped his hand between my thighs and inserted a finger between my swollen lips. "Not as much fun as you anyway."

He pulled his hand out and brought it down on my ass again. "Now are you going to tell me where you got the money?"

Out of sheer stubbornness I bit my lip and shook my head.

"Fine."

Joe continued to spank me, his hand landing on one cheek, and then the other. Blood rushed to my bottom and everything in that area was supersensitized. He switched things up, changing the angle so that some swipes landed on the tender undercurve of my butt. I bit my lip, tears starting to pool in my eyes. Yet, the heat and sting had an orgasm gathering inside me.

Suddenly, Joe stopped. "Stubborn, aren't you?" His hand skimmed over my burning rump and dipped between my thighs. A fingertip brushed against my sensitized clit and my body jerked. "Tell me, Katie."

A soft moan escaped me. I wiggled my hips, trying to press my body against the teasing finger that diddled in my slit.

He tweaked my clit. Back and forth, back and forth. The orgasm inside me gathered power but I couldn't get over the edge. It was the night after he fucked my mouth all over again. I was ready to come, but I couldn't, because he didn't want me to. He knew how to torture me.

"Please, Joe," I whimpered, writhing on his lap.

"Tell me."

"Please," I begged. "Let me come."

He flicked my clit two times, then stopped. "Tell me where you got the money."

The words jumped from my lips. "I won it in a poker game!"

He froze. The sudden silence of the room broken only by my whimpers of arousal.

"A poker game?"

"Yes, yes." I nodded and humped against his leg. A soothing hand stroked my back at the same time two fingers clamped onto my clit and pinched. "Come for me, angel."

My eyes slid shut, every muscle tensed, and fireworks went off inside me. Tremors still shook my body seconds later when Joe shifted me in his arms. He whisked my panties off my legs, sat back on the couch, and lifted me so that I straddled him.

"No." I pushed against his chest. Intense emotions flooded my mind and I didn't want comfort from him right then.

"Shhh," he crooned. His arms wrapped around me and he pulled me close. A gentle hand at the back of my head forced my face into the crook of his neck. "It's OK, angel. It's over. I'm done."

Cuddled up against him, I kept my head down, my hair covering my face and gave in to the urge to let it all out. I sobbed quietly in his arms for a few minutes. When my tears had dried and my sobs were mere hiccups, I tried to pull away again.

"No, Katie." Joe let me sit back far enough that he could look into my face, but that was it. "I'm sorry I hurt you, angel. But I had to know where you got that money."

With my heels tucked under my thighs, my tender butt didn't come into contact with anything but the heat was still there. A presence that kept me on the sexual edge.

Trying to get past the arousal still clamoring around inside me, I raised my eyes to his. I saw concern, remorse, and more tenderness than I ever thought possible coming from him.

"Why?"

24

Pain, arousal, and anger all battled with the curiosity inside me. Joe heaved a deep breath at my question, and let it out slowly. The furrow in his brow told me whatever was going on was serious.

"How well do you know the people you work with?"

I thought about it. "I know most of them pretty well, I guess. I mean it's not like Chadwick is a huge place, so most of us have known each other for years."

His lips tilted up at one corner. "That doesn't mean you *know* them."

"There's not many secrets in a town this size, Joe." Much to my dismay.

"There are a lot of secrets in this town, angel. You're just not seeing them."

I eyed him. "What does that mean?"

"How many people in town know that you have a secret kink for being dominated?"

A flush crept up from my chest. Julie sort of knew, but other than that I hoped no one. Hell, *I* hadn't really even known until that first time with Joe. "No one but you."

"And you don't think that if you have a secret, others don't, too?" His rusty chuckle echoed in the quiet apartment. "What about your mom and your ex, or even Julie for that matter? They have secrets."

I shrugged. He had a point. "Okay, so what's your secret?"

"That's what I've been wanting to talk to you about, but the last week has been one thing after another with you."

"Tell me about it."

When he didn't laugh even a little with me, unease started to build deep inside. "Well, you know the saying, 'When it rains it pours.' Spit it out, Joe."

He had one hand on my hip, and the other was stroking up and down my bare arm, keeping me sensually aware. Yet, it wasn't a sexual caress; I don't even think Joe was aware of its effect on me. When I searched his gaze I didn't see seduction, or lust. I saw a wariness I'd never seen before, and it made my heart clench.

"I'm not really a security guard."

Not a huge surprise there. I'd always known he was more than your average security guard. "And?"

"I work for a private company based in Vancouver."

"And?"

"As a security specialist."

For a guy who wanted to have this conversation, getting information from him was harder than trying to get my mom to admit there was more to life than getting, and keeping, a man. "What are you doing here?"

"Charles Fiddler is a friend of my boss. Casino thefts are pretty small scale for what my company normally handles, but since Fiddler is a friend of Damien's, he sent me down to help him out."

"Casino thefts?"

"There's been a steady stream of money going missing from Black's. Not large amounts, but slow and steady enough that when they did the year-end he realized that the final loss was bigger than they could let by. I'm here to find out who's taking it."

I stiffened. "And I'm a suspect?"

His shoulders lifted and fell. "You have access to all the cash. While your name was on the list of possibilities, you were never a serious suspect. This"—he waved his hand between our chests—"never would've happened if you were."

"Okay. Then why didn't you tell me what you were up to earlier?"

"When would've been a good time, Katie? When I had you bent over the sofa? Or maybe when you were trying on my handcuffs? When we got together I never had the impression you were interested in anything more than what I could make you feel."

It sounded a little harsh when he put it that way. Like I was some selfish brat that hadn't cared to get to know him as a person.

Julie's words came back to me and I felt a tingle of shame. It was true.

When I'd set the seduction wheel in motion I never gave a thought to the future. Even when it became clear there was a unique connection between us, I'd focused on leaving town and not getting tied down. When we were in the kitchen together that one night, Joe had been open to answering my questions. I was the one who hadn't bothered to ask them.

"Don't worry about it." He shrugged. "I'm certainly not complaining about the fact that you enjoy being my sex toy."

I didn't know what to say. What was there to say? Oh, yeah. "So I was on the list of suspects, but you didn't really think I was a thief?"

Joe blew out a sharp breath. "Right. But when I saw all that cash fall out of your purse, I had a brief bit of doubt that my instincts had been wrong." He looked at me and smirked. "For a minute there I wondered if you'd been leading me around by the dick for a reason."

My stomach was starting to cramp and there was a roaring in my ears. I was swamped. Anger, frustration, hurt, surprise . . . they pooled together in my head in large amounts until I felt like I was drowning. Then I reached for one thing that stuck out the most.

He thought I'd been leading him around. Here I thought I'd been chasing him, and he thought I'd been leading? What a mess.

My eyes widened and my jaw fell open. "I haven't been leading you anywhere. I feel like I've been chasing you!"

Joe leaned forward and kissed me gently. "I've been watching and wanting you since I first laid eyes on you." He kissed me again. His lips soft, his tongue gentle as it slid between my lips and rubbed against mine. After a smatter of more small kisses along my jaw to my ear he sat back, and his gaze searched my face.

That would've been the perfect time to talk about our relationship, but I'd had enough emotional shit that week. I just didn't want to go there.

Instead, I had another question. "Tonight, when you saw that money, you thought I stole it from the casino?"

"No." He shook his head slowly. "I didn't want to believe it, but I wouldn't be very good at my job if I just let the sight of that cash go without saying something."

"Saying something?" My temper finally started to simmer. "You did more than say something, Joe. You almost crossed the line there. What the hell is going on?"

"This isn't about the casino." He met my eyes and I saw a maelstrom of emotions there. I could literally see the mental walls starting to crumble. "This is about us."

Shit. *He* wanted to go there.

As much as I wanted to shove off his lap and say, "Screw it, I can't deal with this right now," I couldn't get past the hurt I saw buried deep in his beautiful blue eyes. He had secrets, too. And the pain they were causing him made my chest tighten.

"Okay," I said cautiously. My hands fell to his shoulders and I sat back on his thighs, gingerly. My arousal had dissipated as much as it ever would in Joe's presence, but my bum was still tender. "What about us?"

"That day when you played with yourself in the cash office for me . . . it was like a fantasy come to life."

He stopped for a minute and I watched him struggle to find his next words. "Go on."

"When I was eighteen I was completely idealistic, and I joined the army so I could protect my country. It was great. I got an education, lots of specialized training, and made friends with some of the best people around."

He paused. His grip on my hips tightened perceptibly, but he seemed completely unaware of it. "It seems I have a natural aptitude for some nasty things, and the military was happy to foster those things. I've been in a few foreign countries, seen and done some things most people wouldn't be proud of, but none of it really bothered me. At least I didn't realize it bothered me."

"Two years ago a friend's wife was murdered while we were overseas on an assignment." His hands shifted restlessly, sliding down to the tops of my thighs, the fingers drumming against my skin. "He took it pretty hard. We all did really. It's why Damien started the security company. We realized that while we were fighting overseas for our country, our families were fighting a daily battle at home."

"I'm so sorry, Joe. That must've been hard." I just wanted to hug him, but he was so rigid in his posture that I knew he wasn't done.

"It's hard after that, you know? To see the world in the same way. To look at people and believe that everyone has good inside them. When I first saw you, I swear you had a halo hanging over your head and wings on your back." He gave a dry chuckle. "You shocked the shit out of me."

I blushed, then leaned forward, and gave him a soft kiss. "I shocked myself, too."

"I tried to stay away from you because I'm not good at relation-ships. I'm not good with people, period. I'm good with guns, and tac-tics, and hunting bad guys down. But I couldn't stay away from you." The last of the wall crumbled from his eyes and the intensity of the emotion there startled me. "I'm in love with you, Katie."

25

Shit! Shit, shit, shit.

"Joe . . ." I shook my head and scrambled for something to say. He must've seen the panic in my expression because he just smiled and pulled me to him in a tight hug.

"It's OK, babe. I don't expect you to say anything, and I don't expect things to change. I know you're leaving town, to Vancouver of all places. Did I mention that's where I'm based?" His chest vibrated beneath my ear as he chuckled. "It's all good. I just needed to tell you how I felt, and to say thank you, for helping me see some good in people again."

"Joe." I tucked my head into the curve under his chin. "I care about you so much. I trust you and I respect you, but I just can't think about this right now, okay?"

He tightened his arms around me, brushed my forehead with a kiss, and said, "Perfectly okay."

———————•———————

I must've fallen asleep in his arms because next thing I knew I was facedown on my bed with my alarm clock yelling at me. After slapping my hand on the snooze button, I lifted my head and glanced around the room. It was Saturday morning, the sun was peeping in through my curtains and there was no sign of Joe. A cursory grope of the pillow next to me confirmed that he hadn't spent the night.

It could've meant he'd just left a while ago, but since he'd dropped his final bombshell at 3 A.M., and it was seven o'clock when my alarm sounded. Still, hours ago equals not spending the night.

If there were any doubts that the happenings of the night before were a dream, they disappeared for certain when I sat up in bed. My tender bum assured me that it had felt repeated swats from a firm hand only hours earlier.

I crawled out of bed and did the morning routine thing on autopilot. Once at work I grabbed coffee from Jimmy, but didn't stop to chat. I just couldn't deal with any sort of discussion.

That didn't stop Tom, though.

"Rough night?" he asked when I asked him to keep the music on low.

"I'm not hungover, Tom. I just didn't get much sleep and I have a bit of a headache."

Things were quiet for a bit, then out of the blue Tom spoke softly, "You know, my wife is a really good judge of character."

I didn't bother to lift my head from my paperwork. "Oh yeah?"

"Yeah," he said from his seat by the doorway. "And she really likes Joe."

Pitter-patter went my heart at mention of his name. But I did *not* raise my head or respond.

"He stops by the bakery before it opens for coffee with her sometimes. She said he's changed a lot since he's come here."

"Uh huh." I forgot Tom's wife owned the bakery in town. That would explain how Joe had coffee and muffins the other morning before any place was open.

"Katie," he said.

"Yes?"

"Did I ever tell you I used be in the army?"

That got my attention.

I raised my head slowly. When I set down my pencil and met his gaze, he continued talking.

"Yeah, I did eight years before I met Sonya. The last year I was there a couple of new guys joined our unit. Good men. Young men that believed they were going to make a difference in the world. Joe was a different man back then. When he walked into the casino a couple months ago I almost didn't recognize him. Military life has changed him, hardened him. For a while I thought he was hardened beyond caring again, but Sonya tells me I'm wrong. She's said from the start that he still had a steadfast heart buried inside him somewhere." He pointed at me. "I think you're the one that's got it beating again."

I started to shake my head, but stopped when I saw the knowledge in his eyes.

"I just wanted to say *thank you*. He's a good man, and he deserves to find some happiness."

Talk about pressure.

There was nothing I could say to that. What was I going to tell him? That all Joe had needed was a woman with a submissive streak to make him feel better? I kept my mouth shut and pretended to go back to my work. Tom sat silently in his chair until Hope arrived as first cashier on.

The rest of the morning sucked.

I was tired, I was cranky, and my thought process was completely stunted by the past week's happenings. When it was time for my lunch break I made a quick call to my landlord to tell him I was leaving town early. I'd given him notice on the apartment for the middle of September, but now, I was ready to get out of town as soon as possible. I told Larry I'd pay him full rent for September anyway, but he just told me it was perfect timing. His nephew was moving to Chadwick and needed a place to live so there were no worries.

With that settled I threatened Hope and Susan with bodily harm if they bothered me before my break was over. Then, I shut the office door, turned off the lights, and put my head on my desk.

For forty blissful minutes I had peace. I'd turned the ringer off on the phone in the office and told the girls to answer it and twenty minutes before my break was over, Susan knocked on the door. "It's your mom, Katie."

A sigh escaped as I picked up the phone. "Hey, Mom."

"Katie, dear. I'm calling to invite you to dinner tomorrow night. You didn't really get a chance to eat on Tuesday, and I'd really like for the three of us to have dinner."

I could her the hope in her voice. If that wasn't enough, the fact that she didn't press, or ramble on after the invitation told me that she really, *really* did want this.

"Okay, Mom. I can be there tomorrow for dinner. What time?"

Oh, joy. Sunday dinner with my mom and Brad. The perfect way to cap off the week from hell.

That afternoon, it was business as usual when Joe escorted me down to the bank. I'd expected to feel uncomfortable. After all, it's not every day I get thrown over a guy's knees and spanked. But once again, Joe surprised me. There was no pressure to talk about, or even think about, either our actions or conversation from the night before. He was as arrogant as ever in attitude, but when I looked into his eyes, there was a lightness there. The shadows were still there, too, but he was definitely letting me see more of the real him now.

He acted like all was well and normal, and I realized it really was. He'd needed to tell me how he felt, so he did. What we did in private, what I let him do to me, *was* all well and good, as long as *we* were OK with it. The light went on and I realized that Joe completely accepted me, just as I was. Not as I appeared to be. Before I could open my mouth and blurt out something stupid, he turned to me and asked if I would help him catch the thief.

Of course. Wouldn't you know it? I'm thinking about sex and what was happening between us, and he was thinking about work.

"Sure. But how?"

He shifted his body so that the security cameras couldn't see his face, and spoke in a low voice. "Do you think you could write up a list of possible ways that someone working in the cash cage could be stealing? Ways that would elude both the cameras, and that the paper trail wouldn't catch right away."

The timer clicked on the vault and we opened it up, still conversing in low tones as we worked. "I can try and think of some ways, Joe. But I'm no criminal. My mind doesn't really function that way."

"How do you know? Have you ever really thought about it?"

"Of course not. But doesn't pulling off something like this require some sort of skill?" I stepped out of the vault and watched as Joe pushed the big door closed and sealed it up again. "I mean, you said it's been going on for a while. You've been here almost three months and you haven't figured it out, what makes you think I can?"

He stepped back and gave me a blindingly wicked grin. "I told you, thefts aren't really my specialty."

Wow! Until then I realized I'd never seen Joe grin before. My heart kicked and instant moisture coated my sex.

Joe had always been sexy, but the new, more relaxed and almost playful Joe was devastating. He pulled at my heart, as well as my libido.

"What exactly is your specialty?" I sucked my bottom lip between my teeth arched a brow and him.

Firm hands spun me around and smacked me on the butt on the way out of the room. "I think you know already."

We said good-bye to Fran in the bank and walked side by side down the hallway. My steps light beside his. He walked me all the way to the elevator.

"You know I'll help any way I can." I turned to him in front of the lift doors. My hands twitched and I clasped it around my other wrist, behind my back. My blood was humming through my veins and I had to keep myself from reaching for him then and there. "But what about just putting a hidden camera in the office?"

The sly tilt to his mouth told me he knew what I was feeling, and he was loving every second of it. The lift doors slid open and he nodded in the direction of the empty space. "Go on. We'll talk about it at your place later tonight."

The rest of the afternoon I hid from customers and staff alike in the office and tried to think like a thief.

I wasn't very good at it.

The only devious thoughts flowing through my mind were about the things I wanted to do to Joe when I got him naked again. Something had shifted between us, and not just because of the declaration of his feelings, but because I finally felt like I was getting to know him. The real him, and not just the man that brought my fantasies to life.

And the real man had asked me for help. Well input anyway. If it weren't for Julie's accusations of selfishness still ringing in my ears, I'd call her and ask her for help. I really needed her for something like that. Even when I was the one to come up with a silly prank as kids, she'd been the one that had sparked the idea in me.

She was like my prankster muse.

I looked down at the list in front of me, the one I'd started hours earlier, and saw only doodles.

There were no ideas running around my head. I couldn't think of one way for someone to be stealing money from the office without getting caught. I needed more information. The only thing that kept popping up in my head was the cameras. How could someone be stealing without those cameras seeing it?

A spark of an idea flickered in the back of my brain, but I couldn't quite catch it. It was the same feeling I got when I was watching a movie and trying to remember an actor's name. You know that you know it, but can't quite remember.

I was pushing things around inside my head when Susan called for more twenties up front, and Sara showed up to take over.

Lurching bolt upright on the sofa, I fought the urge to smack myself in the forehead. "I got it."

"Got what?"

Joe was in my kitchen, cooking. He'd shown up at my door just after six, dressed in jeans and a plain white T-shirt, with a bag of groceries. He'd declared he had a craving for beef stir fry, done his way.

When I'd offered to help he'd shooed me out of the kitchen so I'd been napping on the sofa. Until it all clicked.

"I know how they're stealing the money!" I jumped from the sofa and padded over to the kitchen entrance. "You said that Charles figured someone was stealing because the machines weren't balancing with Liquor and Gaming totals, right?"

He set aside the knife he'd been using to chop red peppers and focused on me. "That's right."

"It has to be in the coin." I paced the four-foot section of linoleum, excitement thrumming through my veins. This was it! "It's brilliant in its simplicity, really. Someone, or more than one person even, is shorting the coin bags. They're just taking a handful of coins from a bag a few times a night."

Joe wiped his hands on a dishcloth and leaned against the counter, giving me a small nod. "Go on."

It was August and the evening air was sticky so I had on baggy cotton shorts and a thin tank top. I was braless, and my nipples poked rudely through the top, getting Joe's attention. I ignored the way his eyes roamed over my scantily clad body and tried to refocus.

"The paperwork on every shift is balancing right? Nine hundred thousand at the start, nine at the end right?"

"Right."

"And the paper money has to be there because even if the cash office supervisor doesn't notice a shortage, it would be noticed by the bank downstairs. But the coin bags rarely even go to the bank. They just go in and out of the office. From the floor to the cashier to the office back to the cashier and to the floor to the machine. And once they're counted, that's it. Unless a bag is severely off weight-wise, no one would notice a thing."

Now Joe had that look. The one that said something was on the tip of his tongue, or brain in this case, but he couldn't quite grasp it.

"Sit." I sat at one of the kitchen tables and pointed at the chair opposite me. When he sat I started from the beginning, sketching a flow chart as I went.

"Okay, a bag of loonies is worth a thousand dollars, a bag of quarters, is two hundred and fifty, and a bag of nickels is one hundred. We're not going to look at nickels because a handful of them isn't worth anything. Quarters are a possibility but I'd say they're working the dollar coin."

"Got it." Joe's eyes were sharp on me, making it clear he understood everything so far.

"Do you have a suspect?"

"Yes."

I lifted a brow at him. "Are you going to tell me who?"

He didn't hesitate. "Susan Jordan."

"Susan?" That surprised me. "Why her?"

He leaned back in his chair and crossed his arms over his chest. The pose made his biceps bulge and saliva pooled in my mouth.

"Her spending habits have changed. Charles and Tom agreed that she's gotten flashier with her clothes in the last six months, as well as the fact that both she and her boyfriend have bought new cars in the last six months."

"That's it? That's why you want to accuse her of stealing?"

"That's why we think it's her. We can't accuse her until we have proof, and we haven't been able to figure out how she's doing it." Damn. I liked Susan. But it would be easy for her to pull this off.

"Okay." I started to think out loud. "It's easy really. She's shorting the bags of coin. A handful of loonies can be up to forty or fifty dollars. If she skims that from every couple of bags she counts and hands in at night, she could be walking out with at least two or three hundred dollars every shift."

"She couldn't be taking the coin out every night," Joe replied.

"Coins, especially dollar coins like loonies, are heavy. She would never get them past the security guard at close."

"Just because she's shorting the coin bag doesn't mean she's taking actual coin home with her," I responded. "The cashier's job is to change coin to bills for the customer and to hand out the coins to the floor supervisors to refill the slots. I'm telling you, this is where it's happening."

I jumped up from my seat and started pacing again. The answer was right in front of me. I just needed to see it.

Joe's gaze was steady, piercing almost, as he watched me. He got up from his chair and went back to chopping vegetables at the counter. "Okay. You're going to have to spend some time in the surveillance room with us."

I couldn't stop the grin of anticipation that crept across my face at that statement, and Joe noticed.

He set down the knife he'd just picked up. "You'll be watching her, angel. Not playing around."

"Did I say anything?" I stepped back, creeping around the table.

"We can't see what she's doing because we don't know exactly what we're looking for. But you should be able to catch it." He was stalking me now. Talking about work in a seductive low voice as he got closer, his eyes gleaming with an intent that had nothing to do with casino security, and everything to do my body's safety.

26

I thought you had a craving for beef stir fry?" I asked, keeping the table between us.

"I did." He crept toward the end of the table. "Now I have a craving for something else."

Excitement ripped through me and my tiredness drifted away. I knew what that something else was.

The nap on the couch had helped my mind rest, but my body had still been feeling the effects of the long night before with only a few hour's of sleep. But now, my body was only registering the effects of Joe's presence.

The normal pulse increase and heat of arousal shifted through me. My nipples hardened and my juices started to flow. All normal signs of being in close proximity to Joe.

Only this time, the urge to submit wasn't among them. This time . . . the urge to fight was.

"What if I don't feel like . . . feeding your craving?" While my words implied I wasn't interested, my actions were designed to let him know I was.

I trailed a hand over the curve of my breast, circled the pointed tip with a fingernail, and let out a seductive sigh.

A flame leapt to life in the intense blueness of Joe's eyes and he inched closer around the table. "I don't really care if you want to or not. You're my little slut. I get to fuck you anytime, anywhere, and anyhow I want."

They were rough words. Words that some women would find extremely insulting, yet being called his little slut never failed to make my pussy drool.

Instant moisture rushed to my sex and I fought the urge to bend over and beg him to fuck me. Instead, I met his gaze head on and flashed him a naughty little smile. "Only if you catch me."

And I took off for the bedroom. I made it three steps from the table before a quick hand shot out of nowhere and got hold of my arm.

He spun me around and pulled me against his chest. I wiggled and squirmed against him, my breasts swelling and feeling every bit of the friction through my thin tank top as he walked me backwards. When I was pinned between his hard body and the wall, he shoved a thigh between my legs and pressed it against my core.

"You're saying no to me?" he growled. "You don't want to give me what I want, then I'll just take it."

I struggled against him as best I could. He had my arms pinned to my sides but my hands had some reach and I kept my knees pressed tight together when he tried to get a leg between them.

I bit my lip as we wrestled, trying not to laugh too hard. Joe's words were harsh, and he was being wonderfully gentle in his roughness. I knew if I wanted him to stop all I had to do was stop, and say no seriously. But fighting him was fun.

The feel of his rock-hard muscles pinning me to the wall while he growled in my ear and thrust his hips against me had whimpers of lust escaping as I tossed my head from side to side, searching for a way to prolong the struggle.

In a desperate move I got my hands under his arms and tickled his ribs, up high, under his arms and he jerked away from me. Quicker than lightning I was away from him, but it only lasted a second before muscled arms wrapped around me from behind and lifted me off my feet.

"You're ticklish!" I laughed. Unable to not say something.

Laughter echoed in his voice when he spoke. "It doesn't matter because I've got you now."

With two steps forward he was next to the kitchen table. My arms were pinned to my sides and my feet dangled above the floor uselessly.

When my thighs were flush against the table he let me slide down his body. The second my feet touched the floor he grabbed the elastic waistband of my shorts and whipped them down my legs. I tried to jerk out of his grasp but a firm hand on the back of my head bent me forward over the table.

He kicked my feet apart and then stepped between them. I heard him work on his belt buckle and the loud rasp of metal teeth disconnecting as he undid his zipper.

There was only a light hand on the small of my back so I braced myself against the table's surface and pushed up, struggling against him.

"Oh, no, you don't."

Strong fingers wrapped around my wrists and pulled my arms out. He stretched them out until I was flat against the table again and my arms spanned the length of it. My fingertips were hanging over the edges and he put his hands over mine, curling them there. "I don't want your hands to move from here."

He straightened up off me, only his pelvis keeping my hips pressed to the table. I quickly lifted up and tried to get away again.

"Shit!"

We struggled for another second, his grunts and mutterings mixing with my breathless giggles until he had me bent over the table and he gave me three fast, sharp slaps on the ass.

I howled at that.

My butt was supersensitive because of the spanking the night before and my thin panties did nothing to protect me. It felt like my ass cheeks were on fire and the flames were licking down into my pussy, making it spasm in hunger for attention.

Joe's chest rubbed against my back as he leaned forward and nipped at my earlobe. "I said stay there. Every time you let go, you get five more smacks."

My forehead rested on the cool Formica, my hot breath creating a visible fog as I panted. When his hand slid under my tank top and along my naked spine I arched like a cat in heat. The hand moved smoothly down my back again to my hip, where he gripped the elastic waist of my panties and tore them off with a quick jerk. Fingers dipped between my thighs and into my slick folds, testing me, teasing me.

"I'm going to fuck you like this, and you're going to love every second of it."

My breath caught in my throat at his words. His voice had deepened so that it reverberated through the room and goose bumps appeared on my skin despite the heat. I felt the head of Joe's cock at my entrance and I moaned. He pushed forward, slow and steady until the dusting of his pubic hairs were tickling my sensitive cheeks.

Another moan escaped from me and I pushed back against him. He didn't move. I could feel the full throbbing length of him stretching my insides. My eyes slid closed and I concentrated on my inner muscles. I tightened and released, stroking him without moving.

"Jesus, that feels good, angel."

His hips jerked against me, and his cock twitched inside me. Suddenly, with a low guttural groan he gripped my hips and started to pump in earnest. His hips pumped and his cock slid in and out of my hungry sex. The slap of skin against skin mingled with our incomprehensible passion sounds and the scrape of the table legs against the cheap linoleum floor.

"That's it," I urged. "Fuck me, Joe."

The dirty words sounded foreign coming out of my mouth, but I could feel their effect on Joe. He was losing control, I could feel it. His cock swelled inside me and his fingers tightened on my hips. He was fucking me so hard I wondered if I'd be able to walk the next day. But I didn't want him to stop. I was completely focused on the feel of him sliding in and out, the sound of his labored breathing, and the urge to feel his hot come fill me up.

It was like his coming inside me would make me feel complete, whole.

"Come on, Joe. Come for me." I gripped the table and braced myself. I used every ounce of concentration I had to get my inner muscle sucking at him with every stroke. "Come inside me. I want to feel you come."

"You want me to fill you up? To fill up my little slut." He bent his knees, the angle shifted and he began to chant with each thrust. "My little slut. Mine. Mine. Mine!"

He slammed into me one last time and stayed pressed tight to me as he emptied his seed into my spasming channel. A warm wave of pleasure flowed from my sex outward in a small orgasm. It wasn't physically intense, but emotionally, I was full of bliss because I'd made Joe lose control.

Because I'd pleased my man.

Joe slowly pulled out of me, only to pull me upright, slip an arm under my legs and behind my back. He lifted and I was cradled against his chest as he walked to my bedroom. "I thought you were craving a stir fry?" I mumbled.

"The craving is gone," he whispered. He laid me on the bed, crawled onto the mattress behind me and we spooned. "You've drained me, all I want now is to sleep with my angel."

I sighed and enjoyed the feeling of being held. Then I giggled.

"What?" he mumbled.

"I know your secret."

"What's that?" he asked against my ear.

"You're ticklish. Big bad Joe Carson jumps like a little girl if you tickle his ribs."

Sunday was my day off. And I needed it.

The wake-up process was a slow lazy one with no alarm clock involved. That, in and of itself, was pure bliss. Then there was the big naked male body that was sharing the bed with me.

I was aware of Joe even before I opened my eyes. We weren't cuddled close, it was too hot for that, but his hand was lying possessively on my thigh when I woke up. When I shifted position, the hand shifted to my back, or my stomach. It didn't matter how I lay, the hand remained in contact with me. I opened my eyes and saw that Joe was still asleep, his breathing even, his chest rising and falling smoothly. The territorial way he kept in contact with me was a completely subconscious action.

Finally, I curled on my side facing him and enjoyed the view. His dark hair was mussed and his face soft. I'd thought that his "bad boy" vibe would soften in sleep as well, but it was still there. Maybe it was because of the dark shadow of a beard that appeared overnight, or the multiple scars visible on his body. He looked so strong and tough—he *was* so strong and tough—yet I knew he was capable of such softness. And he was in love with me.

Now that he'd told me, I felt it in his touch, heard it in his voice if not his words. There was no doubt in my mind that whatever he'd seen or done with the army had hardened him. But Tom was right, I could see flashes of a younger, more open Joe every now and then. Like the surprised joy on his face when I'd tickled him.

Tom thought I had something to do with those flashes coming forth. I certainly hoped so. Joe had done so much for me, not just sexually, but emotionally. He'd helped me to see who I really was.

Joe had helped me to see that just because I took my responsibilities seriously, and liked to be in control at work, I didn't have to be that way all the time. He showed me that it was OK to let go with someone you trust. In fact, that it was necessary to have that release, otherwise I'd just make myself miserable.

A sigh escaped and I reached out a hand to play with the soft fur on Joe's chest. Wouldn't you know it? I'd finally found something I liked about Chadwick and it was just in time for me to leave.

I was torn. I admit it.

I'd found a good man, who loved me for me, and I still wanted to leave. It was selfish, but after more than a decade of watching my mother do everything a man would tell her, with the hope that he would take care of her, I wanted to take care of myself. I wanted to go out in the world and be on my own.

For seven years, ever since my nineteenth birthday when Julie and I had spent a three-day weekend in Vancouver, all I'd dreamt about was living there. About finding my own niche in a place where my only responsibilities were to myself. To please myself, to do what I want, when I wanted to. And now it could happen.

It was going to happen.

"Serious thoughts?"

I lifted my gaze from where my finger was tracing a small scar on Joe's abdomen. His piercing blue eyes gazed into mine and I struggled to smile. "I'm thinking about Vancouver."

"You having doubts?"

I shrugged one shoulder. We were almost whispering, heads on pillows, only inches apart. It felt like the right time to let out all my secrets. "Not really doubts. I've wanted this for so long I can't *not* go. I want to go, I really do. But . . . I'd be silly if I wasn't a bit scared also. Right?"

"Don't worry, angel." He cupped my cheek and rubbed his thumb over my bottom lip. "Just say the word and I'll make sure you're looked after."

27

There was a slight feeling of déjà vu when I parked on the street in front of my mom's house. Brad's shiny blue pickup was already in the driveway though, and that told me things were definitely going to be different this time.

I reached for the box of pastries I'd picked up from the bakery for dessert. This time when I got to the front door and knocked, I hesitated. My hand hung over the doorknob when it the door opened and my mom stood there.

"Katie! Why didn't you just come right in?"

"I'm being a proper dinner guest." I gave her a big smile to let her know I wasn't being sarcastic.

In truth, I didn't want to chance walking in on her and Brad kissing or something. While I was OK with them being together, I really didn't think I was ready to actually see that.

Mom stepped back and fluttered her hands in the air. "Come in, come in. I'll take that," She reached for the pink pastry carton. "I'll put them in the kitchen then join you and Bradley in the living room."

Okay, I truly was a guest. I closed the door behind me and gave myself a mental shake.

"Be accepting," I muttered under my breath. "If they're happy, you're happy."

I toed off my sandals and walked barefoot into the living room. Brad was on the sofa with the TV guide spread out before him and the remote control in his hand.

"What's on?" I asked and dropped into the overstuffed chair next to the sofa.

He smiled at me. "Hi, Katie. Glad you could make it for dinner."

I met his gaze and we stared a minute. Everything was fine.

"So?" I prompted again, noticing the blank screen. "What's on?"

"Nothing right now. I'm programming all of Lydia's favorite television shows into the timer on the VCR so they'll tape every week."

"That's so sweet. And smart, too. Then you won't get any panicked calls when she can't figure out how to turn it on."

We shared a chuckle.

"What's so funny?" Mom asked as strolled into the room with a cheese and fruit platter.

"Your relationship with the VCR."

"That thing." She glared at it. "Brad is programming all my shows into it for me. Did he tell you?"

"Yup," I grinned. "I can see he's going to take care of you real good."

Dinner went surprisingly well after that. Mom had made a huge pan of lasagna and we talked, laughed, and ate until we were going to burst. I didn't even save room for a pastry, but left them there for my mom and Brad.

———————

I sat with Tom on Monday night and watched Susan on the surveillance monitor.

It was easy to see why the guards would get so bored in that small room if they had to stay in there for too long. As it was, Tom and Joe alternated every thirty minutes.

Normally the guards rotated positions every fifteen minutes, but with only Tom and Joe knowing why I was there, and what I was doing, it was better to keep it between us.

I didn't catch anything going on that first night. Maybe it's because my mind was on the fact that I was actually spying on a coworker, someone I liked. It felt wrong. Part of me hoped I wouldn't find anything because I didn't really want to believe she was stealing.

On Tuesday, Susan's shift was the three-to-ten. The plan was that when my shift in the cash office was over, I'd say good-bye and head for the basement. I knew it meant missing poker night with the girls, but I only had one week left at Black's, and I was determined to help Joe catch the thief before I left.

Julie came by the cash office that afternoon. There was a lull in the lounge business so she knocked on the cash cage window and motioned me out to chat.

"I'm just making sure you're going to make the poker game tonight." She stood with her feet shoulder width apart, her hands braced on her hips.

"Not this time," I said. I pulled the door to the cash cage closed behind me and moved off to the side so we could talk without being overheard. "I have plans I can't get out of."

Her dark eyes grew stormy. "Used to be the plans you couldn't get out of on a Tuesday night were our poker games."

I knew she was hurt. That she thought I was canceling on the poker night because of our fight the week before. But Joe had said not to tell anyone, so I didn't.

"That's true, but not tonight. I promised to help out a friend and we didn't finish last night, so we're doing it again tonight. I'm sorry, Julie."

She nodded and looked at the floor. Then she raised her eyes and stared straight at me. "I also heard you gave your notice. That you're leaving town on the weekend."

"Yeah, it's time for me to head out."

I waited for her to say something else. I wanted to be mad, I wanted to stay hurt, but most of all . . . I just wanted my friend back. The best way to do that was to show Julie that I was ready to share again.

"I won a lot of money in the poker game Brandon put together."

"Really? You went! I can't believe you went and didn't call me!" Julie's face lit up and she reached for my hands, and just like that, we were on an even keel again.

We might hurt each other, friends do that at times, but in reality, we were spirit sisters, and we would always remain that way. Even when one of us fucked up.

"I went, and you'll never guess who else was there." We huddled together in the corner and I told her about Renee. "It was perfect for her. You should've seen her, the next old rich guy that comes in here is going to find himself married to her, I just know it. Then a month later, he's gonna die of a heart attack in bed or something."

We laughed, we giggled some more, and then I had to get back in the office. But before we parted she agreed that she'd come over and help me pack later in the week.

———————

When my shift ended, I gathered up my stuff, said good-bye to everyone, and joined Tom in front of the security monitors again. Then Joe, then Tom. Around eight-thirty, I finally began to notice something.

It wasn't anything special in and of itself. But Susan seemed to fiddle with her hopper a lot. Now, coins got caught in the hoppers fairly often, the cashiers would give the machine a jiggle. Sometimes coins got stuck and that was all it took to free them.

If a little shake and jiggle didn't get the hopper counting the coins again, the cashier was supposed to call the supervisor. And if the supervisor can't immediately see a problem, then a technician comes to unjam it. Basically, other than giving the coin-counting machine a quick shake, the cashiers weren't supposed to fiddle with them. The machines were too expensive to let an untrained person mess with them.

Susan's machine was getting caught too often. And she wasn't calling the supervisor to unjam them. Instead, she'd stand in front of the machine and dig around in the coins for a minute. And it was always her loonie machine. There was a reason for that.

The gears in my head started to grind and then I saw it. A weird movement when she was counting out some bills to a customer.

It was fast. So fast and smooth I knew it wasn't her first time.

"There! See that?"

"See what?" Tom asked.

"She slipped a bill between the two nickel buckets. Is this taping? Can you rewind it?"

Tom showed me a different screen to watch and rewound the tape. "OK, it's coming up, watch her right hand carefully."

Tom watched.

"Freeze it!"

He pushed a button and stared at the screen. "I'll call Joe."

By the time Joe came into the room fifteen minutes later, I'd found the pattern on the tapes.

"It starts here," I told him. "Watch her hands."

Susan reached over and pulled the ice cream–sized bucket from her loonie machine and dumped it into a cash bag. Then she put the bag on her lap to seal it, and for a brief few seconds, maybe ten seconds, her body had shifted so her hands weren't visible.

"I don't see anything." Tom's forehead wrinkled.

"That's the point," I said. "Keep watching."

I forwarded it a bit, the clock timed it at twenty three minutes later when she did it again. The exact same thing. The coins from the hopper bucket into the bag, the body shift. Her movements were swift and sure, like she knew exactly what the camera could see.

"She's pulling coins from the bags after they've been counted, but before she seals them, and putting them in her cash drawer. When she gets enough coins built up in her little stash, I'm guessing a hundred dollars, she slips a bill into a nickel bucket, and puts another empty one on top of it. That's why she never pulls a bucket from *this* stack." I pointed to the small stack of the little plastic buckets customers used to tote coin around when playing the slot machines.

"That small stack on her left side is hers. She's never once taken one of those containers to give to a customer. Susan always offers to take the trash out at the end of her shift. I know this because Sara loves it when Susan works because she does this. I say she doesn't get rid of the trash. She dumps the containers in the trash, takes the trash outside, and collects the containers, with the bills in between them. That's why you never actually see her pocket the money."

Once I'd gone over the video with Joe again, and explained everything in detail to him, he pulled me aside. "You should go home now."

"I will. Are you going to arrest Susan tonight?" My voice was soft, and it felt like it was an effort to talk. I still couldn't believe Susan was stealing. And that it had been such an easy thing for her to do.

"Not tonight, no," Joe said as he walked with me out of the building. "I've got a small camera I'll put in the cash cage tonight. Now that we know what she's doing, I can place the mini one at the proper angle to catch everything on tape. When we have absolute proof, there's no wiggle room for her to deny that's what she was doing."

Aside from the flood-lights along the building's roof, the parking lot was pitch dark. The air was fresh and had a bit of a chill to it. Even in August, once the sun dropped behind the mountins, it could get cold.

"Do you think there's a good reason for what she's doing?" We got to my car, I leaned against the driver's door and looked up at the stars. "Do you think there's ever a good enough reason to steal?"

Joe leaned against the car next to me, his arm against mine. "I think that people can do surprising things when they have to, and sometimes . . . even when they don't."

It was a weird answer, yet it sort of made sense to my tired mind. Joe leaned down, pressed a kiss to my temple, and steered me into my car. "Go home and get some sleep."

I knew I should've been upset that I wouldn't be around to see them arrest Susan, but I wanted nothing to do with it.

The gossips would have a field day with it all and I had enough complications in my life without that. Joe had said I might need to testify if it went to court, but he doubted it, and I was glad.

28

The rest of the week sped by. On Friday, my last day at work, I made it a point to say good-bye to Jimmy, Tom, and the girls in the cash cage.

That was it.

I knew if I'd given even a hint, they would've made a big deal out of me leaving, but I didn't want the attention. I just really wanted to slip away quietly, and they let me.

Julie and Lillian had spent Thursday night helping me pack and Brad had come over and loaded up his truck with the stuff I wanted to store at my mom's. At dusk on Friday I went downstairs and knocked on Mrs. Beets's door.

"I just wanted to tell you I was leaving tonight, and that Larry's nephew should be moving in on Sunday," I said when she answered the door in her pink floral housecoat.

"Oh, Katie." Her plump hands fluttered at her side. "I can't believe you're leaving. I thought for sure you'd stay now that you have that nice young man hanging around. He rescued Pepper from a tree last week, you know? After you'd already left for work."

"He is a nice guy, isn't he?" For once the fact that my neighbor knew who was hanging around my place didn't bother me so much. "But I had these plans before I met Joe, and I'm not going to let a man change them, no matter how nice he is."

"You young women these days. So independent." She reached out and gave me a hug. "You take care of yourself, Katie. Pepper and I will expect a card from you at Christmas."

Her hug felt good. I gave Pepper a good-bye scratch behind the ears and went back upstairs. I was ready to go.

All I had left to do was say good-bye to Joe.

When eleven o'clock came and went and he still hadn't shown up at my place, I loaded up my car, locked up the apartment, and started out on the highway.

Just outside of town I pulled over at the roadside motel and parked next to the shiny black Charger in the lot. My heart was heavy, my hands were shaking, and a fine sweat was forming on my brow. I got out of the car and knocked on the unit in front of the Charger before I could change my mind.

Before I even dropped my hand back to my side the door opened and Joe stood there barefoot and shirtless. My breath caught in my throat and a minute later trembling started in my insides.

"I got tired of waiting for you," I said.

"I just got out of the shower." He opened the door and ushered me in. "You okay?"

I nodded and perched myself on the edge of his bed. The room wasn't fantastic, but it was clean and neat. There was a small corner kitchen area, a table and chairs, the dresser, television, and a bed.

"It was just time to go. I'd said all my good-byes and I didn't want to stay in the apartment any longer." I took a closer look around the room. It looked like he'd just arrived and hadn't even unpacked yet. "I'll be in a place just like this tomorrow, you know?"

Joe propped the pillow up against the wall, sat down with his legs stretched out, and crooked his finger at me. "Come here."

I straddled his legs and cuddled up against his chest, where it was safe and warm. My head was on his shoulder, my nose pressed against his neck so I could breathe in his scent every time I inhaled. He stroked a hand from the top of my head all the way down my back and cupped my butt gently.

"Do you have a place to stay?" he spoke softly.

"I figured I'd find a hotel when I got there."

We talked quietly for a while, about the city, and where I wanted to go. Joe reached into the bedside drawer and pulled out a small flat piece of metal. It was shaped like a military dog tag with a hole at one end, but no chain.

I looked at it closely, running my fingers over it. There was a 1-800 number on it, and the initials DD. "If you need anything at all, you call this number, tell them who you are, and they'll help you. Okay?"

"What is it? Who's DD?"

"It's a Safety Chit. DD Security Group is the name of Damien's security company. All the members of our team have them, as do their family members. We look after our own."

My heart clenched. Joe was telling me I was still his. Even if we weren't together, he'd look after me. I wanted to tell him I loved him. He deserved to hear it, but only if it were true. And I wasn't sure it was.

Our eyes met and the taste of tears filled the back of my throat. I swallowed and gave him a watery smile. "Thank you."

"You're welcome." He pressed a soft kiss to my lips.

———————

There was no sign that read WELCOME TO VANCOUVER.

I tried not to think of that as an omen. That maybe I wasn't welcome in Vancouver. I'd made my choice, and even though I'd given Mom and Brad my blessing, and made up with Julie before I left Chadwick. I didn't intend to go back for a long time, if ever.

I wished Joe had said he was coming back to the city for sure. That maybe I'd see him again. But he'd said he really liked the peace and quiet of the mountains, and he was thinking of staying there and becoming a security guard for good. He had some choices of his own to make.

I wanted freedom and excitement and acceptance. Oh, and an education. As much as I wanted Joe, and I knew I'd miss him, I couldn't find those things in Chadwick.

The community college was in the city center, so I followed the signs that pointed to Robson Street. Joe had given me the name of a guy who ran an apartment building near the city center campus that rented by the month with no leases, and he said to use his name if the guy gave me a hard time about renting at the last minute.

Julie and I had spent a weekend in Vancouver to celebrate our nineteenth birthdays, becoming legal and all. But my only memories were of dancing, laughing, and a day spent at the aquarium. The city was basically a maze to me.

I'd looked at my map when I'd stopped for a late lunch a few hours earlier and had felt pretty confident then. But now, my heart was racing and my palms were sweaty from the heavy traffic, and I was starting to feel a bit overwhelmed. The plan had been to stop on the side of the road on the outside of the city and refresh my memory, but there never seemed to be any real city limits.

The highway driving had been just fine, then there were more and more lights, and cars, and signs telling me where to go. I passed signs that said Surrey and Abbotsford and kept going, waiting for the one that said Vancouver. My fingers were white knuckled on the steering wheel and I forced air deep into my lungs, then slowly let it out.

Though there was no WELCOME TO VANCOUVER sign, I know I *was* in the city.

Now where did I go?

I pulled into a gas station, dug through my bag for the map I had, and went inside to ask for help. When I climbed back in the car I had a big bag of licorice to calm my nerves and verbal directions. With a deep breath I eased back into the steady stream of traffic and made my way.

It was easy to get distracted by all the lights and stores. Finally I just pulled over into a strip mall with a Starbucks and went inside to sit down. I sat on a stool at the window and did some people watching.

I was there.

I was finally there.

29

Damn, he looked good.

Leaning against a shiny black and chrome motorcycle parked at the curb, his blond waves tousled in the breeze, Karl looked good enough to make heads turn.

In the month since the wet T-shirt contest in Tavers, he hadn't changed much, and I was glad that he'd programmed his number into my cell phone. The first two weeks in the city alone had been exhilarating, but I'd just received confirmation of my acceptance to the full-time financial management program at the college, and I wanted to celebrate.

When I'd called Julie to tell her about my success, she was the one who had reminded me of Karl's number. Mark had told her the whole

group of bikers that had been at Moe's that night were from Vancouver, so if I wanted someone to celebrate with, he'd be a good choice.

She was right, too.

"Hey there, Mr. Purr," I said as I strolled up beside him.

He still looked like an angel dressed in denim and leather, until I
gazed into his eyes. That gleam there made it very clear he had very
naughty things on his mind. And that was fine with me. I was finally
free in a big city and I wanted to revel in that freedom.

He arched a scarred blond brow at me. "Mr. Purr?"

A small chuckle eased from my throat and I realized I actually
sounded sultry. "After you made that promise about being able to
make me purr, it stuck in my head."

"Uhmmm." He nodded. "I stuck in your head, eh?"

I pressed a newly manicured fingertip into his chest. "You did.
Now, you're not going to let me down are you?"

Where had this confident flirt come from? It was like I was channeling Marilyn Monroe. I glanced around the other sidewalk café at
the other customers. I didn't know any of them. At all. And none of
them knew me.

The intoxication of freedom swam through my veins, and I
leaned into Karl. "Take me for a ride?"

"Honey, I'll give you the ride of your life."

I laughed at his blatant arrogance and he gave me a smile that
showed he knew what an outrageous statement it was.

He swung a leg over the bike and handed me a helmet. I pulled it
on and had him do up the chinstrap for me, then climbed on behind
him. At that point I was glad I'd worn my new hip-hugger Capri
pants instead of a skirt. They weren't exactly biker gear, but they were
sleek and they didn't flash the world my butt when I sat on the bike.

Karl kick-started the bike and it rumbled erotically between my legs. I wrapped my arms around his waist and scooted closer, so that his firm ass was cradled between my hips. "I like this already," I said.

My chin was resting on his shoulder, my mouth directly by his ear so he could hear me clearly, and the muscles of his abdomen sook with laughter beneath my fingertips.

"You want to see the real sights, or the tourist highlights?"

"The real sights," I declared. "Show me what Vancouver has to offer!"

He pulled away and we roared down the street. Karl was a safe driver. At first I'd expected to be scared on a motorcycle, but it was amazingly solid beneath me, and even when Karl wove the bike around cars I felt completely secure. The adrenaline from the ride, the hard body of a hot man between my thighs, and the throbbing vibrations of the bike beneath me started my juices flowing.

We prowled the busy streets of Vancouver on that Harley for almost two hours. Daylight wasn't gone yet and people were everywhere. There were buskers playing music on street corners, sidewalk cafés full of an eclectic mix of people. When Karl pulled to a stop in front of a pub and turned the bike off, I was full of excitement.

Reckless heat flowed through my veins. The thrill of the city, of being on a motorcycle with a man that I'd only met once before, in a city where no one knew me, was a turn-on.

"Ready for a drink?" Karl asked when I climbed off the bike.

The pub he'd parked in front of was pretty crowded, but there was an empty table on the sidewalk patio so I sat there, and he went inside to grab our drinks. The city streets were full of people, just like I'd imagined. I watched a couple holding hands walk past, followed by a group of teenagers with jeans down around their butts, underwear hanging out over the top. I shook my head and smiled to myself.

That was the style, I'd seen it on TV and in movies, but If some kids walked around Main Street in Chadwick like that, Mary would come out of the beauty parlor yelling and screaming and demanding they let her fix their pants.

I ignored the couple arguing at the table behind me, smiled flirtatiously at the three jock types that were watching me from two tables away, and soaked up the atmosphere. It was after ten and the sky was starting to darken, the lights and signs from the surrounding business contributing to the eclectic vibe of the area. The sound of musicians warming up came from inside the pub, adding to the noise of conversation and laughter.

"Pear cider, right?" Karl handed me the chilled green bottle, and dropped into the chair next to me, pulling my attention away from the small brick building across the street.

"Perfect." I smiled at him. "Thank you, for the ride . . . and the drink."

"Happy to oblige. I have to admit, I was pretty surprised you actually called, *Caitlyn*."

"Hey! That could've been my full name. I just choose to go by Katie."

He chuckled and slung an arm casually around my shoulders. "Yeah, right. It had nothing to do with being in a wet T-shirt contest, right?"

"Nothing wrong with a girl wanting to play it safe while she . . . played."

Karl took a swig of his beer and set it back on the table. Then he focused all his attention on me. "And what do you want to do now? Play? Or play it safe?"

The band inside had started and music spilled out onto the patio as I considered my options. Karl was a very sexy man, and my body was already humming with the need for some action.

"What's over there?" I asked, nodding my chin toward the brick building and the well-dressed man standing guard in a small

doorway. There was a simple sign over the door that said THE
DUNGEON.

Karl glanced across the street and when he looked back at me his
eyes had a speculative gleam in them. "It's an underground club."

The air between us shifted, tightened. He hadn't said it was nightclub, just a club. My pulse jumped. I had a good idea of what it might
be . . . but I wasn't sure. "What kind of club?"

He lifted his beer to his lips and took a slow pull from it before
setting it on the table and shifting to get a better look at me. "A
BDSM club."

Heat swept through me. "BDSM as in domination and submission?"

His head cocked to the left. "D and S is part of it yes. Does that interest you, Katie?"

My cheeks warmed as I remembered the way I felt when I was
with Joe. The urge to do whatever it took to please him. The pleasure
I got from submitting to him. I shifted in my seat and squeezed my
thighs together.

"Yes, it does." The words were firm and I met his gaze squarely.
He had that lazy arrogant look that had caught my attention that first
night and a light bulb went on in my brain. He was a Dom. That was
why I'd been so attracted to him in the first place.

Heat simmered in his chocolate-colored eyes and I felt it coil low
in my belly. It was as if he were stripping me naked and getting ready
to introduce himself to my body right there and then.

"Do you have experience with D/s play, Katie?" His tone turned
into a seductive purr, and all the background distractions faded away.

"A little bit."

"Do you want more?"

The Marilyn Monroe ghost I'd been channeling was gone, and
in her place was me. A shiver ran down my spine. This was what I'd

wanted. To be in the big anonymous city and have some adventure. Sexual adventure and personal freedom.

"Yes, I do."

***

I was strangely calm getting ready for Karl to pick me up the next night. We'd sat on that patio for quite a while with him asking questions, probing me about my experiences. It was weird, to sit and talk about such intimate acts and thoughts like that, but exciting, too. The whole time we talked, the knot of arousal in my belly grew. When he pulled up in front of my apartment building a couple of hours later, I was more than ready to get naked. But he'd just instructed me to wear a short skirt and a white button-up blouse with nothing underneath, and said he'd pick me up just after nine.

The short black skirt flared a bit at the hem, giving it a flirty look, and the button-up white blouse would've looked demure if only my nipples weren't so clearly visible.

Anticipation made my blood hum as it flowed through my veins and my eyes glow as I looked into the mirror. I'd put my make up on quite heavily, and I didn't really look like myself. I certainly didn't look like Miss Nice Girl from Chadwick. I smiled in satisfaction and went to answer the knock at my door.

"Hey," I said when I swung it open to see Karl standing there. He looked yummy with a black T-shirt molded to his lean chest, covered by a black leather vest, and black jeans tucked into biker boots. Tousled dirty blond curls were at complete odds with the colorful dragon tattoo that peeked out from under his shirt collar.

"Hey yourself," he said, and held out a small plastic bag for me. "I brought you something to wear tonight."

I closed the door behind him and reached for the bag. It was quite heavy for its size and I opened it eagerly.

"What is it?" I asked, holding up a tangle of leather straps. As soon as the words left my mouth I got the straps untangled and it became clear what it was. What they were. "This is supposed to be underwear?"

Karl's lips titled at one corner and he reached for the bundle in my hands. "Lift up your skirt."

Shock went through me. I knew he'd see me naked at some point that night. But right then and there? I hesitated and he repeated his words. This time the command in his voice was clear and I didn't hesitate.

When I had my skirt lifted he got down on one knee and held out the straps for me to step into, just like panties. The leather brushed against my skin and he skimmed his hands up my legs. He maneuvered the straps into place so they rested against my hips, and the leather triangle with no middle framed my neatly trimmed bush. The sides of the triangle swept between my thighs so each small strap pressed against one rapidly swelling pussy lip. The straps then met and blended into one that slipped between my buttocks like a thong.

Karl tightened the buckle on my hip and I gasped. Heat rushed up inside me and I knew my cheeks would be bright red. As he'd done up the buckle the leather had nudged at me intimately. Once it was done and the belt secured, the smaller straps kept my sex spread and exposed, while the place where they joined pressed gently against my puckered anus, making every movement an erotic tease.

"Oh, Lord," I whispered.

Karl stood up, the gleam in his eyes daring me to say I couldn't wear it. When I pressed my lips together he grinned and stepped back to open the door. "Let's go."

30

The ride to the bar on the back of Karl's bike had my insides quivering and an embarrassing wetness growing between my thighs. He parked in front of The Dungeon and helped me climb off the bike.

"Enjoy the ride?" He lifted a playful eyebrow at me when it took me a minute to feel steady on my feet once again.

I rolled my eyes at him and giggled. There was no use pretending. Although I did thank God my skirt had been long enough to tuck under my butt and hadn't left my ass bare for all to see. The fact that Karl knew what the throbbing engines and vibrations from the bike had done to me was enough.

He reached into the bike's saddle bags and withdrew a small satchel before leading the way down the steps to the clubs entrance. At the bottom he nodded to the bouncer that held the door open for us and we continued inside silently. There were more steps, taking us deeper underground. With every breath I took, the sultry throbbing music filled my head and seeped into my body. There was another well-dressed bouncer at the bottom and this one greeted Karl by name.

"Master Karl, I'm sorry to tell you there were no cancellations with the private bookings tonight."

"That's fine, Josh. I didn't really expect there to be. If there's nothing available I understand."

Josh checked the clipboard in his hand and smiled at Karl. "There are no private rooms, but there are a couple of stations still available for use in the Shared Room."

Karl turned his head and his intense gaze met mine, almost as if he were trying to see inside my head. "That'll be fine, Josh. I'm going to show my guest around a little first." He looked back at the man. "Fifteen minutes?"

"Station Six will be ready for you, sir."

Karl placed a hot hand on the small of my back and urged me into the room. He steered me steadily forward as I struggled to take everything in at once. The room was dim, with a slightly blue tinge to the lighting that gave it a warm, comfortable atmosphere. But the crowd was unlike any I'd ever seen.

Almost everyone was dressed in leather, latex, or lace of some sort. The women wore corsets or body-hugging mini skirts and stiletto boots. The men wore leather pants, chaps, and jeans, and a couple even wore what looked like silk suits.

Karl fit in, what with his leather and sort of Biker Dom look, but me in my basic skirt and top didn't quite blend. Strangely enough, it didn't seem to matter. If anything, the fact that it was obvious I had no bra on beneath my white blouse helped. Nobody looked askance at me or made any rude comments, and several people nodded and smiled at Karl. A few people let their gaze run over me before moving on, but that was it.

I wasn't sure if I was excited by that or insulted.

Karl stopped at the bar and ordered a couple of bottles of water. When he handed me mine I raised my eyebrows at him in question.

"No alcohol ahead of time. You can have a drink after if you want." He leaned in close and spoke into my ear. "What do you think?"

I looked around the crowd, felt the thrill of anonymity and freedom shoot through me, and met his gaze. "I think I'm going to have a very good time tonight."

"Do you like what you see on stage?"

The stage was on the other side of the room and I hadn't even noticed it. But once I did, I couldn't tear my gaze away.

There was a naked man bent over what looked like a padded sawhorse, with his hands and feet tied to the legs. A woman dressed in a one-piece shiny black latex suit, and the requisite stilettos, dark hair pulled back sleek and smooth, was standing off to the side looking down at a table. She picked up a riding crop and fingered it before setting it back down. My pulse jumped and my nipples hardened. She picked up a whip that had many tails on it and turned decisively to the bound man.

Karl's hand at my back shifted lower, his thumb running along the bare strip of skin between my top and the waist of my skirt, leaving a trail of fire.

"She's going to tease and play with that man until he begs for release in front of everyone. And he's going to love every minute of it," Karl's lips brushed my ear when he whispered.

The memory of Joe tossing me over his lap and warming my ass with the palm of his hand flooded my mind and I felt a small pain in my chest. Dragging my eyes from the stage I looked at Karl. At the heat in his intense gaze, the small tilt to his lips, the dangerously attractive man. And at that moment all I wanted was Joe.

I shoved the thought of him aside ruthlessly and pressed the palm of my hands against Karl's hard chest. "I'm ready for you to follow through on your promise."

"Which one is that?"

Our eyes met and the throbbing music, the action on stage, the crowd around us faded into the background. "Make me purr."

———————

Station Six was a semi-private cubicle in a room of eight cubicles. By the time we got there, only one other station was empty besides ours. The rest were occupied with people in various forms of undress and restraints. I tried not to stare as we walked to our cubicle and passed the others. I was curious to see what was going on, yet the way the stations were set up, you could only see what was happening in them if you were directly in front of one.

There were two people in the middle of the room, fully dressed in elegant black suits like the bouncers had been, apparently monitoring the activities in the room.

"Safety is a must here," Karl said when he saw me checking out the man and woman in the middle of the room. "They monitor everything to make sure that no one ignores a safe word or is mistreated. They'll see everything I do to you."

My eyes flew to his. He'd warned me that people might be able to see us "play," but it hadn't seemed real. None of this really seemed real. Suddenly, as I watched Karl move about our small cubicle, spraying the super-sized padded X cross with detergent and wiping it down, I wondered what the hell I was doing.

I'd always fantasized about being submissive, and with Joe, it had seemed so natural and freeing. Yet here, this was so . . . calculated.

The leather underwear and the motorcycle ride had me wet and aching. Being in the club, the open acceptance of people and all that was happening, was arousing. Yet, something was off.

"Ready?" Karl stepped in front of me, using a firm hand to tilt my head up so I met his gaze. He cared. I could see it in his eyes. As bad boy as he seemed, as lighthearted and challenging as he was, it was clear he didn't want me to do anything I wasn't comfortable with.

"Yes, sir."

This was something I'd fantasized about. I wasn't about to quit now.

"Step back to the cross and spread your hands and feet."

"Do we need a safe word?" I asked this as I did what he said. Adrenaline pumped through my veins as he secured my right wrist with a padded leather strap, then my left.

"It's not necessary as we're not getting to pain play tonight. But if it makes you feel more comfortable, you can use the basic stoplight system. Yellow means you need a break. Red calls everything to stop." He knelt down and secured my ankles to the cross.

I was spread-eagle, leaning back slightly on the cross, and despite the fact that I still had my clothes on, I felt extremely exposed and hugely turned on. I heard some light rustling noises behind me and then felt Karl's presence at my back.

"This is just an introduction, sweetheart. The start of your training as a true submissive." His hot breath wafted across my ear and a blindfold was slipped over my head. "And this will help you forget that we are surrounded by others. I want you to focus only on me. On my voice, on my hands, on my touch."

At first, when the blindfold slid over my eyes and the world went dark, I became super aware of the sounds around me. The slap of flesh meeting flesh to my left, the ecstatic sighs and moans coming from my right. But I sucked in a deep breath and focused on Karl's voice.

As if he were soothing a skittish horse, he talked to me as he ran his hands lightly over my body. My nipples peaked and my pussy clenched with every touch. When I pressed back against the cross I realized that the joint of the thong pressed against my rear entrance in the most delicious way.

"You have a real adventurous streak, don't you?" He spoke as he started to unbutton my blouse. Cool air hit my bare skin and my nipples tightened almost to the point of pain. I licked my lips, unsure if I was supposed to answer him or not. He flicked a nipple, causing a jolt to go through my system. "I asked you a question."

"Yes. Yes I have an adventurous streak." I tried not to squirm against the restraints. My blood was running hot, and my body was eager for the attention.

Warm fingertips skimmed over my ribcage, across my belly, and up the center of my torso. A small whimper escaped when he circled my breasts. They were so heavy and full. Aching for a firmer touch.

"You need more?" Karl's hand cupped the weight of one breast and he squeezed, earning a grateful sigh from me. "Oh yeah, you like this don't you?"

Then both breasts were being cupped and fondled by both hands. My pulse picked up and I tried to squeeze my thighs together. "More," I gasped out to Karl.

He let go of my breasts and I was lost. I couldn't see or hear what he was doing. Then I felt his hands sliding up my legs and under my skirt. A fingertip teased my exposed labia and he chuckled. "You're extremely wet, sweetheart. It's not going to take much to make you come is it?"

I shook my head, unable to speak and my hips flexed, pressing me more firmly against his finger. He placed two fingers lightly against my exposed clit and leaned into me. His chest pressed against mine briefly and his words puffed across my lips. "Make yourself come on my hand. If you can make yourself come, I'll reward you well."

I pressed my shoulders against my support and flexed my hips.

Karl held his hand still and I did all the work, rubbing and grinding myself as best I could against his stiff fingers, the leather underwear keeping my pussy lips spread for easy access. Every time I thrust forward, my buttocks clenched and the thong pressed into my rear hole.

The stimulation was almost enough, but not quite. A whimper squeezed from my lips and Karl urged me on. "You are so wet, sweetheart. Show me you can do it."

His husky coaxing sent me over the edge and my body trembled as I focused completely on the explosion of pleasure in my core. Before I had time to recover he thrust two fingers deep into my body, and pumped into me. His lips nibbled on my neck for a brief minute before making their way to my breast and suckling on a rigid tip. The palm of his hand pressed against my sensitive clit and his fingers stroked my insides, ripping a cry from my throat and sending me over the edge again.

While I was panting and gasping, Karl's hand gently stroked my side and he murmured in my ear. His stubbled cheek pressed against mine.

I was glad for the blindfold then, because, despite the ripples of pleasure still echoing through my body, I wasn't sure I could look him in the eye.

When I almost had myself under control again, Karl whispered, "Third time's the charm." Then backed away.

My befuddled brain didn't get what he meant until he lifted my skirt and tucked the hem into the top of the leather thong. His breath on the inside of my thigh was the only warning I had seconds before his mouth went to work on my sex.

Thumbs spread me even wider open as he licked, sucked, and nibbled at my over-sensitive flesh. His agile tongue thrust deep and my insides clutched at him. He pulled out, replacing his tongue with a finger while his mouth sealed itself over my swollen clit and suckled. He flicked it with his tongue, then he suckled some more. My hips bucked against him, constant moans and sighs working from low in my belly and out of my mouth. It was torture. The sweetest torture ever, and I couldn't form the words to make him stop.

Did I even want him to stop?

Before any of it registered in my brain, sparks lit up behind my eyelids and an explosion of pleasure ripped through my body. I shuddered, I trembled, I cried.

When I came back to myself, my skirt was back in place and Karl was buttoning up my blouse. When the blindfold was pulled gently from my eyes, he stood before me with a soft smile.

"You okay?" He wiped a thumb under my eye, drying my tears.

I nodded and he pressed a soft kiss to my lips before he bent down to undo the first of the restraints.

———

Two hours later I was curled up in the middle of the bed. Knees pulled up, my arms wrapped around the extra pillow, holding it close to my body. The warmth of my own hands tucked under my chin my only comfort.

Why I needed comfort wasn't exactly clear. I'd just spent the night at a club straight out of my fantasies. No one had known me; no one cared what I did for a living or where I lived. They didn't know or care if they ever saw me again either. The cubicle had given me anonymity, the rules of the club had given me safety in my explorations, and Karl had given me orgasm after orgasm.

Yet, there was an emptiness inside me that was scary.

Karl would give me more. He'd made it clear that he wanted to "train" me. I even trusted that he wouldn't try to extend the power exchange into other aspects of a relationship. Yet the feelings just weren't there.

When the last orgasm had subsided, I was the one that pulled away. Physically and emotionally. I hadn't wanted to stay for a drink or go for a late dinner. All I'd wanted to do was go deep inside myself.

Karl, a true gentleman despite his leather and tattoos, had brought me home, seen me to my door, and left with nothing more than a kiss and the promise of a phone call the next day.

Nothing was working out the way I'd wanted it to. Vancouver was big, and dirty, and loud, and . . . and . . . I missed Chadwick. I never thought it would be possible but I missed Mrs. Beets's nosiness, I missed Jimmy's morning coffee and the fact that the butcher knew I preferred pork over beef. I even missed my mom.

Warm tears rolled down my cheek and I pressed my face into the pillow.

Mostly, I missed Joe.

31

Two days later I did not want to get out of bed.

I'd fallen into a funk for no real reason. Everything had gone right for me since I arrived in the city. I had a decent place to live that was close to the school. I'd called Ray and had gotten a part-time job at one of his restaurants. I even had a sexy lawyer wanting to date me. Who'd have though Karl's day job was as a lawyer? There was definitely more to him than met the eye, yet I wasn't ready to see him either. And maybe date was too strong a word.

The point was, everything was exactly what I had hoped for, what I had expected and looked forward to in the city.

Yet there was an emptiness inside me that was scary.

Karl had offered me exactly what I thought I'd wanted. There were no responsibilities, no promises, and no commitments. I'd loved the motorcycle ride, the pub had been great, the time at The Dungeon had been the exact type of adventure I'd wanted. Yet things just didn't feel as good as I thought they would.

I looked at the digits on my clock, then the sunshine out my window. The new job didn't start for another three days, so I rolled over and went back to sleep.

———————

It was noon when I woke up with a headache.

"Well, no shit, Sherlock. That's what happens when you give in to self-pity."

I turned the shower on and stepped in. I had to focus on the good things. I was just a little homesick is all. The city wasn't that bad, it was just . . . big. It would take some getting used to. Mom and Julie were only a phone call away. Nothing I ever did would chase them out of my life, so it was stupid of me to feel like they'd left me behind. Especially since I was the one who'd left *them* behind.

It also wasn't fair of me to compare Karl to Joe. Joe Carson had been a fantasy come true. He'd known what every hint I'd given him had meant, as if he could read my mind. It wasn't Karl's fault that Joe was the only man I really wanted to submit to. That it was Joe that made everything OK, and not the actual act of submission itself. That would explain why the sight of the naked man restrained had gotten me so hot, too. My palms had itched with the urge to touch and tease him, so maybe I had a bit of the dominant in me.

Jimmy would tell me, "Life is what you make of it." And he'd be right. I could lie around and feel sorry for myself, or move on.

It was time to learn from my mistakes. I'd do things smarter the next time around. Maybe one day I'd even get up the nerve to call Joe again.

I rinsed the conditioner from my hair and turned off the shower.

I needed to go shopping for school supplies, and there was a girl close to my age in the apartment across from me. She'd smiled at me when we passed in the hall the other day. Maybe I'd knock on her door and see if she was interested in going shopping with me.

——— ■ ———

Her name was Sharon, and she was a student at the city center campus too. When I told her I needed to go shopping, she'd been all in.

With an outgoing personality and a huge grin that never left her face, Sharon was great company. She had short dark hair that spiked up in all directions, big brown eyes lined heavily with black eyeliner that matched her black nail polish, and a nose piercing. She looked a bit like a punk rock pixie, and by the time we'd gotten home from shopping I was begging her to sprinkle me with magic energy dust because I was exhausted.

"Where the hell is Chadwick?" she asked as we climbed the stairs, arms laden with shopping bags.

"South, down in the Kootenays. It's really quite beautiful. You'd like it." I laughed. "You'd shock the shit out of everyone there, but you'd like it."

"What? You don't think they'd like my tattoos?" She gestured to the one arm she had almost completely covered in ink. She called it her sleeve.

I unlocked the apartment door and pushed it open. "It's not the . . ."

"It's not the what?" Sharon nudged me from behind. "Get in there would ya, or I'm gonna drop your bags in the hall."

"You'd better come inside, angel. She sounds serious."

"Joe!" I dropped my bags and lunged at the man standing in the middle of my living room.

Strong arms wrapped around me and held me tight as I planted kisses all over his handsome face.

"Uhh, I think I'll be going now. Talk to you later, Katie."

Joe pulled back, "Your friend is leaving, say good-bye."

"Bye, Sharon. I'll see you tomorrow." I called without taking my eyes from Joe's gorgeous face. I heard her laugh and the apartment door close. Then we were alone.

"What are you doing here? How'd you find me?"

He let me go and sat on the overstuffed sofa. The minute he was settled I straddled his legs and sat on his lap.

A dark eyebrow winged up under his hairline. "Miss me?"

" I did." I nodded. "Very much."

"Good to know." His hands settled on my hips and he shifted under me. "I found you easily because I was the one who told you to come here, remember? The building owner is a friend of mine."

"Oh, yeah." Duh! Just seeing him again was short-circuiting my brain.

He chuckled. "How are things going for you here? Do you like the city?"

I couldn't stop staring at him. My hands were petting him everywhere, his arms, his shoulders, and his chest. He was here. That must mean I had another chance. That I hadn't screwed up and lost him by walking away. When I didn't answer him right away he pinched my chin and forced me to meet his gaze.

"Katie, are you okay?"

"I'm okay," I said. "But I miss home."

"That's understandable."

"I know, it just surprised me. I thought once I left I'd never look back. But I was wrong." I cocked my head to the side and gave him a stern look. "Now you. What are you doing here?"

"Well, I decided I wasn't ready to retire just yet. Chadwick is beautiful, and I can see myself retiring there in ten years or so, but I'm not quite ready yet."

"You're going to retire in ten years?"

"I plan to retire young." He gave me wicked grin. "But until then, I was hoping to make my life in the city a bit more enjoyable by, well . . . by getting a life. Starting with a roommate. You know anyone that needs a place to live? I have a very nice condo not too far from here."

My heart stopped and my jaw dropped. "Me? Are you asking me to live with you? Here? In the city?"

He nodded, eyes shining with emotion.

I clapped my hands on his cheeks and kissed him soundly.

When I pulled back I wiggled my butt down on his lap, happy to feel a solid bulge growing there. "I'll do it if you promise me one thing."

He caught onto my playful mood and his eyes sparkled back at me. "Of course."

"I want to be in charge once in a while."

His eyes widened and his lips twitched.

"I'm not joking. Every once in a while I want to be the boss in the bedroom."

"I can live with that," he said, and pulled me close.

I pushed his hands away and scrambled off his lap to stand in front of him. "Starting now. I get to be the one in charge tonight. Your body is going to become *my* personal playground for once."

He stood quickly. So fast that I didn't have to time to get out of the way and we were chest to chest, my eyes level with his chin. I tilted my head, refusing to back up. "You may carry me to the bedroom. Gently," I warned when he swept me up in his arms.

"Just so we're clear," he said when he set me back on my feet beside my bed. "I'm completely open to you being in charge every now and then, but you are nobody's little slut but mine."

Our gazes locked and I was drawn into the blue fire there. I reached up, wrapped a hand around his neck, and pulled his head down. His lips parted and he let me lead. My tongue swept the inside of his mouth, testing, touching, exploring.

"Only yours," I whispered against his lips. When he was in my room, he set me on the bed and started to cover my body with his.

"Uh-uh," I said, and pushed him back. I climbed on top of his body. My knees straddled his hips, my belly and chest pressed against his while my hands roamed his face, his neck, his chest.

I grabbed the bottom edge of his T-shirt and pulled it over his head, but didn't touch his jeans or anything below the waist. My dress was next. The thin summer cotton dress floated to the floor and I was completely naked.

"No panties," he observed.

"It feels naughty." A hot blush crept up my neck and he chuckled.

"Good girl. Katie Long is learning to let the bad girl out to play, huh?"

"Yes, I am. And you're going to love it."

Joe's hands ran up my sides to cup my breasts, but I shook my head.

"No, no, no," I said and pinned his hands at his sides on the mattress. "You can look, but you can't touch until I say so. Do I need to restrain you, sir?"

His lips tilted into a smirk. "That's not necessary. I can control myself."

"Oh, really?" I cupped my breasts in my hands and pointed the nipples at him. "Is that a challenge?"

"Take it however you want to." His eyes gleamed in the dark room.

"You enjoyed it when I masturbated for you once before." I bent forward and whispered in his ear. "But that's not what I have in mind for tonight. Right now, I want free access to *your* body. I want to find all the spots that make your cock twitch and your lips form the word *please*."

The tip of my nose brushed the side of his neck and I inhaled deeply. The clean scent of Joe filled my head and my eyes slid shut. He smelled like leather and fresh air, with the slight tinge of male musk beneath it. My tongue darted out and took a swipe at his neck, tasting the salt of a light sweat.

I swiveled my head and explored the other side of his neck. My body was braced inches above his, I arched my back and swayed. My nipples brushed against his naked chest and pleasure shot from the rigid tips to my core.

Joe's breathing was getting choppy as my mouth worked along his neck, across the top of his shoulder. when I nibbled at the rounded muscle of his shoulder he shivered. I trailed my tongue down the wicked scar there, from shoulder to mid-chest, and he moaned.

My breasts brushed his belly as I slid lower down his body and my mouth began to tease his flat male nipples. When they were hard and pointy like little miniature cocks, I gave each one a sharp nip that made his body jerk on the mattress before pulling away.

Joe's expression was tight, his eyes full of blue flames as he watched to see what I would do next.

With a little giggle I swung my body around so that my knees were by his shoulders, and my face was above his groin. "All the polls with men in magazines say that they love sixty-nine. How do you feel about this position, Joe?"

I watched his fingers curl into the palms of his hands and make a fist. But, he kept his hands by his sides where I'd put them. "It's not my favorite, but it's OK."

A titter escaped from me and I wiggled my hips, spreading my legs and lowering myself a bit more. "Really? I thought you enjoyed licking my pussy."

He growled and the bulge behind the denim grew. I breathed hotly on his stomach and scraped the nails of one hand around his belly button and down the light dusting of hair that disappeared into his waistband.

"Can you smell how turned on I am? See how wet I am?" I traced the outline of his erection through his jeans, then laid my hand flat over it and stroked up and down. "I can feel how hard you are. See how much this is turning you on."

"*You* turn me on," he said. "No matter what you do, or what position you're in."

My heart flipped in my chest. "Do I turn you on enough to make you beg?"

A rusty chuckle filled the room. "I'm enjoying the view from here too much to beg just yet."

I swallowed a laugh and flipped open his belt buckle. I pulled the zipper open slowly and watched as his cock pressed against the thin layer of cotton still keeping it restrained.

"Yummy," I whispered. I slid my fingers beneath the waistband of his jeans and briefs and told him to lift up. With a quick move he was naked to the knees and his cock was dancing in front of my eyes.

I wanted to tease him, to torment him and make him beg, but the sight of his hard length bobbing in front of me, the shiny purple head already leaking, was too much to handle. I circled the base of his shaft with my hand and took him as deep into my mouth as I could.

His moan filled the room and I felt the heat of it against my inner thighs. His hands twitched at his sides and his hips jerked upwards, thrusting his cock deep enough to hit the back of my throat. I wasn't going to last long, but I wasn't willing to give up yet. I sucked at him some more, lifting and lowering my head, my tongue swirling along his shaft and around the head with every stroke.

My pulse raced and my pussy clenched. I wanted him inside me, but it wasn't going to happen until he asked for it. I needed to hear him ask for it.

My hand left his cock and trailed down my own body to stop between my thighs. All my weight was on the other hand on the mattress as I continued to work him over with my mouth. I spread my swollen pussy lips and flicked my aching clit.

"Katie," he growled.

I inched my knees wide and lowered myself another inch closer to his mouth. My fingers slid around my slick heat, nudging my clit a few more times before I thrust two fingers deep into my entrance.

"That's it." Hands gripped my hips and I was flipped onto my back.

Joe's hands spread my thighs wide and his tongue was on me, swirling, licking, nudging my clit. His teeth nipped at me and he sucked at my sex. I moaned around his cock and my hips jerked. My feet were in the air and an orgasm was fast approaching.

I ripped my head away from him and cried out, "No! Stop!"

Joe froze.

His body completely still, his breath panting over my wet sex.

32

"On your back," I ordered.

"Katie," he growled. "Please."

"On your back, Joe."

With a groan he rolled off me and I scrambled around until I was straddling his thighs. I didn't tease anymore, I just gripped the base of his cock, aimed it at my entrance, and impaled myself on him.

"Oh God," I moaned.

"Oh yes," Joe muttered.

I leaned forward, bracing my hands on his muscled chest and looked down into his eyes as I rolled my hips. "I didn't want another orgasm without you inside me."

"Smart thinking, angel." We grinned at each other and I started to ride him.

I was full. The angle, the size of him, the way my insides clenched. I felt every inch of him slide in and out, again and again. His hands skimmed up my sides. They roved over my body leaving a trail of fire wherever he touched. He cupped my breasts, played with the nipples, and thrust his hips under me. Soon I was bouncing up and down on him so fast and hard the bed was rocking.

Inarticulate sounds of passion filled the air as I leaned forward, changing the angle. My clit caught some of the friction and my insides exploded. My pussy clenched around the hard thick length inside me and I sat back, grinding myself against him. Joe's hands left my breasts, gripped my hips, and held me tight to him as his back arched and his hips lifted off the bed. Hot fluids filled my insides and set off another orgasm inside me.

When it was over, I slid off and curled against Joe's side, the occasional tremor still sneaking up on me. A warmth filled my heart at the way his calloused hand stroked absentmindedly up and down my back. I might not be ready to commit to love, but I was ready to accept it.

"Well?" I asked.

Joe cuddled close and kissed my damp forehead. "I could get used to that."